NICOLE CLARKSTON

THE
SHEPHERDESS
and the
SOLDIER

Rogues in Disguise Book Two

PROPER ROMANCE

Cover Design by GetCovers.com
Cover Image Licensed by Period Images
Background image licensed by Shutterstock

Blog and Website: https://nicoleclarkston.com/
Newsletter: subscribepage.io/V5dPFd
Book Bub: https://www.bookbub.com/profile/nicole-clarkston
Facebook: https://www.facebook.com/NicoleClarkstonAuthor
Twitter: https://twitter.com/N_Clarkston
Amazon: https://www.amazon.com/Nicole-Clarkston
Austen Variations: http://austenvariations.com/

Contents

Chapter One

London, December 1811

ANOTHER FREEZING WIND BLUSTERING up the Thames today. Lieutenant Owen North pressed through the snowy labyrinth of London's streets, stamping the cold from his boots and beating his arms against his chest as he approached the looming edifice housing Captain Hunt's present quarters.

Two months prior, their covert unit had executed a clandestine operation, shattering a spy ring that threatened His Majesty's troops in Portugal. They had kept Wellington's men from an ambush—or, rather, helped Wellington spring an ambush of his own. Yet, their triumph remained veiled in secrecy, known only to a select cadre. Only a handful knew even a whisper of it, and even fewer could speak with any authority on the facts.

Now, with Captain Hunt poised to retire into civilian anonymity, North's mind whirled with the prospect of assuming command. Surely, he would be chosen. There was no one else so qualified, no one else who could so easily step into Captain Hunt's boots.

Could even he do it? Lead the others with the same deft hand and steely resolve that had marked Hunt's tenure? The weight of responsibility pressed upon him, a mantle both daunting and exhilarating.

He had been waiting for this day for years. All the work and danger, everything he had given up... indeed, he was young for command, but so had Hunt been. Espionage was not an old man's game. Surely, he would be the one chosen as the captain's successor.

North straightened his posture and quickened his pace, ignoring the bite of the cold. Soon enough, he would know. Hunt had just returned from a meeting with his superiors and had summoned him rather urgently. It could only mean one thing.

Stepping inside the rooming house, he went to the small room at the back and knocked. Hunt kept a room in Town this winter for his own convenience, but he would be giving it up by the end of next week. Giving it up, and returning to Lincolnshire, where his family home was... and where his lady wife Bess Hunt was waiting for his return.

At Hunt's summons, North twisted the doorknob and entered, waiting for his eyes to adjust to the dim light. Hunt sat hunched over a map, his brow furrowed in concentration. Papers littered the rough-hewn desk—missives of alliance and war, no doubt. The weight of command carved deep lines in Hunt's face.

"Sir!" North snapped a crisp salute, his voice cutting through the heavy silence. Pride surged through him at the thought of their recent victory. What fortune had befallen him to place him under the command of an officer he had admired like no other? He was sorry to be losing his captain and had no desire to serve under another. But it left the door wide open for Owen North to add another insignia to his uniform.

"Are you well, North? How fare the others?" Captain Hunt spoke monotonously, without making any effort to look up at him. Hunt was focused on a spot on the map laid on the table. It must be a new mission, a new venture for him to explore and, eventually, enjoy the fruits of glory and success.

"I am perfectly well, thank you, sir, and so is Daniels. I have not seen Wesson since the day before yesterday. Is your rib mending?"

"Slowly, Lieutenant. Too slowly, for my wife is adamant that I should not ride horseback until it is mended. It is a pity there is not some magic potion to cure me at once."

North smothered an insubordinate grin. "I beg your pardon, Captain, but I take Mrs. Hunt's side in the argument. Not because of your injury, sir, but is it even safe to ride that brutish mare of yours when you are whole and well? To say nothing of recovering from broken ribs."

The captain snorted. "That mare is like any other lady, North. A bit of courtliness will take you far." Hunt straightened with a wince. "But in this case, I think it best to heed my wife's advice."

North grunted. If there was a soul alive who could bring Captain Nicholas Hunt to heel, it was his wife. "Sir, I can ask Wesson to bring some therapeutic ointments that might ease the pain."

"No. At the moment, I cannot afford a leisure hour, and I would rather not grant this bit of a trifle any consideration. Look at all this mess, North. It appears this war is never going to end, but even if it does, our work will carry on. Never any end in sight."

"We shall capture the next enemy agent, sir, as well as the one after that. Our troops have the best soldiers, trained for the worst circumstances on the battlefield, and our naval forces are unmatched. They deserve nothing less than our best, ensuring that their secrets are secure."

"Indeed. Spoken like a man who has not yet lost heart." Hunt blew out a sigh. "I assume you are aware of the new assignment."

"Not entirely, sir. Something to do with a smuggling operation in an otherwise commercial port, but I would appreciate more details," North responded while looking straight ahead. Word of that promotion would be welcome, too. Hunt *had* just come from Whitehall, after all.

"Well, I am afraid what I am about to say might disappoint you, North." Hunt now looked directly at him. "There has been an alteration to your orders."

North blinked. "Sir?"

"You are not to be assigned to the next mission as of now, I am afraid. Instead, I am sending you to Yorkshire."

North flinched slightly. "Yorkshire, sir...? But..."

"I know, North. I know. You have not been back for years, and I respect your privacy on the matter. I cannot disclose my reasons for sending you, because this cannot be an order."

"I am afraid I do not quite follow, sir."

Hunt walked around the desk, tapping the air with a folded letter. "I cannot issue the order that would override your previous instructions from Whitehall. I am retiring—I have no say in where you are sent. I can, however, recommend a personal leave for my men before I go, citing the best interests of the unit and the fact that certain of those men have not taken a personal leave in three years or better."

North shook his head. "Sir, I am fit to serve His Majesty."

"I am aware of your willingness, your capabilities, and the fact that you have your eye on a promotion that is well deserved. I see no reason why any of those ambitions ought not to be satisfied, but North, there is..." Hunt broke off, furrowing his brow. "I can say no more than I have my reasons. I desire for you to be sent on one month's leave before reporting to Kingston upon Hull."

North fell silent. Despite the chill from a room with an empty hearth, he could feel his temperature rising—not out of anger, but the sheer disappointment of not being selected for the next mission. "If it is because of any failing on my part—anywhere I have not seen through my duty, sir—"

"Nothing of the kind. Rather the opposite." Hunt paced before him and then stopped, leveling a long look at him. "A bowstring can only be pulled so tightly before it snaps. You are too good of an officer to let that happen, North."

"I am in no danger of that."

Hunt's mouth pressed into a frown. "Hmm. When was the last time you visited your family? Your mother is in Yorkshire, is she not?"

North narrowed his eyes. "Sir... sending me back home, on purpose... well, that is hardly a recipe for relaxation." North's voice shook slightly. He, the man who had ratted out dozens of the worst of characters and risked life and limb more than once in the service of a king he would never meet, and he quaked in his boots at the thought of walking up the street in his home village. "You are not... trying to force me into a retirement along with you, are you?"

"Forgive me. I did not suggest that, North." Captain Hunt could not help but laugh. "Why would I try to undercut one of the finest men who ever donned a uniform? It would be a disservice to everyone."

"Then you have some reason, sir, besides your stated wish for some 'respite' for me. I am afraid I still do not comprehend the underlying—"

"There is nothing underlying; it is as clear as day. Mighty Lord, North, can you not see?" Hunt held that folded letter up once more like a flag.

North hardly needed to glance at it. "That is not the paper used for official correspondence from Whitehall. Nor does it even resemble something from one of your informants."

Hunt chuckled and walked back around his desk. "That is what I like best about you, North. Even when there is no reason to be so, you are constantly thinking, evaluating, making decisions before you even fully understand why. Your craft is second to none. No, this is quite an ordinary letter, I should think. I do not know where your mother would find anything else."

"My mother, sir?" North could barely form the words. What the devil? His *mother*? She... wrote to him?

"You seem astonished. Do you not write to your family on occasion? It is the first time I have seen any letters come for you, but surely there have been some, somewhere."

North shook his head. "In this line of work, sir, writing to my mother can only endanger her."

Hunt grunted. "I see. And why did you become a catcher of enemy agents, North?"

"Forgive me, sir. I do not understand what you are truly asking."

"The Army's ranks are full of enthusiastic youngsters, all signing up to win glory and esteem. But in the line of duty and responsibility, one tends to forget the most important duty of all is to serve your loved ones. Why risk your life for strangers? It is their protection that incited you to join up, was it not? Were it not for those back home, we, none of us, would be here."

North began to breathe a little more easily. "Sir, in all the time I have served under your command, I have never once heard you speak of such things. You... you always said family was a luxury none of us could afford."

Hunt's expression sobered. "Indeed, and it was to my everlasting regret. But I have made my amends, and I tell you, it is a blessing no soldier ought to forego." His gaze grew distant. "To know that someone back at home is waiting for you with open arms..." Hunt stopped himself and shook his head. "I have made mistakes, North. You need not repeat them. Go see your mother and remind yourself what you are fighting for."

"My mother? I..." He shook his head. "To think of the shock I would give her!"

"When was the last time you heard from her?"

"I believe it has been a year or so," North replied vaguely.

"Should you not be concerned?" Hunt poured some beer for North and offered it to him.

"I suppose, but bouncing between duty posts as we do, hardly any notion of where we will be next, I am certain some letters may have been lost and never recovered. Sir, are you certain... We are still at war. I haven't time for a leisurely trip to Yorkshire for Christmas. I believe I must concentrate on the next assignment, and I request you to reconsider."

"Missions are for but a time, but family will be waiting for you when the mission is done. They ought to be able to recognize you when you do hang up that uniform." Captain Hunt poured himself another glass of beer and said, "You need to visit your mother, North."

"May I ask—"

"No, you may not. I know very well what you want, but I have more reasons than merely your personal good for sending you there. I am simply not at liberty to disclose them."

"Sir, I pray, will you please..." He broke off when Hunt pressed that letter into his hands.

"To answer your question before you ask it, no, I do not know its contents. It merely arrived at a convenient moment and answered a need. Or at least provided an excuse. I expect I may hear from you after you have arrived... or I may not. I pray for the latter. You are dismissed."

North nodded in some bemusement and returned to his quarters, four streets away through the icy afternoon. An air of agony had engulfed him, gripping him and his nerves in an uncomfortable embrace. It seemed as though all the cold in the world could not compare to the chills he felt creeping all over his spine.

What a blow! He closed the door of the room he had rented with Daniels and turned to the light from the window to examine the envelope. Why would she write to him now? Well... he *assumed* it was his mother. No one else would...

He paused and swallowed, his hand shaking with the letter. No. No one else from his home village would have any reason to write to him. But his mother had not written to him in more than a year. He scanned the direction again, and his eyes froze the letters. The scribbling was unfamiliar—certainly not her hand in which it was written.

Was there bad news? Had something happened to her? She had seemed well in her last letter, but that had been too long ago to even recall the particulars. His fingers shook a little as he broke the seal and spread out the page.

The contents inside were not numerous pages of maternal love and affection. Nor was it rambling gossip of the neighborhood, which was what she had often written of before. Rather, it was a single page with the bare minimum of words.

Lieutenant Owen North,

It is of the utmost urgency that I bring this matter to your attention. Your family's safety could be at risk. It is imperative that you return home immediately. Time is of the essence, and the weight of the decision lies with you. I urge you not to treat this letter lightly or dismiss it as mere jest. Consider it a genuine plea for caution. Act swiftly.

North's hands trembled, and his heart pounded like a wild animal in his ribcage. What the devil? Was this a joke? A cruel ploy on his sympathies?

Or did his mother truly need him?

He had been victorious on the battlefields, where he had tackled the mightiest, the wisest, the strongest. He had kept his cool when a spy's blade was at his throat, and he had played hundreds of parts to deceive his enemies.

Never, however, had he been forced to hold his nerves and compose himself for fear that harm might come to someone dear to him. Never had he felt like a defeated and weak man; he was a warrior and a fighter.

But, with a single paper, he was smitten and broken to countless pieces. Looking around his quarters, he reached for his sword and his pistol.

Aggression and panic replaced the prior feeling of disbelief. He knew not what manner of plot this was, nor who might have sent such a message. But now that he had read it, his mind was already forming every fear and eventuality. A moment's delay could perhaps cost him his mother's life. He rubbed his eyes and re-read the message, unsure what to make of it. He contemplated the thought of all the mishaps: sickness, accident, or a matter of robbery; what could it be?

There was only one way to find out. He was going home.

A MELIA PULLED HER SHAWL tighter around her shoulders as she stepped out into the biting December wind, the cold seeping through the thin fabric like icy fingers. She paused for a moment on the porch, her keen eyes scanning the farm's horizon. The cows huddled together in the pasture, their breath rising in steamy puffs, while the few remaining chickens scratched hopefully at the frozen ground.

"Ethan, love, come along now," she called, her voice cutting through the boy's vivid imaginings. "We've a long day ahead, and daylight's a-wasting."

Ethan's blonde head popped up from behind the woodpile, his cheeks flushed with the cold. "Coming, Mama!"

The old barn door creaked as Amelia pulled it open, the weathered wood rough beneath her chapped hands. Ethan darted inside ahead of her, his breath puffing in the cold air.

"Mama, can I help with the milking today?"

Amelia smiled down at him, her heart swelling with love and pride. "Of course you can, love. Just mind you're gentle with old Bessie. She's not as young as she used to be, and she doesn't take kindly to rough hands."

As they moved down the line of stalls together, the rich scent of hay and animals enveloping them, Amelia's mind began to wander. The familiar routine of milking and feeding was soothing, almost meditative, and she found herself slipping into memories of trundling behind her father when she was Ethan's age. How vividly she could see, even now, his strong, weathered hands guiding hers as he taught her to coax milk from a reluctant cow. He'd been a man of the earth, her papa, his face lined with laughter and his heart full of gentle wisdom.

"You've got to be patient, Amelia girl," he'd always said. "Animals can sense if you're hurried or anxious. They need a calm hand and a steady heart."

He'd always been kind to her when she was young. It was later... when... well, when things changed, that he had seemed to weary of the sight of her. Her fault... mostly... She could not bring herself to regret the reasons she had fallen out of her father's favor, but she still missed him.

Amelia blinked back sudden tears, her hands faltering on the cow's warm flank. It had been nearly a year now since they'd laid him to rest on the hill behind the house, his body wasted by the fever that had swept through the village. A year of shouldering the burden of the farm alone, of trying to fill the void he'd left behind.

Some days, the weight of it all felt like it would crush her. The endless toil, the constant worry over crops and animals and coins. But then she'd look at Ethan, at his bright, curious eyes and his calm smile, and she'd feel that weight lift, just a little.

He was her heart, her purpose. The reason she rose with the sun each morning and worked until her bones ached and her eyes blurred. She'd promised her papa, there at the end, that she'd keep the farm going, that she'd make sure Ethan had a roof over his head and food in his belly. And she'd be hanged if she'd break that promise, no matter how hard it got.

Shaking herself from her reverie, Amelia turned her attention back to the task at hand. The cows wouldn't milk themselves, and there were a hundred other chores waiting. But for just a moment, she let herself lean into the warmth of her son beside her, into the quiet strength of the animals under her hands. Let herself breathe in the scent of hay and life and home.

They would make it through this winter. Through this winter and the next, and the one after that. As long as they had each other, their animals, and the land beneath their feet, they would find a way. It was, after all, the only choice they had.

Ethan trailed behind her, peppering her with his usual fanciful questions. "Mama, do you think the fairies have homes like ours? With barns and cows and such?"

Amelia smiled, pausing to ruffle his fair hair. "I reckon they might, love. Though theirs would be a sight grander, I'd wager. With walls of spun sugar and roofs of gingerbread."

The boy's eyes widened with delight. "And stables full of unicorns?"

"Aye, that they would. And fountains flowing with honeyed mead, no doubt." She chuckled, turning back to her work. If only life were as sweet as a child's imaginings. But pregnant ewes needed hay, icy water troughs needed to be broken, younger animals needed a bit of molasses cake—

"Mama, look!" He was crouched in the corner of the barn, his hand outstretched toward a tiny, mewling kitten. "She's so little! Can we bring her inside?"

Amelia hesitated, her practical nature warring with the pleading in her son's eyes. She'd found the mother cat only yesterday—poor thing had been torn by a fox or a stray dog, and she had not found any surviving young. Trust Ethan to find the lone kitten from that litter and ask to keep it in the house. Another mouth to feed, when they could barely feed themselves... But the thought of that tiny creature shivering in the cold was too much to bear.

"Oh, I suppose," she relented, "but you'll have to take on the responsibility of caring for her. She'll need milk and warmth and lots of love."

Ethan nodded solemnly, cradling the kitten to his chest. "I will, Mama. I'll take the very best care of her."

As they walked back to the cottage, the kitten tucked snugly inside Ethan's coat, Amelia stopped at the wicket gate to look over her herbs. Hopefully, the coverings over them had prevented any frost during the night, but now they needed daylight to thrive as well as they could in the cold months.

Ethan's weak lungs were a constant worry, the fear of illness always lurking at the edges of her mind. That was where her herbs came in—the lunaria to soothe his breathing, the thyme and rosehips to keep his immune system strong. The apothecary in town, Mr. Sommers, had taught her the basics, and in so doing, had probably saved Ethan's life more than once.

"Mama, can I help with the herbs today?" Ethan asked, as if reading her thoughts.

"You mind that kitten first, love, and then you may help. I was just thinking I needed to check on them. Make sure they're holding up against this cold."

They spent the next hour in the garden, brushing snow from the delicate leaves and stems. Amelia showed Ethan how to mulch around the base of the plants, insulating them against the chill. As they worked side by side, Amelia felt a sense of peace settle over her. Yes, the days were long, and the work was hard. Yes, there were times when she felt the weight of her responsibilities like a physical ache in her bones.

But in moments like these, with Ethan's laughter ringing in the crisp air and the promise of spring waiting beneath the frozen ground, she felt not a moment's regret for all she'd given up for him. This... Well, it was not the life she had expected, but it was the one she wanted.

As the day lengthened and gardening chores wound back into barn chores, then later to her domestic duties, she found herself watching her son with a wistful ache in her heart. He had his father's eyes—that same dreamy, faraway look that spoke of a mind forever wandering.

A fanciful man, he had been, a lover of books and poetry, but that was a side of himself he had shown only to her. To others, he was a practical man, a man of courage and honor who protected his own, more at home with a blade and pistol in his hand than the handle of a plow. She'd loved that about him once—still did, truth be told. But fancies didn't put food on the table or coins in the purse. That duty fell to her now.

With a sigh, Amelia set down her mending, flexing her cramped fingers. "Ethan, love," she called, a sudden thought striking her. "What say we take ourselves into the village? See if old Mr. Cummings has any new books in?"

The boy leaped up, his eyes shining. "Can we, Mama? Truly?"

"Aye, we can. You've been a right good help today, and that deserves a reward." The book would be dear, but the joy on his face would be worth the cost. If she had to take on extra mending or sell a jar of her precious preserves, so be it. Her boy would have his book.

She squeezed her son's hand as they set off down the lane. "Now then, my little dreamer, tell me more of these fairy folk and their sugared halls..."

Chapter Two

OWEN NORTH STOOD BEFORE the weathered door of his childhood home, his heart pounding against his ribs like a caged bird. The chill December wind whipped through the deserted village streets, but he scarcely felt it, so consumed was he by the sense of unease that had dogged his steps since he'd received that cryptic letter.

He raised a fist to knock, the rough wood biting into his knuckles. Once, twice, three times he pounded, the sound echoing hollowly through the stillness. But no welcoming footsteps sounded from within, no warm voice called out in greeting.

Stepping back, North scanned the windows, hoping for a glimpse of movement, a flicker of lamplight. But the panes stared back at him blankly, dark and lifeless.

"Lieutenant North? Is that you, lad?"

North spun at the sound of the unfamiliar voice. An elderly man stood at the gate of the neighboring cottage, squinting at him uncertainly. At his side was a younger man, perhaps a few years North's junior, his expression clouded with suspicious curiosity.

"Aye, it's me," North replied, striding forward to meet them. "Forgive me, but have we met?"

The old man's face creased into a smile. "Nay, not formally. But I knew yer mother, God rest her soul. Finest woman I ever met, she was."

North felt the words like a physical blow, driving the air from his lungs. "My mother? What do you mean, 'God rest her soul'? Where is she?"

The younger man stepped forward, his eyes filled with compassion. "I'm sorry, Lieutenant. Your mother, she... she passed on, near a year ago now. The fever took her."

North staggered back, his mind reeling. It couldn't be true. It had to be some sort of cruel jest, a misunderstanding. His mother, gone? Then who wrote to him?

"I don't... I don't understand," he managed, his voice sounding distant to his own ears. "I received a letter, saying she was in danger. I thought..."

The old man shook his head sadly. "'Tweren't no danger, lad. Just the sickness that swept through the village. Took a lot of good folk, it did."

North turned back to the house, his vision blurring. He half-expected to see his mother appear in the doorway, her apron dusted with flour, a warm smile on her face. But the door remained firmly shut, the windows dark and empty.

"Come, sir," the young man said, laying a hand on North's shoulder. "Let's get you inside, out of this cold. I'm Elliot, by the way. Elliot Barrow. And this here's my father, Thomas."

North allowed himself to be led into the neighboring cottage, his feet moving of their own accord. Inside, the fire crackled merrily in the hearth, the room tidy and well-kept. But to North, it all felt surreal, like a dream from which he couldn't wake.

"Sit yourself down," Thomas said, guiding him to a chair. "I'll pour us a pint. Reckon we could all use one."

Elliot pressed a mug into North's hands, the ale sloshing over the rim. "We moved in next to your mother two summers past," he explained. "Lost our farm to Lord Ashwood, may he rot."

"Ashwood?" North's head jerked up.

"Aye, you know the blighter, do you?"

He looked down and shook his head. "No. Not anymore, anyway."

The older man leaned back in his chair with a sigh. "Not worth your notice, I say. We had to sell everything just to keep food on the table."

North nodded numbly, scarcely hearing the words. His mind was filled with memories of his mother—her gentle hands, her warm laughter, the way she'd hum as she kneaded bread. The thought that he'd never see her again, never hear her voice... somehow, he had always just assumed she would be here waiting for him when his service to the crown ended.

"She spoke of you often," Thomas said, settling heavily into the chair opposite. "Said you were off fightin' for king and country. She was so proud, she was."

North swallowed hard against the lump in his throat. "I should have been here," he rasped. "I should have..."

"You were where you needed to be," Elliot said firmly. "Serving your country, just like she wanted. There wasn't nothing you could've done, even if you had been here."

But the words were little comfort. The grief bubbled up in him, choking and visceral. He'd faced death a hundred times on the battlefield, stared it straight in the eye without flinching. But this? This wound would never heal, a loss so profound, it defied comprehension. If only he had been less concerned with his precious duty...

He drained his mug in one long swallow, the ale bitter on his tongue. The two men sat with him in silence. They were practically strangers, but to a man who had faced the battlefield, all that was necessary to make another his brother was a shared understanding of sorrow.

One thing seemed abundantly clear—these were not the men who had sent that letter. Someone was playing on his sympathies, trying to gain something from him. What the devil for? He ought to be out searching for the answer.

For now, though, all he could do was mourn. Mourn, and try to find the strength to face a world that would never be the same again.

THE CHILL DECEMBER WIND nipped at Amelia's cheeks as she and Ethan navigated the bustling streets of the market town. The scent of roasting chestnuts and spiced cider mingled with the sharp tang of chimney smoke, a festive counterpoint to the gray sky overhead.

Amelia adjusted her grip on the basket hanging from her elbow. An hour ago, the glass jars of jam and preserves had clinked softly with every step she took. Now, though, she had an empty basket and a pocket full of shillings. This year had been a good one for berries, and she was hopeful the extra provisions would continue to fetch a fair price. Every penny counted, especially with more cold months looming.

"Mama, can we visit the bookshop?" Ethan asked, his hand tucked securely in hers. "You promised we could, after we sold the jam."

Amelia smiled down at him, his cheeks bright beneath his woolen cap. "Of course, love. A promise is a promise."

She led him through the winding lanes, sidestepping the clumps of dirty snow and the slick patches of ice. The bookshop was a tiny, cramped space wedged between the haberdasher's and the candlemaker's, but to Ethan, it was a palace of wonders.

As they stepped inside, the bell above the door jingling merrily, Amelia breathed in the familiar scent of leather and paper. Ethan dashed ahead, his boots thumping on the creaky floorboards, his hands already reaching for the colorful spines lining the shelves.

The shopkeeper, a stooped old man with a pair of spectacles perched on his nose, glanced up from his ledger. "Ah, young Master Grey! Back again so soon?"

Ethan grinned, his cheeks flushed with excitement. "Yes, Mr. Hanley! Mama said I could choose a new book as a Yuletide gift."

The old man chuckled, his eyes crinkling at the corners. "Well then, you'd best take your time and choose wisely. A good book is a treasure beyond price."

As Ethan began his careful perusal of the shelves, Amelia wandered over to the section reserved for ladies' novels and penny dreadfuls. She had little time for such frivolities herself, but it amused her to imagine the scandalized whispers if she were ever seen purchasing one, especially on her meager income.

As she browsed the shelves, lost in thought, a sudden commotion near the front of the shop caught her attention. She looked up to see old Mr. Jameson, the village blacksmith, standing in the doorway, his face flushed, and his eyes slightly glazed.

"Well, well, Mistress Grey," he slurred, his voice carrying across the small space. "Surprised to see you in town, I am. Thought you preferred to keep to yourself out there on the moors."

A prickle of unease raced up her neck at his tone, but she forced a polite smile. "Good day, Mr. Jameson. I'm just here to sell my jams and do a bit of shopping, same as anyone else."

The blacksmith snorted, swaying slightly on his feet. "Aye, your jams. I were thinking of your lambs. Why weren't you hit with the pulpy kidney last spring, what wiped out 'most everyone else?"

She looked away, thinning her lips and moving to put the shelf of penny dreadfuls between herself and Jameson. "Our farm has been blessed, not seeing much of either that or the husk. We did lose some to the sway-back, so, you see, we are not entirely free of troubles."

"Oh, aye. Funny, isn't it, how a single woman like yourself manages a healthy flock when others are losin' their own? One might wonder if you have some sort of help."

A few other patrons glanced up at his words, their expressions ranging from curious to disapproving. Amelia's cheeks burned, but she kept her voice level. "I assure you, Mr. Jameson, I manage quite well alone. And even if I did have help, why would I be ashamed to own it? There is nothing untoward at work. Now, if you'll excuse me..."

She started to turn away, but the blacksmith's next words stopped her cold.

"Of course, there's some as might say it's not natural, a woman living alone like that, with a flock what's protected by some magic or luck. Especially with a child what don't look like no one else in the village. Makes folks wonder, it does."

Amelia's heart clenched, her hands tightening convulsively on the basket handles. It was an old hurt, the whispers and sidelong glances, the unspoken questions that hung in the air like smoke. She had borne them stoically for years, refusing to let the petty cruelties of narrow minds poison her love for her son.

But to hear it spoken aloud, in a public place, with Ethan standing just a few feet away... It was almost more than she could bear.

She drew herself up, fixing the blacksmith with a steely glare. "I fail to see how my private affairs are any concern of yours, Mr. Jameson. Or anyone else's, for that matter."

A few of the other customers murmured in agreement, casting disapproving looks at the blacksmith. He flushed darker, his eyes narrowing.

"You want to watch that tongue of yours, Mistress Grey," he growled. "There be some strange doings hereabouts lately. Folks might start to think you've got something to hide." With that, he turned and stumbled out of the shop, leaving a tense silence in his wake.

Amelia stood rigid, her heart pounding and her throat tight with unshed tears. Jameson's words were nothing more than the drunken ramblings of a foolish old man. But they preyed on the deepest, most secret fears of her heart—that someday, someone would start asking questions. And there were no answers she dared give them.

"Mama?" Ethan's small hand slipped into hers, his voice tremulous. "Why was that man saying those things?"

Amelia forced a reassuring smile, giving his fingers a gentle squeeze. "It's nothing to worry about, love. Did you find a book you wanted?"

Ethan nodded, holding a used book out for her inspection. "It's a book of stories, about brave knights and kingdoms. The shopkeeper said it's one of his favorites."

Amelia took the book, running her fingers over the worn cover—a book with tattered edges that made it affordable, but the stories inside were immortal and timeless to a boy of five. A shiver ran down her spine. *Brave knights*—noble men who marched off to serve king and country... leaving everything else behind.

Suddenly, the cozy shop felt claustrophobic, the air stale and oppressive. She wanted nothing more than to snatch up her son and flee, to retreat to the safety of their little cottage on the moors.

But she forced herself to take a deep breath, to steady her racing heart. This—none of this—was new to her by now. There had been rumors for years, and they were only intensified whenever misfortune befell her neighbors but somehow did not touch her. It was not as if she did not have her own share of hard luck, but no one cared about that.

"It looks perfect," she said, handing the book back to him with a smile. Hopefully, the book was not *too* costly. She put her hand in her pocket, giving the coins in there an experimental toss to decide if she had enough. "Why don't we purchase it, hmm? But I am a little tired, so perhaps we will not stop at the baker's afterward. Here. Take these and go buy your book."

Ethan beamed as she pressed several coins into his hand. And the smile she gave him in return must have been convincing, because he trotted merrily off to the counter with his prize.

Chapter Three

OWEN NORTH STOOD BEFORE his mother's grave, his head bowed and his heart heavy with grief and regret. The headstone was simple—crisp and fresh, compared to his father's beside it, which was weathered by twenty years of the harsh Yorkshire weather. He was used to seeing that one, but the words carved into this fresh surface struck him like a physical blow.

Emma North

Beloved Mother and Friend

May She Rest in Eternal Peace

He knelt, heedless of the cold seeping through his breeches. With trembling fingers, he laid a small bouquet of wildflowers at the base of the stone. They were a poor offering, a paltry gesture after all the ways he had failed her, but they were all he had.

"I'm sorry, Mother," he choked. "I'm sorry I wasn't here. I'm sorry I..."

What else was there to say? He had taken her for granted. The regret was a living thing inside him, gnawing at his heart like a hungry beast. If only he had thought to write to her more often. Oh, he always told himself that it was not safe, sending her too many letters. People would find him, or find her. But hang it all, she was his mother! She deserved... better than what she got.

Owen closed his eyes, breathing deeply of the crisp winter air. He could almost hear his mother's voice on the wind, feel the warmth of her embrace. But when he opened his eyes, there was nothing but the bleak expanse of the graveyard, the bare branches of the trees reaching towards a leaden sky.

With a heavy sigh, he pushed himself to his feet, his hand lingering on the rough stone for a moment longer. There was no point in empty promises to the wind. His mother was gone, and whatever that cryptic letter was, it was clearly someone's idea of a joke. Or a threat. Or... well, whatever it was, it meant nothing. There was nothing here for him anymore. He would just tell Hunt that he was coming back to his regiment.

He turned, his boots crunching on the frosty ground as he made his way back towards the village. As he walked, he pulled his collar up around his ears, hoping to avoid recognition. The last thing he wanted was to be accosted by well-meaning neighbors, their eyes full of pity and their mouths full of platitudes. He couldn't bear the thought of their questions about where he had been for so long, their murmurs that he had failed his mother. Not now, when the wound was still so raw.

And then there was the other reason for his desire for anonymity—the fear that he might encounter *her*. The woman he had once loved with every fiber of his being, the woman he had left behind when duty called... for both of them. The thought of facing her now, after all that had happened, made his stomach churn with dread.

Lost in his dark thoughts, he almost didn't notice the man hurrying towards him until he called out his name. "Lieutenant North? Is that you?"

Owen looked up, his eyes widening in recognition. It was Elliot Barrow, his mother's neighbor. The younger man had a long coat like the merchants wore over a neat suit of clothes, a crisp top hat on his head and a second hat clutched in his hand.

"I thought that was you," Elliot said, slightly out of breath. "I was just locking up the bank for the day when I saw you walking by. I had to run out to give Mr. Thompson his hat. The daft bugger forgot it on the counter again."

He smiled, but there was a hint of something else in his eyes—concern, perhaps, or curiosity. "I'm headed home as soon as I catch him up, if you'd like to walk with me."

North hesitated. Company was the last thing he wanted, but hang it all, they were walking the same direction. It would be a little too awkward to refuse to walk with the man. "Aye, that would be grand," he said at last, falling into step beside the other man. "Lead the way."

It was only a moment before Elliot had caught up with the hatless man on the street, just getting into his carriage. North watched with some detached interest as Elliot passed off the article, and in such a modest way that he made it sound as if it were his conversation that had made Mr. Thompson forget his hat, and not some level of senility on the part of the other. It was kindly done, at least, and North quite liked the younger man's manner in the affair.

"There, and that is finished. Have you any errands in town, Lieutenant?" Elliot Barrow returned to him with a wide grin. "I can point you to the best baker, or perhaps you would like a pint on your way.

"No, nothing like that, thank you."

Elliot gave a jerk of his head. "Then, onward with us."

As they made their way through the village, North couldn't shake the feeling of unease that prickled along his spine. He could feel people's eyes on him, curious and speculative. Hushed conversations seemed to spring up in his wake, the words lost to the wind but the tone unmistakable. Well, he was now a stranger in town. New folk always attracted notice and gossip. Did any of them recognize him? Someone would, eventually.

He quickened his pace, eager to be away from the scrutiny. But even as they left the market behind, the sense of wrongness persisted. It was like an itch between his shoulder blades, a nagging awareness of something just beyond his grasp.

"I must say, Lieutenant, it's good to see you back in the flesh. We didn't want to pry, what with... everything. But it is a fine thing, you know, to see you well. I hope the questions about town do not trouble you."

"No trouble," Owen replied as lightly as he could manage. "I am sure I am something of an object of curiosity."

"Well, to be sure. We've all been wondering where you've been off to these past few years. With the Army, of course, but you must have seen a great deal. Were you cavalry?"

There was a twinge of discomfort at the question, but he forced a casual smile. "Oh, yes. In a manner of speaking. But I have been a bit of everything."

Elliot nodded, his eyes still alight with interest. "I can only imagine. I've heard tales of the wars on the continent, the great battles and campaigns. It must be quite the adventure."

North huffed a laugh, but there was little humor in it. "Adventure is one word for it, I suppose. But the reality is often far less glamorous than the stories make it out to be."

"Oh?" Elliot quirked an eyebrow. "Do tell."

North hesitated, weighing his words carefully. There was so much he couldn't say, so many secrets he was bound to keep. But Elliot had been a friend to his mother. He and his father had probably been the ones to find her when... North swallowed. Elliot deserved some measure of truth, at least.

"There's a lot of waiting, for one thing," he said at last. "Long stretches of boredom punctuated by moments of sheer terror. And the conditions can be... challenging, to say the least. Mud, blood, disease."

Elliot let out a low whistle. "And me, here in my clean suit, all because I had a bit of a limp when I was younger. An old leg break, you see, but I manage well enough now. You can hardly tell."

North tilted his head to watch the other walk, and he nodded in agreement. "It is faint, but I regret to tell you that it is not unnoticeable, for I saw it the first moment. But that is my job, do you see—I notice things."

"Oh? To what purpose, if you don't mind my asking?"

North shrugged, trying to affect a casual air. "A little bit of everything, really. Training the men, leading patrols, overseeing supply lines. And of course, engaging the enemy when the time comes."

It was a vast oversimplification, of course. His true duties were far more complex, far more dangerous than he could ever let on. But it was enough to satisfy Elliot's curiosity, or so he hoped.

The other man nodded thoughtfully, his gaze distant. "It sounds like a heavy burden to bear. I can't imagine being responsible for so many men, making decisions that could mean the difference between life and death."

Owen felt a pang of something like gratitude at the words. It was rare to find someone who understood, even in part, the weight that he carried. "Aye, it's no easy thing," he agreed quietly. "But someone has to do it."

They walked in silence for a few moments, each lost in their own thoughts. Owen found himself studying the other man out of the corner of his eye, taking in the crisp, if not luxurious, attire, and the air of quiet competence that seemed to surround him.

"And what about you, Barrow?" he asked. "How did you come to be a banker?"

Elliot chuckled, a rueful smile tugging at his lips. "Well, that's a long story. Father wanted me to take over the farm someday. Suffice it to say, I had dreams of my own, making my fortune in London or some nonsense like that, but life had other plans. When we lost the farm, it was up to me to make my way in the world and put a roof over his head like he'd done for me all my life. So, Perkins at the bank brought me on as a clerk, and now I am assistant manager."

"I thought bank managers made good wages." North tipped his chin toward the end of the village, where his mother's cottage stood. "Why do you still live in the weedy end of town?"

"Ah." He chuckled. "That would be Father. He got used to his little room where it is, and he says he won't get used to another and he means to die in someplace familiar. He wanders about at night, sometimes, lost or asleep. You know how it is. And I haven't a wife, but I've given the idea some thought. Someday, perhaps, I'll buy me a snug little cottage and woo a pretty girl to cook for me."

Owen studied the ground as they walked. "We are not so different, Barrow," he mused. "Except that when faced with the same question—what to do with yourself with few options before you—you stayed with your family, while I ran."

"What is this?" Elliot moved a few paces ahead of him, turning somewhat to walk backward and look him in the face. "Regrets, Lieutenant?"

North held his breath for a moment. *Regret...* that word did not begin to scratch the surface. But he just shook his head. "I suppose we saw duty differently. I answered my country's call."

Elliot shrugged, but there was a hint of something like wistfulness in his eyes. "And I took the easier path, you might say. It's not a bad life, really. Quiet, but honest. And I like to think I'm doing some good, helping folks manage their money and plan for the future."

"That is the very definition of good," he said sincerely. "Truly. Using your position and your talents for the benefit of others. A pity there are not more honest chaps like you."

"Indeed! And what makes you so certain that I am honest?"

Owen cracked a smile. "Because I know the look of a *dis*honest man. That is not you."

Barrow ducked his head, a pleased flush coloring his cheeks. "I cannot say I am as good as I ought to be. But I do my best."

They lapsed into a comfortable silence, the sounds of their footsteps echoing through the nearly empty streets as they left the market and square behind. North found himself relaxing incrementally, the tension that had coiled in his gut beginning to unwind.

But just as he was starting to feel something like ease, Elliot's next words sent a chill down his spine.

"Did you hear about those prisoners who went missing?" he asked. "A few of them, all working on farms around here. Vanished into thin air, like they never existed."

North's steps faltered. He took a deep breath, forcing his voice to remain steady. "Missing prisoners? When did this happen?"

Elliot shrugged. "A week ago, maybe two. It's got folks talking, that's for sure. Frogs, you know, all captured somewhere and forcibly lodged wherever the crown pleases until the war is over. Half the farms 'round here had at least one dropped at their door, and right worked them to skin and bones for the favor. You'd think they'd be happy to be rid of the extra mouths to feed, but now they're just complaining about losing their free labor."

North's face contorted with thought. "No one saw them go? Surely, they would have left tracks in the snow. Was there a mail coach they might have stowed away on? How many?"

"Half a dozen, I think. A few folk say more like double that, but I believe that is an exaggeration. Some say they just ran off, but others..." He trailed off, his expression troubled.

"Others what?" North pressed.

"Others say there's something darker at work. Something... unnatural."

"Oh, poppycock. One thing I can say after several years in the army is that the folks hereabouts are the most superstitious lot you'll ever meet. There is always an explanation that does not involve black magic and goblins or elves."

"Try telling them that!" Barrow laughed. "No, no, I'm of the same mind as you, but all the same, it's dashed odd. Folk don't just up and vanish."

"No..." North agreed. "They don't." Perhaps... Well, perhaps that merited a bit of a look. They were prisoners of war, after all. Men who might carry secrets, and secrets were Lieutenant Owen North's stock in trade.

As they reached the cottages, he turned to Barrow. "Thank you for joining me. I expect it has been some while since I talked to a man merely for the pleasure of his company." His cheek flinched a little. "Softens the blow, you know."

Elliot's eyes widened slightly, but he nodded. "Of course. I am truly sorry about your mother, North. We thought you knew, but... well, that is silly, of course, because how would you? If there's anything else I can do to help, just say the word."

North clasped his shoulder briefly in thanks, then turned and strode towards the house. He probably ought to have told Elliot that he had meant to depart on the first mail coach the next morning, but... perhaps he could stay *one* day longer. Just out of curiosity.

Chapter Four

A MELIA SAT BY ETHAN'S bedside, the flickering candlelight dancing eerie shadows over the ticking clock on the mantel. She glanced at it and grimaced—it was after three in the morning, and nothing had improved since Ethan's first cough at half-past ten. In her hands, she cradled a bowl of steaming water, the fragrant scent of herbs rising in tendrils of vapor. Gently, she guided her son to lean forward, urging him to breathe deeply of the soothing mist.

"That's it, love," she murmured, her voice low and comforting. "Nice and slow, in and out."

Ethan's breaths came in shallow, ragged gasps, his small chest heaving with the effort. Each inhale was a battle, a desperate struggle for air that left him spent and trembling. Amelia watched helplessly as he fought for each precious lungful, his face pale and slick with sweat.

Minutes crawled by with agonizing slowness, marked only by the labored sound of Ethan's breathing and the pounding of her own heart. Her knuckles on the bowl were white with the force of her grip. The herbs had always worked before, had always eased the tightness in his lungs and soothed the inflammation. But now, as she watched her son suffer, doubt began to creep in, insidious and cold.

What if the herbs weren't enough this time? What if Ethan's lungs, already weakened by so many bouts of illness this winter, simply couldn't recover? The thought sent a spike of pure, icy terror through Amelia's veins, and she had to bite back a sob of despair. If only she had the means to move him somewhere else—live somewhere warmer, without the constant bother of dust and hay and animals that made his breathing worse.

"Breathe, my darling," she whispered, her voice cracking with emotion. "Just breathe. Mama's here, Mama's got you."

But Ethan couldn't seem to hear her, lost in the throes of his own struggle. He gasped and wheezed, his small body wracked with the effort of drawing air. She could see his pulse fluttering wildly at his throat, could feel the heat of his fever through the damp cloth she pressed to his brow.

Seconds stretched into minutes, and still Ethan fought for breath. Amelia's panic rose with each passing moment, a clawing, desperate thing that threatened to tear her apart from the inside out. She wanted to scream, to rage against the unfairness of it all—against the cruel twist of fate that had left her son so frail, so vulnerable.

"That's it, my brave boy," she crooned, her voice a thin, reedy thing in the stillness of the room. "Just keep breathing, just keep fighting. Mama's here, Mama's got you."

And then, just when she thought she couldn't bear it a moment longer, just when the panic had risen to a fever pitch and threatened to consume her entirely, Ethan's breathing began to ease. It happened gradually, almost imperceptibly at first, but slowly, surely, the harsh, ragged gasps evened out, settling into a steadier rhythm.

Amelia watched, scarcely daring to hope, as her son's chest rose and fell with greater ease. The pain and fear were still there, etched into the lines of strain around his mouth and eyes, but there was something else too—a flicker of relief, a hint of color returning to his pale cheeks.

"That's it," Amelia breathed, tears of gratitude welling up to blur her vision. "That's my brave, strong boy."

The worst of the crisis had passed, the danger had been averted—for now. But as Amelia sat back on her heels, the bowl of now-tepid water forgotten at her side, she knew that this was only a temporary reprieve. Ethan's lungs would always be weak, always be susceptible to the cold and damp and the myriad illnesses that lurked in every dusty hay loft and moldering corner. And winter was the worst, with its knife-like gulps of air that froze his lungs with every precious breath.

It was a battle they would have to fight again and again, a war with no end in sight. But for now, in this moment, Amelia let herself savor the small victory, let herself bask in the relief of her son's steady, even breaths. She began to hum softly, an old lullaby her own mother had sung to her as a child. The melody wove through the quiet room, mingling with the crackle of the fire and the soft whisper of Ethan's breaths.

As she stroked his hair, his eyelids grew heavy, fluttering closed as sleep claimed him at last. Amelia watched him, her heart aching with a fierce, protective love. In the dim light, his features seemed to shift and change, the planes of his face taking on a hauntingly familiar cast.

With a start, she realized who he resembled... his father. And for the first time, she saw it in more than just his eyes. It was there, in the shape of his chin, the set of his jaw. He was a perfect miniature of the man who had been her dearest friend since they were younger than Ethan was now. The man she had loved with a passion that had consumed her, body and soul. The man who had left her, all those years ago, to chase glory on the battlefield, because she had been pledged to another.

"Owen," she breathed as she stroked her son's hair.

The name broke something inside her, like the shattering of a magic spell. She had not uttered those syllables in almost six years and had vowed never to do so again. But with that one whispered word, all the memories flooded back. The way Owen's eyes had crinkled at the corners when he smiled, the warmth of his hands on her skin, the dreams they had whispered to each other in the dark that one night—impossible dreams of a future together, of a family and a home of their own.

But that future could never come to pass. It was a horrid, horrid mistake, that was all. What was supposed to be a simple farewell between friends—for they had never permitted themselves to become more—had instead become a brief, stolen moment of joy, a flash of passion that had burned bright and hot and then guttered out, leaving her alone and adrift.

Amelia closed her eyes, her heart constricting with a pain that was all too familiar. In the years since Owen had left, she had tried to bury those memories, to push them down deep where they couldn't hurt her anymore. But seeing his face in her son's, seeing the echo of his spirit in Ethan's bright, curious eyes—it brought it all rushing upon her, sharp and bittersweet.

What might have been? It was not the first time she wondered that. If Owen had stayed, could they have found a way to be together? Her father would not have approved. He had wanted stability for her, distinction and an easier life, all of which she would have had by marrying Lord Ashwood. And all things she gave up when she discovered what that one night with Owen had left her with.

Would things have been different if she had ever told him? Would Ethan have grown up with a father's love, a father's guidance? Or would he still have left her for his duty to the crown, because he had no way of keeping a wife and family? Yes... that was what he would have had to do. His enlistment papers were already signed, and he had vowed he would never be a farmer like her father. If she had married Owen, she would have been a soldier's widow from the first day of her marriage, whether her husband was dead or alive.

Amelia shook her head, pushing the thoughts away. There was no use dwelling on what-ifs and might-have-beens. The past was the past, and she had to focus on the present—on the child who needed her, the son who was her whole world.

Gently, she tucked the blankets around Ethan's slumbering form, her fingers lingering on his soft, round cheek. He looked so peaceful in sleep, so innocent and unburdened. It was her job to keep him that way, to shelter him from the harshness of the world for as long as she could.

Even if it meant keeping secrets, even if it meant bearing the weight of her choices alone. Ethan was all that mattered, and she would do whatever it took to keep him safe and happy.

With a sigh, Amelia leaned forward and pressed a tender kiss to her son's forehead. The candle sputtered and flickered, shadows dancing on the walls, and outside, the wind howled through the eaves like a lost and lonely soul.

NORTH HOVERED IN THE doorway of his childhood bedroom, his heart heavy with a weight that had nothing to do with the musty air or the dust that layered every surface. The room was just as he'd left it, all those years ago—the narrow bed neatly made, the shelves lined with books and boyhood treasures. But it felt smaller somehow, like a relic from a past that no longer quite fit.

He stepped inside, his boots leaving imprints on the faded rug. Slowly, almost reverently, he let his fingers trail over the spines of the books, the smooth wood of the desk. Each touch brought back a flood of memories, a rush of emotions that threatened to overwhelm him.

And then his gaze fell on the small wooden box, tucked away in the corner of the bottom shelf. His breath caught in his throat, his heart stumbling over a beat. He knew that box, knew the secrets it held.

With trembling fingers, he pulled it out and carried it to the bed, sinking down onto the threadbare quilt. The hinges creaked as he lifted the lid, revealing a jumble of papers and mementos—a pressed flower, a smooth river stone, a scrap of ribbon.

But it was the letter that drew his eye, the creamy parchment standing out against the darker hues. He picked it up gingerly, unfolding it with a care that bordered on reverence. The words swam before his eyes, blurred by the sudden sting of tears. He blinked them back, forcing himself to focus on the neat, familiar script.

My dearest Owen,

I have news. I hope you shall be happy for me, for I am happy for myself, or at least I am persuading myself to be. Papa received Lord Ashwood today and has accepted an offer for my hand. I cannot know why...

That was as far as he ever got. There was more, but he had not the heart to read it, all those years ago when she had first dropped it in his hand. He'd been walking in the market, waiting for a glimpse of her, to be truthful. But her father had never liked him, and even less so when it became obvious to everyone that the poor boy from the village who did odd jobs for all the farmers had lost his heart to the fiery, red-headed Amelia Grey.

And so, they had been careful. Friends, and no more, because they both knew...

Well. They both knew. There was no future for them. They could never be anything other than the sort of friends who shared secrets and dreams, and no more. The knowing made it more painful than doubt and hope could ever have been. Mr. Grey stopped hiring him for work, and the only time they ever saw each other was on market day, when he might get lucky and cross gazes with her while her father was bartering his fleece and milk.

But that day, a letter had found its way into his hand—a brush against his fingers, and she had vanished, leaving only these wretched words for him to torment himself over.

He never got farther than those first few sentences because he had... egad, *what* he had done. He'd run up that cut in the Dales in the dead of the night—well over an hour's walk for a cool head, but that wild dash up the mountain had been but half an hour's worth of madness for him. Too short a time for his ardor or his grief to cool. Not long enough for him to think through what he meant to do or say...

But he hadn't meant to do what he did.

North closed his eyes, the memories washing over him in a tidal wave of emotion. He could see her face as if she were standing right before him—the blaze of her hair in the light of the lantern, the wide, luminous eyes, the soft curve of her smile. Could feel the warmth of her skin beneath his fingers, the gentle swell of her form against his chest.

He'd begged her to renounce the engagement. Run away with him, do anything but marry Lord Ashwood, who was surely twenty years her senior. What could Lord Ashwood want with her, anyway? She had no money, no connections to lure a nobleman. She had only her beautiful spirit, her sweet face, and a figure that would make a goddess jealous.

That was far more than Ashwood deserved, a thing North had shouted back at her with tears in his eyes.

But she would not be moved. Through sobs and agony, she had pleaded with him to understand—she had no choice. It was her father's wish, and she had already given her promise.

So, he'd lied to her, claiming he'd made a promise of his own... to the Army.

It was not as if he had not been considering it. Where else could a lad without a penny to his name find a chance at honor? How else could he escape the monotony of slopping pigs and shearing sheep for farmers who only paid him in ale and milk?

So, that night, he told her that he had already made his pledge—after all, why not? She was promised elsewhere, and there was nothing he could do about it. The last thing he would do was stay in that village and watch her riding to town in Lord Ashwood's carriage. Bouncing his bairns in her arms.

When he told her that, she'd pleaded with him to change his mind... to be safe... and then she had kissed him. There, in the hayloft of her father's barn, with her face streaming tears and her voice quaking—begging him not to go. He had kissed away her tears and whispered promises into her hair, vows of love and devotion that he knew he could never keep. And then...

How was it possible that the most exquisite moments of his life were now the ones that caused him the most pain? He'd known it was wrong... that he should have stopped... but for that moment, he had let himself believe the lie that he could live the rest of his life on that stolen moment. That it would be enough...

He'd promised to write to her, but even in that, they both knew it could never be. She was to be married by the end of the season! What business had a married woman in receiving letters from her illicit lover? No... that, too, was a lie.

Now, sitting in the quiet of his childhood room, the weight of his choices pressing down on him like a physical thing, his heart surged with bitter remorse. What had he been thinking, leaving her like that? Leaving the only woman he'd ever loved, the only future he'd ever truly wanted? He might have made a fair farmer, if it had ever come to that. He could have found a way to stay, if there had been any hope of being with her.

But she had sworn there was not. So, rather than fighting for her, the one thing in his life he'd held as worthy of fighting for... he had thrown it all away, and for what? For glory and adventure, for the chance to prove himself a hero?

He was no hero. He was just a man, a man with a heart full of regrets and a past full of mistakes. Mistakes he dared not unearth now—not after all these years. What if he saw her in the market? Lady Ashwood, with fine gowns and no doubt a passel of hook-nosed barns she'd never wanted, pulling at her skirts and squabbling in the carriage. He just... he couldn't be the one to see what she had become.

That was why he meant to leave on the first mail coach tomorrow.

Chapter Five

AMELIA HURRIED THROUGH THE bustling market square, Ethan's small hand clutched tightly in her own. His little body was swaddled and bundled in every scrap of warm clothing she could find in the house, including her own scarf and heavy wool coat. The winter wind nipped at her cheeks and nose, turning them a rosy red, but she barely felt the chill.

What she did feel was the way Ethan's feet were dragging as he tired from their long walk, but what choice did she have? She could not leave him home alone, and she couldn't put him on a horse. She'd sold the plow horse last autumn when she'd needed to buy molasses cake to save some of her struggling lambs. The only way to town was on their own two feet.

"Just a little farther, my love," she mumbled. A few steps later, she stopped to scoop him back up on her shoulders. She could save his legs and the stress on his lungs a little, at least. Hopefully, the apothecary would have some medicine to forestall Ethan's next bad spell.

She could feel the eyes on them as they wove through the crowds, the curious glances and hushed whispers that always seemed to follow in their wake. The villagers had never quite known what to make of her—the unmarried mother with the strange, dreamy child. But Amelia held her head high, her jaw set with stubborn pride. Let them talk and let them stare. It wouldn't change anything she meant to do, even a whit.

The apothecary's shop was a welcome respite from the cold and the scrutiny. The air was thick with the scent of herbs and spices, the shelves lined with jars and bottles of every shape and size. "Ah, Mistress Grey!" Mr. Sommers looked up from his mortar and pestle, his lined face creasing into a warm smile. "And young Master Ethan, too. What brings you in today?"

Amelia approached the counter, her hands twisting nervously in her skirts. "It's his chest," she said softly. "That same old cough, but it's getting worse. I've tried everything I know, but nothing seems to help."

The apothecary's brow furrowed with concern, his keen eyes taking in the pallor of Ethan's skin, the dark circles beneath his eyes. He reached beneath the counter, producing a small jar of pale green ointment.

"This should do the trick," he said, pressing the jar into Amelia's hands. "Rub it on his chest and back, morning and night. It will ease the inflammation and help him breathe easier."

"And... how much is it?"

"Six pence."

Amelia reached for her reticule, her fingers trembling as she counted out the few meager coins she had managed to scrape together. But it wasn't enough... not nearly enough. She should never have bought him that book...

"I'm sorry," she whispered, her cheeks burning with shame. "I only have three with me. If you could just give me a few days, I can try to—"

But Sommers waved away her apologies, his smile never faltering. "Do you know, just the other night, I had a hankering for a bit of jam, but blast if my cupboard was not nearly bare. I don't suppose you have any you might part with?"

The tears spilled over then, trailing down Amelia's cheeks in hot, salty streams. "I do. I'll bring some this very afternoon, and—"

"No, no need for that." Sommers took back the ointment and put it in a little burlap sack, into which he also stuffed a satchel of eucalyptus. "Next market day will be soon enough."

"Thank you," she managed, her voice choking with emotion. "Thank you so much."

Beside her, Ethan was lost in his own world, his fingers tracing patterns on the polished wood of the counter as he hummed softly to himself. The apothecary's eyes twinkled as he watched him, a hint of affectionate amusement in his gaze. "No need for thanks, Mistress Grey. Best start for home before the snow hits."

As they stepped back out into the cold, the jar of ointment clutched tightly to her chest, Amelia felt a rush of conflicting emotions. Relief at having the medicine Ethan so desperately needed, gratitude for the kindness of the apothecary. But beneath it all, a nagging sense of unease, a reminder of just how precarious their situation truly was.

What if the apothecary had been less than kind? She hated to think of it, but... when she ran out of extra jams and jellies to sell before shearing season, it might come down to selling some of Ethan's books to keep medicine in the cupboard and food on the table.

The sound of hoofbeats and wooden wheels startled her from her thoughts, and she looked up to see a grand carriage pulling to a stop beside them. The coat of arms on the door was achingly familiar, a sight that sent her heart leaping into her throat. She knew that crest all too well—the rampant lion, the crossed swords, the motto "Honor Above All" emblazoned beneath in flowing script.

"Miss Grey!" Lord Garrison Ashwood leaned out the window, his noble face split in a roguish grin. "What a pleasant surprise!"

"Lord Ashwood," she managed, dipping into a curtsy. "I didn't expect to see you in town."

Ashwood's eyes flickered over her, taking in the old cloak she wore, the faded dress beneath, and probably the tell-tale redness of her nose and cheeks. Something like confirmation flashed in his gaze, but it was gone as quickly as it had come.

"I had some business to attend to," he said airily. "But never mind that. You two look half-frozen. Allow me to give you a ride home."

Amelia's heart stumbled, her eyes widening in surprise. "Oh, no, my lord. That's very kind, but I couldn't possibly—"

But Ashwood was already opening the carriage door, his smile brooking no argument. "Nonsense, Amelia. I insist. It's the least I can do."

She hesitated, her mind racing with excuses. "My horse and buggy are just tied up by the livery stable. We wouldn't want to inconvenience you."

Ashwood's laugh was rich and confident, sending a shiver down her spine. He sounded much too friendly. "Come now, Amelia. We both know you sold that old plodder months ago. Please, let me do this for you. Good heavens, what does a gentleman have to do to show a little kindness to a neighbor?"

'Neighbor,' was he? Not a spurned suitor? A wealthy widower with little to do but... well. Best she did not think about that too long.

There was no graceful way to refuse, no polite way to extract herself from the situation. With a sigh of resignation, Amelia allowed herself to be handed into the carriage, Ethan clambering in beside her.

The interior was sumptuous, all plush velvet and gleaming wood. It was a far cry from the rough-hewn benches of her farm cart. As the carriage set off, the horses' hooves clattering against the cobblestones, Ashwood turned his attention to Ethan. "And how are you today, young man?" he asked, his tone jovial. "Keeping your mother on her toes, I'll wager."

Ethan blinked up at him, his milky blue eyes wide and guileless. "I was just thinking about the fairy king I heard about in a story Mama read to me," he said solemnly. "And I thought up more about him. He lives in a castle made of starlight and spider silk, and he rides a dragon with scales like rainbow glass."

Ashwood's brow furrowed, a flicker of confusion crossing his aristocratic features. "I... I see," he managed, shooting Amelia a questioning glance.

Amelia felt her cheeks heat, a mixture of embarrassment and defiance welling up inside her. "Ethan has a very active imagination," she said, a hint of warning in her tone. "He likes to read and dream up stories."

Ashwood nodded slowly, his smile a bit forced. "Of course. What child doesn't love a good fairy tale?"

"No child I want to know," she replied stoutly.

Ashwood tugged at his cravat. "Naturally, naturally. Does a lad good to fancy heroics and what not. I'd wager you would make a capital soldier one day, lad."

Ethan shook his head. "I want to own a press, so I can read books all day long."

His Lordship furrowed his brow and cleared his throat. "I see. Books, eh? Ah... that is interesting."

The rest of the ride passed in awkward silence, broken only by Ethan's occasional bursts of chatter and Ashwood's strained attempts at small talk. Amelia could feel the weight of his gaze on her, could sense the unspoken questions and the simmering tension that hung in the air between them.

When they finally pulled up outside the cottage, Amelia was quick to usher Ethan out, her thanks to Ashwood stilted and formal. She could see the questions in his eyes, the unspoken intent to say more, but she hardened her heart against it. There was nothing she had that could possibly interest Lord Ashwood now—which was a relief.

As the carriage pulled away, leaving them in the swirling snowflakes, she ushered her son back inside. "But Mama, the ewes," he protested tiredly.

"Not today for you. You have been too long in the cold already. Back inside, and once we have the fire nice and warm, you will rest with this nice ointment. Tonight, will be better, you will see."

OWEN STOOD AT THE edge of the market square, his eyes fixed on the road leading out of town. The mail coach was delayed today, they had told him. It should have been and gone an hour earlier, and in London or any other half-civilized borough, the driver would have undergone a tongue-lashing and probably been dismissed. But here, no one seemed to care.

He spun around with a hiss of impatience. The longer he waited there, the greater the possibility of encountering someone who might recognize him. He could ill afford that... but the delay did put in mind some rather unpleasant business that he ought to attend before he left.

Perhaps he should walk down to the bank and speak to Elliot Barrow about his mother's cottage. He seemed an honest enough chap, and it appeared as though North would need to sell the property. Elliot could keep the money, as far as he was concerned, but...

That was when he saw *her*.

Amelia.

She was there, not in some distant dream, but in the flesh, just a few paces away, through the glass of the apothecary's shop. Her red hair peeked out from beneath a brown hooded cloak, her cheeks flushed with the cold. North's heart stuttered in his chest as he watched her, drinking in every detail like a man starved for water.

She was haggling with the apothecary, her voice muted by the window as she gestured to a small jar in her gloved hands. North couldn't make out the words, but he could see the tension in her shoulders, the worry etched into the lines of her face.

She was... well, she was just as beautiful as she had ever been. He might have believed that not a day had passed since he last saw her—she still carried herself with that same willowy grace, still had that same careful way of leaning into a conversation, as if the person she was speaking to were the only person in the world. Perhaps that was why he had fallen for her from the first moment he ever saw her as a boy—she was the only one who made him feel as if he mattered.

What if...? Should he speak to her? Would she even care to hear what he had to say? He had promised her when he left that he would never bother her again... but he had also meant never to return home. Yet, here she was, almost within reach, with her cheeks rosy and her—

But the thought shattered when a small hand tugged at Amelia's skirts. Owen blinked and his gaze fell to her side... and the child standing there. It was a boy of no more than four or five. His head barely reached her hip, so he must be young, and most of his face covered by a warm hat and a thick woolen scarf. The child said something and Amelia smiled, her face softening with a love that pierced North's heart like a dagger.

Of course. It had been years since he had left, years since he had walked away from the only woman he had ever loved. She had a child now, a family. And it wasn't with him.

Dazed, Owen watched as Amelia took the boy's hand, leading him out the door and away from the apothecary's shop. He could not help but follow them as they wove through the crowded street. The boy's steps lagged, and she paused once, as if offering to carry him. But she never picked him up, because a moment later, a carriage pulled up to the kerb for them. A carriage emblazoned with a coat of arms North knew all too well.

Lord Garrison Ashwood. The man Amelia was meant to marry. The man who could give her everything he never could—stability, security, a future.

North's vision blurred, his chest tightening with a grief that stole the very breath from his lungs. He watched as Lord Ashwood handed Amelia into the carriage, his hand lingering on her arm in a gesture of easy familiarity. The boy clambered in after her, his laughter ringing out like a bell across the snowy street.

And then they were gone, the carriage rattling away into the gathering dusk. North stood there, frozen, as the first flakes of snow began to fall, clinging to his eyelashes and melting on his cheeks like tears.

He had to leave. Had to get away from this place, from the memories that haunted every cobblestone and alleyway. He couldn't bear to be here a moment longer, to see the life Amelia had built without him, the happiness he had thrown away in the name of duty and honor.

With a shuddering breath, North turned on his heel, his boots crunching through the freshly fallen snow as he fled. He didn't know where he was going, didn't care. All he knew was that he had to put as much distance as possible between himself and the aching, yawning chasm his choices had carved in his heart.

Chapter Six

H
E HAD BEEN A fool to come back here, to think that he could face the demons of his past without being torn asunder. All he wanted now was to put this place behind him, to lose himself in the familiar rhythms of military life until the ache in his chest faded to a distant throb.

With a final, determined stride, North marched back to the mail coach station, only to find the yard empty and the ticket window shuttered. A small, hand-lettered sign tacked to the door delivered the crushing news: the coach would not be arriving until the morrow, waylaid by the impending storm. When did that ever happen?

North cursed under his breath, his hands clenching into fists at his sides. The thought of spending even one more night in this town, with its suffocating memories and haunting regrets, was almost more than he could bear.

But what choice did he have? To wander the streets, risking an encounter with someone he knew—or worse, with Amelia herself? The very thought made his stomach churn with a sickening mixture of longing and dread.

No, he needed solitude, needed space to clear his head and gather his thoughts. And so, with a last, frustrated glance at the empty station, North turned on his heel and strode out of the village, his boots crunching through the freshly fallen snow.

He walked for what felt like hours, his mind churning with a maelstrom of emotions. Anger, regret, despair—they swirled together in a dizzying whirlwind, threatening to sweep him away entirely. And a sort of mania began to overtake him, demanding answers to questions that he had once deemed unanswerable.

How could he have been so foolish, so blind? How could he have thrown away the only thing that had ever truly mattered, all in the name of duty and honor? Hang the fact that she had been pledged elsewhere. He could have... *Should* have...

What? What in blazes was he supposed to do but what he had already done? Retire from the field with a shred of dignity, or at least the semblance of it.

It was not as if he could have run away with her. That would have been even worse, for how could he have kept her? What, made her a camp wife, following the drum in Spain, enduring whatever hardship came their way? Unthinkable.

His head hung in defeat as the village fell away behind him, the frozen landscape seemed to mirror the desolation in his heart. The trees stood stark and skeletal against the leaden sky, their branches reaching up like grasping fingers. The river, once a rushing torrent, lay still and silent beneath a layer of ice, its secrets locked away beneath the frozen surface.

In a secluded spot along the riverbank, Owen finally allowed himself to give voice to the frustration and pain that had been building inside him. With a wordless howl, he lashed out at a nearby tree, his fist connecting with the rough bark with a satisfying crack.

Again and again, he struck the tree, his breathing ragged and his vision blurred with unshed tears. The physical pain was a welcome distraction from the ache in his heart, the emptiness that threatened to consume him whole.

But even as he raged against the injustice of it all, a small, distant part of his mind remained alert, ever watchful. Too many years on the field, perhaps, but he could not snuff it out, even if he tried. And so, when a flicker of movement caught his eye, Owen's head snapped up, his senses instantly on high alert.

There, in the distance, two figures were running across a snowy field, their forms little more than dark smudges against the stark white landscape. They were heading towards a small copse of trees, their movements furtive and hurried.

His brow furrowed as he watched them. Who were they, and what could they be doing out here in the middle of nowhere, in the dead of winter? His military instincts, honed by years of training and combat, screamed at him that something was amiss.

As the figures disappeared into the trees, North caught sight of a third man, this one standing beside a coach at the edge of the field. He seemed to be waiting for the other two, his posture tense and alert. Why, that... that looked like the blooming mail coach! He started forward in a run, raising his hand to hail the driver, but in the next instant, the coach was turning back with its new passengers aboard and the driver not sparing the lash.

What could it possibly...? The prisoners Elliot had mentioned tickled his mind. Could those elusive figures be more French, running for an escape? But where would they possibly go? For a moment, North was torn. Part of him, the part that had dedicated his life to the service of his country, urged him to investigate further. But another part, the part that was still raw and bleeding from the shock of seeing Amelia, wanted nothing more than to turn away, to flee this place and all its painful memories. He'd have chased after that coach and begged them to take him with them, if he'd been fast enough.

In the end, it was a moment of sudden, startling clarity that decided him. He stood in the stillness of the winter landscape, his breath clouding in the frigid air as his thoughts churned. Running away had never brought him peace. All it had done was leave him haunted, forever chasing the ghosts of his past.

And what was it Captain Hunt had said? Keep his eyes open... notice things.

Owen lowered his head and banged it against the tree. *Blast!* This was one thing he could have happily done without noticing. Now, even if he *could* flee town on the mail coach today, there was no hope of doing so without practically violating orders.

No, if he wanted to find any measure of solace or purpose or satisfaction, he would have to search out what was truly going on. And perhaps, if he were very fortunate, he would solve the nagging curiosity of that fool letter that had brought him back here in the first place.

With a curse under his breath, North squared his shoulders and set off across the field, his boots crunching through the snow with renewed purpose.

THE PALE WINTER SUN had barely begun to peek over the horizon when Amelia stepped out into the frigid morning air, her breath puffing in clouds before her face. The farm lay still and silent, blanketed in a layer of fresh snow that glittered like diamonds in the weak light. Last night's snowstorm had raged and howled over the countryside until the shutters rattled and gusts leaked around the cracks in the windowpanes, but now all was calm and still, with the silvery light of day making everything sparkle.

Amelia paused for a moment on the porch, her eyes drifting to the window of Ethan's room. The events of the previous day weighed heavily on her mind—the trip into town, the visit to the apothecary, the unexpected encounter with Lord Ashwood. She couldn't shake the feeling that she had made a terrible mistake, that by exposing Ethan to the cold and the excitement, she had somehow worsened his condition.

The memory of his labored breathing, the way his small body had shaken with the force of his coughs—it was enough to make her heart clench with fear and guilt. If anything happened to him, if she lost him...

With a shuddering breath, Amelia pushed the thought away. She couldn't afford to dwell on such dark possibilities, not when there was work to be done. And so, with a final, worried glance at Ethan's window, she stepped off the porch and into the waiting day.

The morning passed in a blur of familiar chores—feeding the chickens, milking the cow, breaking the ice in the water troughs for the sheep. It was hard, physical labor, but she welcomed it, relished the burn of her muscles and the sting of the cold air in her lungs. It kept her mind from wandering, from fixating on the fears that lurked at the edges of her consciousness.

She was just finishing up with the sheep, her hands red and chapped from the icy water, when the jingling of harness bells broke the stillness of the morning. Amelia looked up, her brow furrowed in confusion. Who could possibly be visiting at this hour, and the morning after a storm?

As the sleigh drew closer, the coat of arms on the door became clear, and Amelia's stomach dropped. Lord Garrison Ashwood. What in blazes could he want with her again so soon? He could not be thinking that her acceptance of a ride in his carriage yesterday was anything more than a desire to spare Ethan another long walk... could he? What could he possibly want with her now, after all these years?

Amelia watched, her heart in her throat, as the sleigh glided to a stop before the house. Lord Ashwood himself was driving the team, and he tipped his hat to her as he looped the reins and stepped down. His tall, broad-shouldered form cut an impressive figure against the snow-covered landscape.

Though he was broaching his early fifties now, he was just as handsome as ever, with his chiseled features and piercing blue eyes. But there was a new gravitas to him now, a sense of purpose and authority that spoke of the years that had passed since her father had first pledged her hand to the man.

"Amelia," he said warmly, striding towards her with an arm outstretched. "What a pleasure to see you again."

"Lord Ashwood," she managed, dipping into a perfunctory curtsy. "This is... unexpected to see you again so soon."

Ashwood chuckled. "Please, Amelia. We are old friends, are we not? Call me Garrison."

Amelia swallowed hard, her throat suddenly dry. "Garrison, then. To what do I owe the pleasure of this visit?"

Ashwood's smile softened, his gaze turning almost tender. "Why, to bring you and your son a bit of Yuletide cheer, of course. I come bearing gifts, as any good friend ought to do."

He gestured to the carriage, where a footman was unloading a series of packages and parcels. Amelia's eyes widened as she took in the bounty—a thick, woolen cloak in a rich shade of green, a stack of leather-bound books, a basket overflowing with exotic herbs and spices.

"I... I can't accept this," she stammered, her cheeks flushing with a mixture of embarrassment and unease. "It's too much, too generous. You have no connection to us—it is not proper."

Ashwood waved away her protests with a dismissive gesture. "Nonsense, my dear. It's the least I can do, after... well, after everything that has passed between us."

There was a weight to his words, a hint of something deeper lurking beneath the surface. Amelia felt a shiver run down her spine, a prickle of awareness that had nothing to do with the cold.

"I know that things ended badly between us," Ashwood continued, his voice low and earnest. "And for that, I take full responsibility. I was too hasty, too demanding, and you were but a lass of seventeen. Rather brutish of me, I think, expecting you to be happy to marry a man so much older than yourself. I always wondered what might have come if... well. If I had been more patient, and only waited long enough to learn..." He cleared his throat, tipping his head toward the house.

Amelia ducked her face. No, she had not told him why she was breaking off their engagement. Nor had she told her father... until the truth became obvious to everyone. "I doubt time would have altered your feelings on the matter, sir. I tried to spare you the disgrace."

"Disgrace?" He took a step closer, his eyes searching her face. "No such thing. I want you to know that I bear you no ill will, Amelia. That I only wish for your happiness, and for the well-being of your son."

Amelia's heart clenched at the mention of Ethan, her mind flashing back to his pale, exhausted face as he slept by the fire. The herbs, the books—they were practical gifts, things that could bring comfort and healing to her ailing child. Could she really afford to refuse them, to let her pride and her unease stand in the way of Ethan's well-being?

"I... thank you, Garrison," she said at last, her voice thick with emotion. "Your generosity is... it's appreciated, truly."

Ashwood's face split into a wide smile, his dark eyes sparkling with something like triumph. "Think nothing of it, my dear. It is my pleasure, truly."

He reached out, his gloved hand brushing against her arm in a gesture that was at once familiar and unsettling. "I only hope that, in time, we can rebuild what was once between us. That we can be friends again, as we used to be."

Amelia forced a smile, her skin tingling where he had touched her. "Of course," she said, the words feeling hollow and false on her tongue. "Friends. I... I would like that very much."

Ashwood's grin widened, his hand lingering on her arm for a moment longer than was strictly necessary. "Excellent. Then I shall take my leave, and let you get back to your day."

He bowed, his eyes never leaving her face. "Until next time, Amelia. Take care of yourself, and of young Ethan."

And with that, he was gone, striding back to his sleigh with a jaunty wave.

She watched the sleigh out of sight as the bells jingled merrily on the harness, but it was not from some sense of fascination or delight. She was... well, she was grateful, surely, particularly on Ethan's behalf.

But what did Ashwood really want from her? Once, he had wanted her youth and innocence, but those things were hers no longer. He already had his heir—a man grown and living in London, the last she heard. He did not need a young wife to bear him another. With his wealth, if he wanted for company, he could have any woman he desired, heiress or mistress or anything in between. So, why would he want *her*, a poor single mother who had already refused him once before? And what would be the price of accepting his generosity, his friendship?

Amelia shook her head, trying to clear her thoughts. There would be time enough to worry about such things later. For now, she had a sick child to tend to, and a farm to run. And so, with a final, troubled glance at the retreating sleigh, Amelia gathered up the packages and made her way back to the house.

Chapter Seven

NOTHING. A WHOLE BUSHEL of nothing.

That was what he had been able to discover so far. Owen had followed the wagon tracks leading away from the village as far as the turnpike, but from there, the roads were glare ice, all packed down from the passage of other carriages and hooves. He had hiked up to a nearby slope to try to spy out the cart in the distance, but it was as if it had simply vanished. How could that be possible? It was no gentleman's gig, no fine sleigh that could slip over the icy terrain at any speed. Good heavens, even the horse, if he had caught sight of it properly, was no gallant steed but a hoof-dragging plug.

So where could the cart, with its evasive passengers, have gone?

He'd paced down the south road about a mile, until the coming storm drove him back. A Dales snowstorm was nothing to trifle with, and he was already frozen to his marrow. Best turn back, before his bleeding curiosity killed him. Heavens, he did not even know if there was anything to be found! Two men riding in a cart was not against the law.

It was just dashedly interesting, in light of other considerations.

Hours later, Owen had kicked off his boots at the door of his mother's cottage and retired. He needed to eat something, but he needed sleep more. When was the last time he'd had more than two hours? An officer short on sleep made poor decisions, but rest seemed elusive. His mind was a whirlwind of questions and possibilities, and the cryptic letter only added to his restlessness.

He paced back and forth in his dimly lit room, the flickering candlelight casting dancing shadows on the walls. The chill in the air seeped through the windowpane, but he hardly noticed. Eventually, he edged onto the bed, scrubbing his face with his hands and trying to order the jumble of his thoughts. He needed answers, and he needed them soon, so he could leave this miserable village behind for good.

But fatigue eventually got the better of him, for his thoughts were no longer his own to master. Before a moment had passed, they drifted to that other matter—the one that had been plaguing him for years. The thing that had kept him away from home for far longer than he'd initially intended.

Amelia.

The woman he could not dare to love.

If he had left her with a broken heart, she had wrenched his from his chest and cast it into the sea. He never should have... it was a mistake. One that no amount of time could erase.

But he wasn't sure he really wanted to forget. That one moment, when she was his, would have to be his consolation forever.

It was probably a sin to think about another man's wife like that. She was married to someone else now, for heaven's sake! Someone who could do better for her than a wandering lieutenant, who never had a home that he did not abandon. She was better off, happily married with a home of her own and a husband who was there every night—a fact that gnawed at him every time the sun set on another day.

He closed his eyes and called to mind the way she had looked today—the ruddy wisps of her hair catching the pale sunlight, her face as gentle and peaceful as it had ever been. But what ached most was the sight of her with a child, a little boy holding her hand.

It was a sight that tore at his very soul. A mother... she was a *mother* now, and that meant she was as far from him as she could ever possibly be. He'd been away for so long, and their separation had been bitter. Still, seeing her with another man's child was a stark reminder of all that he had lost.

North lay back on his bed, staring at the ceiling, his mind a battleground of emotions. The mystery of the letters and the strange visitor could wait; for now, his heart was consumed by the ache of lost love and the haunting image of Amelia, the woman he could never forget.

A MELIA SAT AT THE kitchen table, the old ceramic money jar before her on the table like a silent sentinel, its contents a meager testament to the hard work and sacrifice that had become her daily existence.

With a heavy sigh, she reached for the jar, her fingers trembling slightly as she removed the wooden lid. The sight that greeted her was a disheartening one—a handful of coins, their dull surfaces seeming to mock her with their scarcity. It was barely enough to cover the most basic of expenses, let alone the looming costs of the upcoming lambing season.

In only a few months, she would have to hire help for shearing and lambing. And buy more molasses cake for the lambs, because early in the spring, the fields of her farm carried something deadly, infecting the lambs until they coughed out their little lives with husk. Her father had learned years earlier that they could not pasture their lambs early in the spring, and that was why the Grey farm thrived when some did not. She bore the expenses of feeding bought food instead of the free grass, until her lambs were stronger, and the grass had lost whatever toxic qualities it carried in the spring.

But in order to preserve this year's flock, she would have to buy more cake and hire more help—all things she would not be able to afford after the expenses of winter.

Amelia's mind raced as she mentally calculated the funds she had compared to the bills that needed to be paid. The farm's needs were endless—feed for the animals, repairs to the barn, repairs to tools and the shed roof, and probably even an animal leech in case the lambs took ill. And then there was Ethan, who required medicines and warm clothing and a thousand other small comforts that she could scarcely afford.

How was she to manage it all on her own, with a sickly child to care for and a farm that demanded every ounce of her strength and attention?

Unbidden, her gaze drifted to the lavish gifts that sat on the nearby sideboard—the elegant woolen cloak, the stack of leather-bound books, the basket overflowing with exotic herbs and spices. Lord Ashwood's generosity, while undeniably useful, left a bitter taste in her mouth, a reminder of the life her father had always wanted for her.

He had been so certain that marrying into Lord Ashwood's wealth and status was the key to happiness for her, the only path worth pursuing. And when she had rejected that path, had chosen to cling to what little dignity remained to her when she had discovered her pregnancy, rather than grasping for the security and comfort of a quick and advantageous marriage... well, Papa had been quick to voice his disapproval.

Even now, more than a year after his passing, Amelia could still hear his words echoing in her mind, sharp and cutting as a winter wind. "You've thrown away your future, girl," he had said, his eyes cold and unforgiving. "Ruined yourself for a moment's pleasure, and now you'll pay the price."

And pay she had, in a thousand small ways and a few larger ones. The sting of her father's rejection still lingered, a wound that had never fully healed. She could still remember the way he had looked at her after Ethan's birth, the disgust and disappointment that had clouded his features as he turned his back on her and her newborn son.

Amelia's heart clenched at the memory, a hot rush of anger and sorrow rising up to choke her. She had shamed him—he had never forgiven her for having a child out of wedlock. Indeed, it was the last thing she would have thought herself capable of, behaving with such impropriety that such a thing could ever be, but she had never been able to feel sorry for the outcome. She would take Ethan and all the disgrace her father and others might heap upon her a thousand times over, rather than contemplate marriage to Lord Ashwood.

She'd begged her father not to pledge her hand to the man in the first place. How she had wept and pleaded! Perhaps it *was* selfish of her to fall into Owen's arms in consolation, but she still stoutly swore that if her father had not forced her into an engagement she never wanted, things never would have gone that far. She never would have...

Well. It hardly mattered now.

A soft whimper from the adjoining room pulled Amelia from her bitter musings, and she rose swiftly to her feet. Ethan lay on the narrow bed, his small face pale and pinched in the weak light. She perched on the edge of the mattress, her hand resting gently on his forehead as she checked for fever.

His skin was cool to the touch, thank the heavens, but the persistent rattle in his chest as he breathed sent a spike of fear through her heart. How much longer could his frail body withstand the constant strain of illness, the unrelenting toll of a life lived in skimmings and hard work?

Amelia closed her eyes, fighting back the hot sting of tears. What kind of mother was she to bring a child into a world so fraught with struggle and pain? What kind of life could she hope to give him, when every day was a battle just to keep food on the table and a roof over their heads?

Perhaps... perhaps she could show a little friendliness to Lord Ashwood. Just out of gratitude for his recent kindnesses. It might not be the *worst* thing she had ever done.

O WEN HUNCHED OVER THE small writing desk, his pen poised above a blank sheet of paper. He had intended to write a report, to document the strange events that had brought him back here. But as the minutes ticked by, he found his thoughts drifting, pulled inexorably towards the one subject he had tried so hard to avoid.

Amelia.

The mere whisper of her name was enough to send a shiver down his spine, to conjure a flood of memories that he had spent years trying to suppress. The curve of her smile, the melody of her laughter, the silken warmth of her skin beneath his fingertips—they all came rushing back, as vivid and visceral as if she were standing right before him.

No!

With a grunt of frustration, North shoved back from the desk, the chair scraping harshly against the rough wooden floor. He couldn't afford to indulge in these sentimental musings, not when there was work to be done. He had a mission to complete, a mystery to unravel. And dwelling on the past, on the love he had lost and the future he had thrown away, would do nothing but distract him from his purpose.

So... what *was* his purpose? Why was Hunt so keen on sending him back here instead of letting him take the next assignment immediately? He racked his memory.

Something to do with smuggling. A commercial port at Kingston upon Hull... not the usual place for smuggling, particularly anything having to do with the French. It was not practical—too few coves in which to hide, and the route would take any ships directly past naval shipyards. A fool's errand, trying to smuggle out of there. Unless the cargo was something that did not look like contraband.

That was, of course, assuming that there was some connection between the mission he had expected to receive, and this goose chase Hunt had sent him on. There probably wasn't. Probably...

Owen sighed and paced to the window, where he could overlook his mother's snow-covered garden and stare right into Elliot Barrow's kitchen window. The young man was pouring a kettle, and never even noticed Owen staring at him.

Dash it all, he was going to have to investigate that rumor Elliot had told him about. With those men running off in a snowstorm and that odd little reluctance of Hunt's to tell him more than to keep his eyes open, how could he do aught else? And there was still the matter of that wretched letter that had proved the excuse to send him here in the first place.

He needed information, needed to find out who had sent that cryptic letter, warning him of his mother's safety a year after her death. And the only way to do that was to get out there and start asking questions, to probe the seedy corners of this village until he found the answers he sought.

Elliot Barrow knew people. He probably knew everyone in town. Who else could he talk to? The village blacksmith, the publican, the apothecary... all people who knew how the folk in town really lived. Who ate at their board, who was causing problems in town. Gossips... he needed gossips.

North grabbed his coat and hat from the hook by the door. He would start with the pub, the place where gossip and rumors flowed as freely as the ale. If there were secrets to be uncovered, the local tap was always the place to look.

Chapter Eight

Amelia clutched Ethan's hand more tightly as she hurried through the bustling market square, the basket on her other arm almost making her elbow go numb with the weight of her precious jams.

She had been saving these jams for months, hoarding them away like a squirrel preparing for a long, harsh winter. This was the last of them—her emergency stash, her final line of defense against the lean times that always seemed to come, no matter how hard she worked or how carefully she planned. But now, with hay for the ewes dwindling and the debt she owed the apothecary for Ethan's medicine, she had no choice but to sell them. It was that or be tempted to let Lord Ashwood help... and though it presented a simple solution to so many problems, she could not bring herself to that. His help would not come freely.

As she approached the bookseller's shop, she felt a pang of guilt, a twinge of unease at what she was about to ask. Mr. Hanley was a kind man, a gentle soul who had always had a soft spot for Ethan and his precocious love of learning. But she hated to impose on his goodwill, to ask for favors when she had so little to offer in return.

Taking a deep breath, she pushed open the door, the tinkling of the bell above her head announcing her arrival. Mr. Hanley looked up from the book he was reading, his eyes crinkling in a warm smile as he saw her.

"Mistress Grey!" he exclaimed, setting the book aside and rising to greet her. "Back again so soon? And how is young Ethan today?"

Amelia's throat tightened, her eyes stinging. "He's... he's doing as well as can be expected," she managed, her voice rough. "But the cold air, it's hard on his lungs. I was hoping... I hate to ask, but I must go to the market, and I was wondering if he could sit here for a while, just to keep warm?"

Mr. Hanley's face softened. "Of course—be right glad of the help, to be truthful. He can help me organize some shelves."

A rush of gratitude warmed her, a wave of relief that threatened to bring her to her knees. "Thank you," she choked. "Thank you so much!"

She hurried back outside, to where Ethan was waiting patiently by the door. "Come on, love," she said, taking his hand and leading him inside. "Mr. Hanley says you can stay here for a bit while I go to the market."

Ethan's face lit up, his eyes sparkling with excitement. "Really? Can I pick out a book to read?"

Amelia ruffled his hair with her free hand. "I am sure he would not mind that very much. He might even help you with the big words, if you will be a good lad and earn your keep while you are there."

"I will!" he promised.

She watched as Ethan scampered off, his small form disappearing among the towering shelves of books. Then, with a final nod of thanks to Mr. Hanley, she slipped back out into the cold.

The market was already in full swing by the time she arrived, the stalls packed with shoppers haggling over prices and vendors hawking their wares. Amelia made her way through the crowd, her basket clutched tightly to her chest as she searched for a likely buyer.

She had just begun to despair of ever finding someone willing to pay a fair price for her jams when a voice called out to her from across the square.

"Oi, Mistress Grey! That's some fine-looking preserves you got there!"

Amelia turned, her eyes widening as she saw Mr. Wallis, the owner of the village pub, waving at her from his doorway. He was a large man, with a ruddy face and a booming voice that carried easily over the noise of the crowd.

"How much for the lot of 'em?" he called, gesturing to her basket with a meaty hand.

Amelia hesitated, her mind racing as she tried to calculate a fair price. She didn't want to seem too eager, too desperate for the sale. But at the same time, she couldn't afford to turn down a good offer, not when her need was so great.

"Two shillings for the basket," she said at last, her voice ringing out clear and strong. "And not a penny less."

The publican's eyebrows shot up, his mouth twisting in a considering frown. For a moment, she thought he might refuse, might try to haggle her down to a lower price. But then he shrugged, a grin splitting his face from ear to ear.

"Fair enough, missus. Bring 'em inside, and I'll get you your money."

Relief surged so strongly it nearly brought tears to her eyes. All sold in one shot for a fair price! And one still secreted in her pocket for the apothecary! She followed the pub owner inside, blinking as her eyes adjusted to the dim, smoky interior.

The pub was nearly empty at this hour, with only a few regulars nursing pints at the bar. The owner led her to a small table in the back, gesturing for her to set her basket down.

"Wait here," Wallis said, disappearing into a back room. "I'll be right back with your money."

Amelia sat down, her hands twisting nervously in her lap. What luck! Could it really be this easy? She just wasn't used to things going to plan or hope. But when the publican returned, he had a small pouch of coins in his hand, and a smile on his face. "Two shillings, as agreed," he said, pressing the pouch into her hand. "You look right done in, Mistress Grey. I'll have Millie fetch you a cuppa before you go."

"Oh, no, really, that is not—"

"And if you ever care to sell more, come straight here first. I'll give you a fair price. Pleasure doing business with you, missus."

Amelia stammered out a thank you, her fingers closing around the pouch with a sense of disbelief. She had done it. She had sold her jams, had earned enough money to keep them afloat for a little while longer. She wanted to hurry back to Ethan, but the publican was already sending the barmaid to fetch a kettle, and... well, it would be rude to just leave.

She found a seat at the small table at the back of the pub, clutching the pouch of coins in her lap. The pub was crowded and noisy, the air thick with the scent of smoke and spilled ale. She kept her head down, her eyes focused on the worn wood of the table in front of her. She didn't want to draw attention to herself, didn't want to invite the curious stares and whispered speculations of the other patrons.

But a hot mug of comfort—tea with a little something "extra" added to it—that sounded heavenly before she had to take that long walk back home. She could afford to stay a little longer, surely.

But even as she tried to make herself invisible, she could feel the weight of someone's gaze upon her, a prickling sensation that made the hairs on the back of her neck stand on end. Slowly, almost reluctantly, she raised her head, her eyes scanning the room with a sense of growing unease.

And then she saw *him*.

He was standing by the bar, his broad shoulders and tall frame unmistakable even in the dim light of the pub. His hair was a little longer than she remembered, his face a little more weathered and careworn. But there was no mistaking those piercing blue eyes, the way they seemed to look straight into her soul.

Owen North... *Lieutenant* North now, if the rumors were true, though how he could have earned such a rank with no sponsor or property of his own was the subject of derision anytime it was brought up. *She* had never been surprised to hear it, for if anyone could make something of himself, it was Owen... the man who had haunted her dreams and her memories for so long—the man she had never thought to see again.

For a moment, Amelia couldn't move, couldn't breathe. The world had tilted on its axis, as though everything she thought she knew had been called into question by the mere sight of him. Memories rushed back, unbidden and unwanted—those stolen kisses in the hayloft, whispered promises under the stars, the feel of his hands on her skin and the taste of his lips against hers.

She had loved him once, had given him everything she had to give. And he had left her, just as she had meant to leave him. The pain of that betrayal still stung, even after all these years. Which of them had abandoned the other first? It was probably her, but... well, hang it all, *he* was the one who disappeared off the face of the earth after that night.

His eyes were already fixed on her, his mouth opening slightly as if he were trying to form the letters of her name. He took a step towards her, his expression unreadable as one hand raised in greeting. Oh, no, no, she could not permit this!

Abruptly, she stood, scraping her chair loudly across the floor as she scrambled to her feet. She had to get out of here, had to put as much distance between herself and Owen North as possible. She couldn't let him see the truth in her eyes, couldn't let him know the secret she had kept hidden for so long.

But before she could take more than a step, Mr. Wallis appeared at her elbow, a steaming mug of tea in his hand. "Leaving so soon, Mistress Grey? And here I thought you might stay a while, warm yourself by the fire. Come on, love. This one's on the house."

Amelia froze, her heart pounding in her chest. She could feel North's eyes on her, could sense the weight of his curiosity and confusion. *Mistress Grey*... indeed, Owen had heard. And the questions in his eyes now burned to a fever pitch.

"I... I really must be going," she stammered, her voice sounding small and uncertain even to her own ears. "But thank you for the tea, and for your kindness."

The publican shrugged, a genial smile on his ruddy face. "Suit yourself, Mistress Grey. But you know you're always welcome here."

Amelia nodded, her throat tight. She could feel Owen North's presence behind her, could hear the soft scuff of his boots against the floorboards as he approached. She wanted to turn, to face him and demand answers to the questions that had haunted her for so long. But she couldn't, because he would demand answers of her, too. Answers she dared not give.

"Amelia?" North's voice was soft, almost hesitant.

She froze. *Oh*, what it was to hear her name in his voice again! Her hand quaked on the bag of coins and she pulled them to her chest, clutching that delicious terror close. No, no, no... she could not look him in the eye! But she did swallow and murmur, in a voice that seemed scarcely her own, "Lieutenant."

"I thought... I mean, I assumed you were married. Lady Ashwood now."

Amelia closed her eyes, a wave of pain washing over her. If only he knew the truth, if only he could understand the choices she had made and the sacrifices she had endured. But how could she tell him, how could she bear to see the look in his eyes when he learned of the child she had borne in secret, the son she had raised alone?

"I... no. I am not."

He caught her elbow, tugging gently. "Amelia... I have missed you," he whispered.

She sucked in a breath and jerked away from his hand, more forcefully than she had meant to. "I really must go. Please, Owen. Don't make this harder than it already is."

She could sense his confusion, his frustration, but she couldn't bring herself to look at him, to see the hurt and accusation in his eyes. Instead, she squared her shoulders and pushed past him, her steps quickening as she made her way towards the door.

The cold air hit her like a slap in the face as she stepped outside, the wind whipping at her skirts and sending a shiver down her spine. But even as she hurried down the street, her heart pounding and her eyes stinging with unshed tears, she couldn't shake the feeling of his gaze on her back, couldn't forget the sound of her name on his lips.

Owen North. The man she had loved, the man she had lost. The father of her child, though he would never know it.

And now he was here, in the same village, the same pub. So close, and yet so impossibly far away.

Amelia's mind raced as she made her way back to the bookseller's shop, her thoughts a jumbled mess of fear and longing and bitter regret. She had spent so long burying her past, so long trying to build a new life for herself and her son. And now, with a single chance encounter, it all threatened to come crumbling down around her.

Chapter Nine

OWEN BURST THROUGH THE door out into the street, her name on his lips and one hand outstretched, as if he could stop her. But she was already gone—out of his reach, unless he wanted to run her down like a criminal or an enemy. She was no such thing.

But she had to stop somewhere. Indeed, he was sure that was the sweep of her skirt disappearing around the door of the bookshop. For a moment, he was tempted to follow her, to demand the answers to the questions that burned in his mind. But what would that accomplish? As if he had ever been able to change her mind once she set it.

He didn't want to frighten her, didn't want to force a confrontation that she was clearly trying to avoid. And yet, the revelation that she was still going by her maiden name, that she had never married as he had assumed... it was like a punch to the gut, a startling twist that he hadn't seen coming.

What could it mean? Had the rascal Lord Ashwood used and abandoned her? North would not put it past him. He never understood what Ashwood wanted Amelia for, anyway, save for... the obvious. And if he found a way to get what he wanted from her and still marry some heiress, well...

It would be a simple enough question. Everyone in town knew, surely, who was presently mistress at Ashwood Estate. They probably knew everything there was to know about Amelia Grey and that child he'd seen beside her. Perhaps she was minding the lad for someone else. A neighbor's child, perhaps, or she might have become a governess for one of the wealthier families in the area. Surely, that... that had to be it.

But he could not bring himself to ask the questions. There were some things a man just... could not bear to hear. Not unless it came from her lips, and she clearly had no desire to speak.

What was more, he had made too much of a scene already, blazing across the pub to talk to a woman who fled his sight. Any hope he might have had today of lingering casually and provoking some ale-sodden local to gossip was dashed. He would have to try somewhere else, another day.

With a heavy sigh, North turned and made his way back home, his thoughts churning with a thousand unanswered questions. He had come back for a simple reason—because Captain Hunt wanted him to "visit his mother". But now, it seemed, there were even more mysteries to unravel, even more secrets lurking in the shadows of his past.

As he reached his door, a familiar voice called his name. He looked up to see Elliot waving at him from across the garden fence. "Lieutenant North!" Elliot beamed, a friendly grin on his face. "I was just about to sit down to some stew. Father has gone to the pub for the evening, but I'd a hankering for some company. Care to join me?"

Owen hesitated for a moment, his mind still preoccupied with thoughts of Amelia and the child he had seen with her. But the growling of his stomach reminded him that he hadn't eaten all day, and the thought of a warm meal and some company was suddenly very appealing.

"That would be grand, Elliot," he said, mustering a smile.

"Jolly good. It's my good mutton stew, been simmering all day. Thought Father would be chomping at the bit to sup, but I guess his pint was calling louder." Elliot held the door as Owen came around the little garden gate and up the path to the cottage. "I hope you've still a taste for mutton, after traipsing all over the Continent."

Owen smiled tightly as he hung his hat inside the door. "Never lost it. And I never saw much of the Continent."

"Oh? Thought I heard... well, never mind."

Owen turned. "What was the rumor?"

"Something about you saving some general when his horse was shot from under him in Spain. But, you know, that's only speculation. There's blokes, you know, what cannot fathom how a common fellow like one of our own became a Lieutenant."

Owen accepted the chair Elliot offered him and braced his forearms on either side of the bowl the younger man set before him. "That much of the rumor is not entirely untrue.

But it was not a general. He was a lowly lieutenant, and I merely a plain corporal, by dint of... ahem... rather precise marksmanship skills."

Elliot sloshed some stew into a second bowl for himself and turned around with a quizzical look. "Well, that doesn't match what folk say."

Owen chuckled and picked up his spoon to sample the stew. "I'd imagine not. No, that lieutenant was sponsored by a rather powerful fellow—I am not privy to his name. The lieutenant was put out of action, so he was sent home and given a promotion in rank and a new assignment. When he learned who it was who saved his life, why, he went to this sponsor of his and saw to not only my promotion, but my reassignment. I served the next four years under his command, and a truer, nobler Englishman I've yet to meet."

"Oi, now that's a fine tale." Elliot settled into his chair with satisfaction. "One does like hearing such. And where is this fine officer now? Back in London in some fancy office, I shouldn't wonder?"

Owen shook his head as he swallowed a bite. "Married and retired from service, just this November past."

"Blimey, that's a rum 'un. And now who's to take his place? You?"

"I can hope. But..." Owen cleared his throat and addressed the bowl before him in silence for a moment. "There are complications. Delays. Nothing to bother yourself with, I'm afraid."

"Oh, aye, I understand." Elliot nodded earnestly. "Nothing you can talk about, there it is. And I'm not the man to put my nose where it might get lopped off."

Owen gave a tight smile. "Something like that."

"Right, then. Shall I catch you up on all the village gossip? Must be some reason you've stuck round, after... well, after learning about your mother."

Owen leaned back in his chair, cocking a half-smile at the cheeky fellow. "And what sort of gossip do you fancy might interest me? Any more local farms missing their forced laborers?"

"Not that I've heard, but then, most farmers only come to the bank when they've cash to pay their loans. Rest of the time, it's us trying to chase them down. They've sure a way of up and vanishing come the end of market day."

North chuckled, stirring a rather large chunk of carrot around his bowl in thought. "Indeed. No word on why that mail coach was delayed the other day, is there? I'd a thought of leaving on it, but it never came."

Elliot shrugged vaguely. "Probably a horse threw a shoe. Mail's gone right spotty the last year or so, always some excuse or another."

"Hmm. That would never be tolerated closer to London. I've a mind to make a report about it, but I fancy there's some as don't mind a little less work to be done when the mail is less frequent."

"That, there, is the fact," his companion replied with a wink and a pull at the mug near his hand.

North nodded and let out a sigh before taking another meditative bite of stew. "Elliot," he said after a moment, his voice carefully casual. "What can you tell me about Mistress Grey? The woman who sells the jams in the market?"

Elliot looked up from his bowl, his brow furrowed in thought. "Mistress Grey? Not much, I'm afraid. She keeps to herself, mostly. Doesn't socialize much."

North nodded, his heart sinking. But he couldn't let it go, couldn't shake the need to know more. "And she never married? Never took a husband?"

Elliot shrugged; his expression bemused. "Not as far as I've heard. But there's talk, you know. About that boy of hers."

So, the boy *was* hers. His stomach knotted. "What kind of talk?"

"Oh, you know how folks are around here. Superstitious, like. Some of them say the boy's a changeling, that he's a sickly lad and he's not quite right in the head. But I think it's all bunk, myself. Just a bunch of old wives' tales and gossip."

North swallowed hard, his throat suddenly dry. "And the boy... how old is he? Do you know?"

Elliot thought for a moment, his brow furrowed in concentration. "Can't say for sure, but I'd reckon he's about five or so. Maybe a bit older. Little scrap of a thing, small for his age, I think. They say he can read like a lad twice his age, though, and that's another reason folks are edgy about him."

Five years old. The words echoed in North's mind, a sickening realization dawning with a force that left him reeling. If Amelia had never married, if she had a son of the right age... could it be? Could *he* be the father of her child? It was but a few moments of holding her! But... but it would have been enough, if...

A wave of nausea washed over him, a dizzying sense of panic and confusion that made the room spin. He barely heard Elliot's next words, barely registered the concerned look on the other man's face as he asked if North was feeling ill.

"I'm well enough," North managed, his voice sounding hollow and distant to his own ears. "Just a bit tired, that's all."

"Nothing a bit more stew won't mend." Elliot ladled another generous helping into his bowl, and North smiled gratefully, but could not bring himself to touch it. Aye, if his stomach could do anything but twist and rumble right now, the hot meal would do him good. As it was, though...

He prodded the stew with his fork, forcing himself to focus on Elliot's chatter, to nod and make the appropriate noises of interest as the other man spoke of his work at the bank, of things like gossiping with Widow Westby and arguing with Mr. Boothe about his mortgage that broke up the monotony of his days.

"Oh, that's one." Elliot swallowed, his head dipping in his haste to blurt out the words that must have just come to his mind. "I clean forgot about it a moment ago. Why, you might think working at the bank is all stamps and coins and shuffling paper, but we'd a particular odd thing happen today."

Owen was still dizzy, his skin prickling with fear and awareness as he tried to recall each detail he had observed of Amelia and that boy. The boy had been covered in so many coats and scarves, he'd barely been able to make him out, but Amelia was shivering slightly. She must have given the lad her warmest coat. Odd...

But Elliot seemed not to notice Owen's distraction, and he rattled on with his tale of banking intrigue. "Strangest thing. A large transfer came through, but there was no proper name attached to the account. There are protocols, you know. Rather serious ones, but when I showed it to Perkins, he acted as if it were nothing at all. Tucked the paper into his waistcoat and hurried off to his office."

North finally shook the fog from his head enough to focus his eyes on Elliot. "How large a sum are you talking about?"

"Tremendous. Some fifteen thousand pounds. Had to be an error of some kind."

Owen narrowed his eyes. "That much money is likely tied to some family inheritance, or the sale of a large property."

"Aye, that's probably what it was. Someone slipped up in the clerical process. But Perkins has got it now, and there's a mercy. I should hate to have it laid at my door that I lost someone's fortune." He grinned, leaning forward conspiratorially. "See? Banking can be just as dangerous as soldiering, in its own way."

North forced a laugh, the sound ringing hollow in his ears. But his mind was already racing, already grappling with the implications of Elliot's story. A large, anonymous transfer? In a village like this, where everyone knew everyone else's business? It was strange, to say the least.

But even as he tried to focus on the puzzle, on the mystery that had brought him here in the first place, he couldn't shake the image of Amelia's face from his mind, couldn't forget the way she had looked at him in the pub, with a mixture of fear and longing and bitter regret.

What had happened to her, in the years since he had left? What secrets was she hiding, what burdens was she carrying all on her own?

And the boy... the child who *might* be his son, the living reminder of the moment they had once shared. What kind of life had he had, growing up without a father, with a mother who was shunned and gossiped about by the very people who should have been her support and her solace?

His head pounded with a sudden, overwhelming sense of guilt, a sickening realization of all that he had missed, all that he had thrown away in the name of duty and honor. He had left Amelia to face the consequences of their actions alone, had abandoned her to a fate that he couldn't even begin to imagine.

And now, here he was, stumbling back into her life like a ghost from the past, dredging up all the pain and the heartache that she must have tried so hard to bury.

He couldn't leave things like this, couldn't walk away from her again without at least trying to make things right... assuming he was the one who had wronged her. But how could he even begin to bridge the chasm? Would she even confess the truth of who the child's father was if he went to her again?

But a worse notion tickled his mind. What if he was *not* the father? She had never married, and she was not wanton... Had some other man harmed her and left her? The stew he'd managed to force down his throat felt like a rock. Any thoughts of leaving Yorkshire at once, before unburying his past were now dashed. He owed it to Amelia to at least learn if he was the one who had failed her.

Chapter Ten

THE WIND WHIPPED THROUGH North's hair as he rode the hired horse towards Amelia's farm, his heart pounding in his chest with every hoofbeat. The notion that he *might* be a father, that Amelia had borne his child in secret, had consumed his every waking thought since his conversation with Elliot. He couldn't rest, couldn't focus on anything else until he knew the truth.

As he approached the small, weathered house, a rush of memories flooded his senses. There was the fence, over which they had talked for the very first time when they were scarcely out of leading strings. His mother used to take in washing, and Mr. Grey had just become a widower, his daughter too young to tend such tasks on her own. It was Owen's mother who had taught Amelia how to mind the house when she was but a girl. For three years or better, Mr. Grey hired Owen's mother to come to his smallholding a couple of times a week and put the house to rights, make up some bread, and tend the washing, while Owen and Amelia tagged after her.

By the time Amelia was capable of minding the house on her own, Owen was strong enough to work, too. And so, Mr. Grey had hired him. Owen's throat tightened as he inspected the boards he'd nailed to the side of the cow shed, all those summers ago. Amelia had handed him the nails as he worked, and they'd talked and dreamed, and said any number of silly things it would be best not to recall.

He dismounted, tying his horse to the fence with shaking hands. The door opened before he could even raise his fist to knock, and there she was—Amelia, with her burnished hair hanging wet around her shoulders after a washing, and her blouse damp with the drippings. Her eyes were the same color he remembered—greenish grey, with flecks of gold sparking in them, and her lips softly parted in surprise. She was just as beautiful and just as haunted as she had the day he left.

"Owen," she breathed, her eyes wide with shock and something like fear. "What are you doing here?"

"I had to see you," he said, his voice rough with emotion. "I couldn't just leave, after seeing you in town. I thought... Amelia, I... I've missed you so much."

She shook her head, her hands trembling as she clutched at the doorframe. "You can't be here. Please, Owen, you have to leave."

But before he could argue, before he could beg her to let him in, to let him explain, the sound of a child's coughing echoed from inside the house. Amelia's face paled, and she turned to rush back inside, but North was faster. He caught the door before it could swing shut, his heart in his throat as he stepped over the threshold.

And there, sitting by the fire, was a boy. A boy with Amelia's fiery hair and his own wintry blue eyes. A boy who could only be...

"Mama?" the child asked, his voice curious and a little afraid. "Who's that man?"

Amelia's eyes darted between them, her expression torn and desperate. "Ethan, this is... this is Lieutenant North. He's an old friend of Mama's."

"Nice to meet you, Ethan," Owen said, his voice cracking with emotion. He knelt down before the boy, searching his face for some sign, some confirmation of the truth he already knew. And as he looked into those eyes, those achingly familiar eyes, he knew. There was no doubt in his mind, no question.

This was his son. *Their* son.

Ethan studied him for a long moment, his little brow furrowed in concentration. "Do you like stories?" he asked at last, his voice hesitant but hopeful. "About kings and heroes?"

Owen felt a smile tug at the corners of his mouth, even as tears stung at the back of his eyes. "I do," he said softly. "I like them very much. And I would be honored to tell you one or two, if you'd like."

Behind them, Amelia made a small, choking sound, her hand coming up to dash away a tear. She turned away, moving to the kitchen as if to hide her face, but North couldn't take his eyes off Ethan, off the miracle of his existence.

"I'm sorry," he said to the boy, his voice rough with regret. "I must speak with your mother for a moment. But I promise, I'll come back and tell you those stories. Have we a deal?"

Ethan nodded, his face alight with excitement and anticipation. And as North rose to his feet, as he followed Amelia into the small, cramped kitchen, a swell of love and grief and bitter, aching regret rose up to choke him.

Her back was to him, and one hand was covering her eyes as her shoulders shook. "I told you," she whispered. "You should not have come."

"Why not?" he demanded in a hushed voice. "Because of *him*?" He gestured over his shoulder at the boy, who was playing with a wood carving of a horse.

Her head tipped backward and her back arched, as if she were pleading the heavens for some inspiration. "Him... you... me... a thousand reasons. Why are you here?"

When he did not respond immediately, she tipped her chin around, fixing those green eyes on him with the same sort of gravity she used to employ to force him to tell her all his secrets. And like when he was a lad, he was helpless against her.

"I..." He swallowed. "I had a letter. I think it was about... about my mother."

"She's passed on. A year ago, last November, like my father."

"I know." He eased half a step closer to her. "That is, I did not know about your father, too. I am sorry."

"Sorry does not change the fact that you were not here for her," she accused softly.

"Would that I had been! I was..." He broke off with a hiss. "I cannot even say where I was."

She turned a little more. "Because you cannot recall? A true man of the world now, aren't you?"

"I recall," he growled, his fist clenching despite himself. "I cannot say because I *cannot*, but I recall every frozen bivouac tent, every third-rate coaching inn, every lonely highway and perfumed ballroom. I recall a thousand places and faces—none of them pleasant or by my choice, but all necessary."

"Necessary for what?" She arched a brow. "You certainly earned your accolades, Owen North. Congratulations. Is that what you came here to hear? I am duly impressed with all you have accomplished. My father would be spinning in his grave if he knew. Are you happy now?"

"No! I..." He closed his eyes and forced his hands to unclench. "I came here to see you. To ask you... By heaven, I do not even know where to begin!"

"Most people begin with an invitation. A proper introduction back into the neighborhood circles. They do not gallop up to someone's house after being away for years, just as if they were old friends."

He blinked, studying her. "I thought we *were* old friends."

She shook her head slowly and turned away once more. "Not for many years now. Please, Lieutenant North. There is nothing left for you here."

"That, I am not so sure of. Amelia," he whispered, his voice raw and vulnerable. "Is he... is Ethan... my son? Our son?"

She didn't answer, didn't turn to face him. But he could see the truth in the hunch of her shoulders, in the way her hands shook as she gripped the edge of the worktable. And in that moment, North felt his entire world shatter, felt the weight of his failures and his mistakes come crashing down upon him like a physical blow.

He had failed her. He had failed them both, had left them to face the cruelties of the world alone. And now, standing here in the home she had built without him, he had never felt more lost, more unworthy of the love and the trust she had once placed in him.

AMELIA'S HEART RACED AS she stood at the worktable, her back turned to the man who had once been her entire world. Owen North, here in her home, face to face with the son he had never known. It was a moment she had dreamed of and dreaded in equal measure, a reckoning that somewhere in the dark recesses of her heart, she had always known would come.

She could feel his eyes on her, could sense the weight of his shock and his grief and his desperate, aching need for answers. But how could she give them to him, how could she put into words the years of longing and heartache and bitter, stubborn pride that had kept her silent for so long?

She heard his footsteps, felt the warmth of his presence as he came to stand behind her. And when he spoke, his voice was gentle, almost pleading.

"Amelia, please. I know I have no right to ask, but... why did you never tell me? Why did you keep this from me?"

She closed her eyes, a single tear escaping to trail down her cheek. "Would it have changed anything?" she asked, her voice barely above a whisper. "You had your duty, your honor. And I had mine."

"But I would have helped you," he insisted, his hand coming to rest on her shoulder, warm and solid and achingly familiar. "I would have been there for you, for Ethan. You must know that."

"How? You were a thousand miles away!" She sniffed and lifted her chin, her gaze fixed on the rooster pecking wheat kernels she'd tossed outside in the snow. Her throat knotted around the words, and they came out garbled. "You can have no possible idea... there is no way you could have helped."

"I could have had my pay sent to you..."

"And not to your mother? She depended on what you sent to her to live. You must know that."

She felt the heat of his chest closing in behind her, his voice low in her ears. "Blast it, Amelia, I would have found a way! I thought you were married, out of my reach! And now I learn you were living in disgrace this whole time because of *my* actions? Aye, I think I'd a right to know that I'd done you a righteous disservice."

"To what end?" She whirled on him, catching sight of Ethan sitting by the fireplace and immediately checking her voice. "What would you have done, Owen? Renounced the claims of king and country, come back here and married me? You could not have, even if you had wanted to. Even if I would have permitted it."

Something fractured in his eyes. "Are you saying you would not have accepted me, had I asked?"

"No. I would not have."

He sucked in a shuddering breath and swallowed. "May I know why? I can only assume you managed to spurn Lord Ashwood because he found you with child and discarded you."

"I refused him before he knew about..." her brow creased. "Any of that."

"But why would you have refused me, too? Am I not good enough for you, Amelia? Good enough for a roll in the hay. A tearful farewell. But not good enough for—"

"Stop it!" she snapped, then immediately regretted raising her voice when Ethan's head swiveled her way. "Oh, bother. Ethan, love? Will you fetch Mama some eggs from the coop?"

Ethan's brow puckered. "But we fetch eggs in the morning. I already—"

"Just see if Brownie has laid another one. I heard her clucking a moment ago. Yes, that's a dear. Look carefully, now, and be sure none are hidden in the straw."

Ethan closed the door behind him, and Amelia's expression hardened as she turned her attention back to the soldier standing before her, with a heaving chest and clenched fists. The bounder was not going to leave without an explanation—she knew that all too well. She might as well let him have it.

Owen stepped away, raking his fingers through his hair and taking a moment to breathe, to scrub his face with his hands, before turning back to her. For an instant, no more, his face was everything she had ached for, all these years. The light in his eyes, the concern etched on his forehead, that sweet expressive mouth of his and the strength in those broad shoulders—shoulders she had wept on, so many times.

"Amelia, I did not come up here to cause you trouble," he said as he approached once more, his hands raised in a gesture of truce. "But tell me honestly. You know—you must know—that I heard your name in town, learned you were not married, and saw your child. What would you have thought of me if I had *not* come to talk to you? If I had just brushed it all off and left, as I planned?"

She rolled her eyes and snorted, covering one cheek with her hand. "Oh, Owen, you are good. You always were good. You reason me right into admitting whatever it is you want me to say, and then I wonder how you ever managed to talk me into it."

He edged a step closer. "Is that what happened that night?" he whispered. "I... *talked* you into it?"

Amelia held her breath for a long pulse, then dropped her head. "No. That was me, as much as it was ever you. I will give you that much, Owen North."

"Then give me the right to do what I may. Let me claim my son."

She stiffened. *Claim him?* He could not mean...

"Amelia, you look frightened. Do not think I would take him from you! I only want to give him a name—the name that ought rightfully to be his."

She dropped her shoulders and shook her head, a bitter laugh bubbling up in her throat. "And what kind of life would that be for him, Owen? The bastard son of a soldier and a fallen woman?"

"How is that worse than what he has now? No one claims him now, do they?"

"But people are used to him as Ethan Grey. Heavens, half the old folk around here still think he's a changeling that just appeared on my doorstep. No one questions it anymore, and I don't want them to start all over again."

"You cannot be serious. In a community of farmers, where rams are prized for the quality of their offspring, you cannot tell me that no one ever looked at his eyes and traced a resemblance to me."

She wet her lips. "My... my father did. He'd have tried to kill you if you ever showed your face here while he lived. But he was as happy as anyone to perpetuate old wives' tales and superstitions. I think he added to them with fairy tales of his own, just because his mates bought him drinks at the pub when he set to talking."

Owen stepped boldly closer now, his voice threaded with heat as he dared to reach for her hand. "Superstition and wives' tales might be all well and good here, but when he thinks of becoming a man, he'll want to know what sort of man he might become. I know I always wanted that. Never had it until... well, until I found one I could look up to. Will you not let him have it?"

Amelia hesitated. "But that would mean telling him... things he is not ready to know. I couldn't do that to him. I couldn't bear the thought of him growing up with that shame."

"The only shame is mine," Owen said fiercely, his grip tightening. "The only disgrace is the way I left you, the way I failed to be the man you needed me to be."

"We both made mistakes," she said softly. Oh, she knew better, but just for a moment, it was like the old days, when she could not resist reaching up to cup his cheek with a trembling hand. "We both have our share of guilt to bear."

For a long moment, they simply looked at each other, the years of separation and longing and unspoken regret hanging heavy in the air between them. And then Owen was pulling her into his arms, his face buried in the crook of her neck.

"Forgive me, Amelia!" he wept, his voice shaken. "I beg you, forgive me! I've never stopped loving you for a day, but I've hurt you more than anyone in the world. Please, I... let me make this right!"

Amelia clung to him, her heart aching with the bittersweet joy of having him here, of feeling the strength and solidity of him against her once again. But even as she savored the moment, even as she allowed herself to be swept up in the tide of their emotions, she knew that it couldn't last.

"Owen," she murmured, pulling back to look him in the eye. "You can't stay. You know that."

"I'm not leaving you," he said fiercely, his hands coming up to frame her face. "Not again, not ever. I will do whatever it takes, Amelia. I will make this right."

She wanted to believe him, wanted to trust in the conviction she saw burning in his gaze. But the practicalities of their situation, the harsh realities of their world, could not be ignored.

"And how will you do that?" she asked, her voice trembling with a mixture of hope and fear. "You are under oath, a man bound by duty to do... well, heaven knows what. How long before you must go back to wherever it is you have been?"

He swallowed, stepping back as his head drooped. "Soon... almost immediately."

"Then what can you possibly do but bring more complications to our lives? You cannot stay here, Owen. What do you think to do? Announce to the world that you are Ethan's father, then leave again? We would be worse off than before."

"I would..." He surged forward, reaching for her hands again. "I would give you both my name, Amelia. You could hold up your head."

"I do already. Oh, I am counted indecent for it, but what good do you think you can do now? The harm is done already, and tongues will only wag the more for it, should you try to do the 'honorable' thing now."

"Is that so? You truly need nothing, do you?" He glanced around the small, sparsely furnished room, his expression darkening as he took in the signs of her struggle, of the hardships she had faced alone. And then his gaze fell on the pile of gifts from Lord Ashwood, the fine fabrics and delicacies that she had not yet found the heart to use or dispose of. Then his eyes flicked back to her, a graven question in them that burned her insides with the accusations she found there.

"Owen, it's not what it looks like," she murmured.

"I saw you," he said, his voice low and tense with some emotion she couldn't quite name. "Getting into Ashwood's carriage the other day. Is that lecherous old dog still sniffing after you, even now? Is that how you mean to secure your future, by accepting him at last?"

A hot flush of shame and anger rose up to choke her, a swell of hurt and indignation that made her draw herself to her full height and survey him coldly.

"How dare you," she hissed, her eyes flashing with a fire that had long been banked, but never extinguished. "How dare you question my choices, my actions, after all this time? You gave up your right to have a say in my life the day you walked away from me."

For a moment, Owen looked stricken, his face a mask of guilt and regret. But then his expression hardened, his jaw clenching with a stubborn resolve that she recognized all too well.

"So, I did," he said, his voice cold and clipped. "And I will regret that choice until my dying day."

And with that, he turned on his heel and marched out of the house, leaving Amelia standing alone in the kitchen, her heart shattered and her soul aching with the weight of all that had been lost, and all that could never be regained.

Chapter Eleven

THE MORNING LIGHT FILTERED through the grimy window of North's long-ne-glected room, casting a pale, sickly glow over the scattered papers and empty ink bottles that littered his desk. He had been up all night, his mind churning with the revelations of the past few days, with the weight of the choices that lay before him.

Amelia. Ethan. The family he had never known he had, the life he had left behind in his pursuit of duty and honor. They haunted his every waking thought, their faces floating before his eyes in the flickering candlelight. He could not leave them, could not abandon them to the cruel vagaries of fate once again. But Amelia had made it clear that she wanted no part of him, that she would not accept his help or his presence in her life.

And so, he had thrown himself into his work, into the mystery that had brought him back to this place. He had been making inquiries around the village, listening to the whispers and the rumors that seemed to swirl like fog through the narrow streets and crowded taverns.

Elliot was not the only one to mention strange doings. North had heard it in the pub again this afternoon—two old men hunched over their mugs, talking of French prisoners of war disappearing without a trace from the farms where they had been sent to work. Families woke to find their charges vanished, their beds empty and their belongings untouched. It was as if they had simply evaporated into the ether, leaving no clue as to their fate or their whereabouts.

And he never had got a satisfying answer as to the mail coach, the one that had been expected three days ago. Someone said the postmaster had been beside himself all that day, ranting about lost letters and delayed parcels, but the next day and every day since, the coach had arrived on time with no explanations or excuses offered for the oddity of the missing one.

But it was what Elliot had told him about the bank that truly set North's mind racing, that made the hairs on the back of his neck stand on end. A large sum of money, transferred without explanation or accounting, then vanishing into the void as if it had never existed at all.

With a heavy sigh, North reached for a fresh sheet of paper, his quill poised above the creamy surface. He had to write to Captain Hunt, had to share his suspicions and his fears with the one man who might be able to help him make sense of it all.

But he could not risk putting his thoughts into plain words, could not chance the letter falling into the wrong hands. And so, he wrote in code, in the careful, deliberate language of secrets and subterfuge.

"The flocks are restless this winter," he began, his pen scratching against the paper. "Three local farmers have reported their sheep vanished in the night, with no trace of the beasts to be found."

It was a risk, using such a transparent metaphor. But he had to trust that Hunt would understand, that he would read between the lines and grasp the true meaning of his words.

"And old Widow Sterling is in a right state," he continued, his mouth twisting in a grim smile. "She's been asking everywhere after her lost bag of coins, certain that some light-fingered rogue has made off with her life's savings. But like as not, the blind old bird has simply misplaced it in her dotage."

The reference to the bank transfer was even more oblique, but Hunt would catch the implication. The man had a nose for financial irregularities, for the kind of underhanded dealings that so often lurked beneath the surface of seemingly respectable transactions.

As he folded the letter, a rare moment of vulnerability washed over him, a flicker of doubt and uncertainty that he rarely allowed himself to indulge. If, indeed, any of these peculiar things were connected, then he was in over his head, he knew that now. The mystery that had brought him here, the secrets that lurked in the shadows of this quiet, unassuming village—they were bigger than he had ever imagined, more dangerous than he could hope to face alone.

He needed Hunt's guidance, needed the seasoned commander's wisdom and experience to help him navigate the treacherous waters that lay ahead. He could only pray that his former commander would understand the urgency of his coded message, that he would read between the lines and come to his aid before it was too late.

With a final, resolute nod, North sealed the letter and set it aside, his mind already racing ahead to the next step, the next move in whatever game he had unwittingly stumbled into. He had to find a way to protect Amelia and Ethan from his own folly, and hopefully shield her from her unwanted suitor... assuming Lord Ashwood was still "unwanted." She had refused to tell him.

He couldn't shake the image of Amelia's face from his mind, couldn't forget the hurt and the betrayal he had seen in her eyes. He had failed her once, had left her to face the consequences of their love alone. He would not make that mistake again. No matter the cost, no matter the risk, he would find a way to keep her safe, to give her and their son the life they deserved. And heaven help anyone who stood in his way.

A MELIA'S HANDS MOVED WITH practiced efficiency as she chopped vegetables for the stew, the rhythmic sound of the knife against the cutting board providing a steady backdrop to her wandering thoughts. She grabbed a handful of carrots, their bright orange a stark contrast to the dark, well-worn wood of the countertop.

As she worked, her mind drifted back to her childhood, to the early days of her friendship with Owen. She had been a young girl then, all skinned knees and wild curls, running through the fields of her father's farm with laughter on her lips.

Owen had come into her life like a burst of sunshine. While his mother taught her the things her own mother never had a chance to, Owen became like a brother, a best friend. The one she chased rainbows and caught frogs with. He had been a few years older, with gangly limbs and a mop of unruly hair, but his grin had been infectious and those sky-blue eyes of his had sparkled with mischief.

Amelia smiled softly at the memory, her knife slowing as she lost herself in the past. They had become inseparable, Owen and she, spending every spare moment exploring the woods and streams that bordered the lower pastures. He had taught her how to skip stones across the glassy surface of the pond, his larger hands guiding her own until she could make them dance and leap with a flick of her wrist.

In turn, she had shown him all her secret hiding spots, the places where she would go to escape the watchful eyes of her father. Together, they had built a world of their own, a place where the only thing that mattered was the laughter they shared and the adventures they dreamed up.

As they had grown older, that easy friendship had blossomed into something deeper, something that made Amelia's heart race and her cheeks flush whenever Owen was near. Stolen glances and brushing fingertips had given way to gentle kisses on the cheek and whispered promises, the two of them wrapped in a cocoon of young love and endless possibility.

Amelia sighed, setting down her knife and reaching for an onion. The pungent scent filled her nostrils as she began to chop, her eyes stinging with more than just the acrid fumes.

For as much as she had loved Owen, as much as she had believed in the future they had planned together, she had always known that it could never truly be. Her father had made that clear from the moment he had caught wind of their growing affection, his disapproval a palpable thing that hung heavy in the air between them.

"He has no place here, Amelia," he had said, his voice cold and unyielding. "You've better expectations than that."

Amelia had bristled at his words, her chin lifting in defiance. "What expectations? A farm that is too large for me to manage on my own?"

But he never would say more. He always rattled on about how she was too good for any farm boy or village laborer. Hah! She wondered sometimes if he knew how much money they had in that kitchen jar, because there was nothing about their circumstances that should have made her feel like she was "too good" for anything. Quite the opposite, in fact.

Still, he had refused to let anyone approach her, and most especially Owen North. "You won't be settling for one of these lazy fellows without two copper coins to rub together," he'd said. A bitter laugh bubbled up in her throat as she tossed the onions into the pot, the sizzle of them hitting the hot broth a distant sound to her ears. Her father had been right, in the end. Her future had been decided, but not in the way he had intended.

For it had been Lord Ashwood who had truly sealed her fate, his leering gaze and grasping hands making it all too clear what he desired from her. One moment with someone who loved her... that was all she'd asked for for herself. Just once, to know the embrace of the one man she could love in return, whose kisses she desired, before consigning her fate to a man who would only use her for his own pleasures.

Well... that was how she had fallen. The rest, she had never intended... had even tried to persuade herself she could keep a secret from Ashwood, just to save face for herself. There was a week or two of doubt, when the fear of the unknown loomed before her in the night... when she thought, *perhaps*...

But it was no use. From the moment she knew, for an absolute certainty, that her reckless abandon to Owen's embrace would leave her with a lifetime of memories, she also knew that she could never live a lie as Lady Ashwood. Smiling as a man she did not even like laid claim to every part of her, including her child... no, there had never been a possibility of that.

She stirred the stew with a wooden spoon, the rich aroma wafting up to fill the small kitchen. Ethan had been the result of that passion, the living, breathing proof of the love she and Owen had shared. But he had also been her downfall, the final nail in the coffin of her girlish dreams and hopes for the future. For what respectable man would want a woman with a bastard child, a woman whose reputation had been forever tarnished by the scandal of her own making? Amelia knew the answer to that all too well, had seen it in the pitying looks and whispered gossip that followed her wherever she went.

But even as the weight of her shame threatened to crush her, even as the memories of all she had lost threatened to pull her under, Amelia forced herself to keep moving forward. She had a child to raise and a life to build, and she would not let the mistakes of her past define her future.

With a final stir of the pot, Amelia wiped her hands on her apron and moved to set the table for supper. The stew would be ready soon, and Ethan needed his strength. But as she carried the bowl to the rough-hewn table, as she called for Ethan to come and eat, she couldn't help but let her mind wander one last time. To a future that might have been, to a love that still burned bright and true, even after all the years and all the heartache.

And for just a moment, just a single, fleeting instant, Amelia allowed herself to recall how it was to feel Owen's arms around her once more. That impulsive embrace, the choked pleas in that dear voice she had never thought to hear again...

It was a dream, nothing more. For in the end, it was all she had left. The memory of a love that had once burned brighter than the sun, and the hope, however faint, that it might one day be rekindled.

But as the months had turned into years, as the whispers and the sidelong glances had grown more pointed, more vicious, Amelia had been forced to accept the bitter truth.

Owen was gone, and he was never coming back. She was alone, a fallen woman with a bastard child, a pariah in the eyes of the world.

And so, she had retreated to the small, dilapidated farmhouse on the edge of the moor, had thrown herself into the backbreaking work of survival with a grim, desperate determination. She had poured all of her love, all of her shattered hopes and dreams, into her son, into the precious, innocent life that had become her sole reason for being.

Even if it meant burying her own dreams in the cold, hard ground of reality.

Chapter Twelve

A SHARP RAPPING AT the door jolted Amelia out of her reverie, the sound harsh and jarring in the quiet of the kitchen. She felt a flicker of unease, a prickling sense of foreboding that made her heart skip a beat. There were few who would come calling at this hour, fewer still who would be welcome in her home. *Please, not Owen...* Not so soon, when she was still fragile from her last encounter with him! All it would take would be a smile, a murmured apology, and all her resolve would be as dust.

But when she opened the door, she found herself face to face with a sight that made her stomach churn with a mixture of dread and resignation. Lord Ashwood stood on her doorstep, a basket of lavish gifts cradled in his arms, a smarmy, unctuous smile plastered across his face.

"Mistress Grey, I hope I'm not interrupting your evening repast. My cook had an extra ham smoked, and I could think of nothing but how well it would grace your table. I do hope you will accept it."

Amelia forced herself to smile as he fairly thrust the basket into her hands. "That is too kind of you, Lord Ashwood. Ah... will you not come in?" But even as she set it aside, even as she invited Ashwood in with a gesture that felt like a betrayal of everything she held dear, she could feel the weight of his gaze upon her, could sense the calculation and the cunning that lurked beneath his pious facade.

As Ashwood settled himself at her table, his eyes roving over the humble furnishings and the stack of gifts he had brought earlier in the week with barely concealed interest, Amelia busied herself with the tea things, her hands shaking slightly as she poured the fragrant brew into chipped, mismatched cups.

She knew why he was here, knew what he wanted from her. It was the same thing he had wanted all those years ago, when he had first set his sights on her as a young, innocent girl. He saw her as a prize to be won, a trophy to be claimed and displayed like a shiny bauble on his arm. But why was he back so soon after that last display of... whatever it was?

Amelia set a cup of tea before Lord Ashwood, her movements stiff and formal. She took a seat across from him, her hands clasped tightly in her lap. "I must thank you for the ham, but to what do I *truly* owe the pleasure of your visit, my lord?" she asked, her voice carefully neutral.

Lord Ashwood smiled, his eyes glinting with amusement. "My dear Amelia, you misunderstand me. I seek only to offer my friendship and support, nothing more."

Amelia took a sip of her tea, her expression guarded. "Your friendship is appreciated, Lord Ashwood. But I assure you, Ethan and I are quite content with our simple life. We have no need for lavish gifts which must certainly put you out a great deal more than our desserts."

He leaned forward, his voice low and persuasive. "But think of how much easier that life could be, with a little help. I have connections, resources. I could open doors for you, provide opportunities you've never dreamed of."

She set down her cup, her hands folded primly in her lap. "And what would you expect in return for such generosity, my lord?"

Ashwood spread his hands, a picture of wounded innocence. "Nothing at all, my dear. Can a gentleman not offer his assistance to a lady in need, without ulterior motives?"

"In my experience, men rarely give without expectation of reward. Especially men of your station and influence."

He chuckled, leaning back in his chair. "You wound me, Amelia. I had hoped we could be friends, that you would come to see me as someone you could trust and rely upon."

She met his gaze steadily, her chin lifted. "Trust is earned, Lord Ashwood. Not bought with trinkets and pretty words."

For a moment, something hard and cold flashed in his eyes. But then it was gone, replaced by his usual mask of charming affability. "Of course, of course. You are a woman of principle, and I respect that. Perhaps, in time, you will come to see the purity of my intentions."

He rose to his feet, straightening his coat. "I won't overstay my welcome, Mistress Grey. But know that my offer stands. Should you ever find yourself in need of a friend, my door is always open."

Amelia stood as well, escorting him to the door with a polite smile. "Thank you, Lord Ashwood. I will keep that in mind."

As he stepped over the threshold, he turned back, his hand brushing against hers in a gesture that lingered just a moment too long. "Until next time, my dear."

She inclined her head, fighting the urge to pull away from his touch. "Good day, my lord."

Amelia watched him go, his tall figure stepping into his carriage and the vehicle receding down the path until it disappeared from view. She let out a breath, her shoulders sagging with relief.

That had been a narrow escape. Ashwood's attentions were becoming rather pointed, his overtures more difficult to deflect without giving offense. She would have to tread carefully, to find a way to discourage his interest without provoking his ire.

She glanced at the basket he had left behind. It was not merely a single ham, but rather stuffed with all manner of delicacies from Ashwood Manor's kitchens—extravagant offerings that sat so incongruously in her humble cottage. Perhaps she could sell them, use the money to shore up her meager reserves. It galled her to accept anything from Ashwood, but practicality outweighed pride in this instance.

But even as she unpacked the delicacies, she couldn't shake the feeling that there was something deeply wrong, something rotten and festering at the heart of Ashwood's newfound generosity.

Why now, after all these years of silence and neglect? Why such extravagance, such ostentatious displays of wealth and favor? It made no sense. He could have married again, after she turned him down. Yet he never had, and she'd assumed he never meant to.

Amelia sighed, her shoulders slumping under the weight of her thoughts. She felt trapped, caught between the devil and the deep blue sea, between the gnawing hunger in her belly and the sickness in her soul.

There was no way around it. She did need help, or... or she did not know what was going to happen. She could sell the farm, but she wouldn't get enough from it to go anywhere else. Not enough to support Ethan, to keep him healthy and safe.

There might, indeed, come a day when she had little choice but to accept some man's advances. If only Owen North could truly be what he said he wanted to be for them!

But he was probably more bound by his circumstances than she was. And how had life changed him in the years they had been apart? No, trusting her future and her son's to Owen North was... well, it was even more foolhardy than letting Lord Ashwood bring her gifts.

And if it came to it, if she truly did face a day when she had no other means of providing for Ethan... She set her jaw and stared at the carriage retreating down the snowy lane. She would make that decision if she were forced to. She'd give anything, *do* anything for Ethan's sake.

Even if it meant selling her soul to the devil himself.

T HE COLD, DAMP AIR clung to Owen's skin as he walked the narrow path that wound through the moors, his eyes fixed on the distant outline of Amelia's cottage. He told himself that he was merely checking on Ethan, that he needed to see for himself that the boy and his mother were well and cared for. But deep down, he knew that it was Amelia who drew him like a moth to a flame, Amelia whose presence he craved with a desperation that bordered on madness.

As he drew closer to the cottage, he caught a glimpse of her through the kitchen window, her auburn hair gleaming in the pale morning light. She was kneading bread, her strong, slender hands working the dough with a practiced ease that made his heart ache with longing.

He remembered those hands, remembered the way they had felt against his skin, the way they had clung to him. The regret was a physical thing, a weight that pressed down on his chest until he could scarcely breathe. If only...

Before he could think better of it, North found himself striding towards the cottage door, his heart pounding in his chest. He raised his hand to knock, but before he could make contact, the door swung open, revealing Amelia's startled face.

"Owen," she said, her voice carefully neutral. "I didn't expect to see you again so soon."

He swallowed hard, his carefully rehearsed speech deserting him. "Amelia, I... I wanted to apologize. For yesterday, for the way I barged in and presumed..." He trailed off, swiping off his hat and running a hand through his hair in frustration.

"You mean... like you just barged in again?"

Owen's shoulders sagged. "Uh... Yeah." He swallowed. "Like that. Is he... is he here?"

She sighed. "He's in the barn loft with a kitten he found."

"So... May I speak with you for a moment? Please, Amelia. I shan't stay if you wish me to leave, but just for a moment?"

Amelia's expression softened slightly, but she made no move to invite him in. "What do you want from me? We can't just pick up where we left off, as if nothing has changed."

"I know that," he said quickly. "And I'm not asking for... for anything you're not willing to give. But Amelia, please. All I'm asking for is a chance to know my son. To be a part of his life, in whatever way you'll allow."

Amelia hesitated, her fingers tightening on the doorframe. "Owen, I don't know. Ethan, he... he's sensitive. He feels things deeply. I can't let him get attached, only to have his heart broken when you leave again."

He was stabbed with a pang of guilt, sharp and sudden. "I'm not going to leave, Amelia. Not unless you send me away. I want to be here, for Ethan and for you. I want to make things right."

She searched his face, her eyes dark with conflicting emotions. "And what happens when your commanding officer calls you back to duty? When the Army decides they need you more than we do?"

Owen met her gaze steadily. "Then I'll resign my commission. Or I'll find another way to serve, one that doesn't take me away from my family."

Amelia blinked, clearly taken aback by his declaration. "No, you won't. You think you will, but Owen... We don't even know each other anymore."

"Then let me... let me know you again. Let me know Ethan. You don't have to tell him anything you don't want to, but please... I cannot just leave, knowing what I know now."

For a long moment, she simply stared at him, her expression unreadable. Then, with a sigh that seemed to come from the depths of her soul, she stepped back, opening the door wider. "Come in. We'll talk. But I'm not making any promises."

He nodded solemnly, stepping over the threshold. "I understand, Amelia. And I know how to follow orders."

She gave him a thin smile as she led him to the kitchen table, gesturing for him to sit as she busied herself with the tea things. There was a tension in her movements, a brittleness that spoke of old hurts and long-buried pain.

"Tell me about Ethan," Owen said quietly, watching her hands as they measured out tea leaves. "What is he like?"

Amelia paused, a faint smile touching her lips. "He's... he's everything, Owen. Bright and curious and kind, with an imagination that knows no bounds. He sees the world in a way that most people have forgotten how."

He felt a swell of pride, of longing so acute it stole his breath. "I want to know him. I know you... you said you don't want him to be hurt. But how can I...?"

She set a cup of tea before him, her eyes searching his face. "I don't know, Owen. How do you see this playing out? What do you want from me?"

He met her gaze steadily, his voice low and fervent. "I want a chance, but..." He shook his head. "Never mind. I've no right to ask that."

Amelia was silent for a long moment, her fingers tracing the rim of her teacup. "I can't promise you anything, Owen. But... but I'm willing to let you talk to him. For Ethan's sake. He..." Her brow furrowed. "Someday he might ask about you, and I could at least tell him that he met you once. But please don't frighten him, Owen."

A weight shifted in his chest. "Thank you. I won't."

She smiled then, a small, tentative thing that nonetheless set his heart to racing. "I hope not."

And as they sat there, sipping their tea in the quiet of the cottage kitchen, a flicker of hope kindled in his chest. It was a fragile thing, a tiny spark amidst the darkness that had consumed him for so long. But it was there, and it was real, and for now, that was enough.

Chapter Thirteen

O WEN FOLLOWED AMELIA OUT to the barn, his heart pounding with anticipation and trepidation. This was the moment he had been both longing for
and dreading—his first real encounter with the son he had never known.

As they entered the dim, musty space, he caught sight of Ethan perched in the
loft above, his small form hunched over something in his lap. At the sound of their
footsteps, the boy looked up, his eyes wide and curious.

"Ethan," Amelia called softly, "there's someone here who'd like to talk to you."

The boy climbed down from the loft with the agility of a squirrel, a tiny kitten
cradled gently in the crook of his arm. He approached them cautiously, his gaze
darting between his mother and the tall, unfamiliar man at her side.

"You remember Mr. North from yesterday?" Amelia said, her hand resting lightly
on Ethan's shoulder. "He's... an old friend of mine."

North crouched down to the boy's level, a warm smile spreading across his face.
"Hello, Ethan. It's a pleasure to make your acquaintance."

Ethan studied him for a moment, his head tilted to one side. "Are you a soldier?"
he asked, his voice filled with innocent curiosity.

"I... yes, I am. Or at least, I was. How did you know?"

Ethan shrugged, a small smile tugging at his lips. "You stand like a soldier. Straight
and tall, like a knight."

North chuckled, a swell of pride and affection blooming in his chest. "Well, you're
a very observant young man, aren't you?"

The kitten in Ethan's arms chose that moment to let out a plaintive mew, drawing the boy's attention back to his furry charge. "I found her in the loft," he explained, gently stroking the kitten's head with one finger. "She was all alone, and she looked hungry. I'm going to take care of her."

Owen's heart clenched at the tenderness in Ethan's voice, the gentle way he cradled the tiny creature. This was a child who knew what it meant to feel lost and alone, to yearn for love and protection. "That's very kind of you," he said softly, reaching out to scratch the kitten behind the ears. "Every living thing deserves to be cared for, don't you think?"

Ethan nodded solemnly, his eyes shining with a wisdom beyond his years. "Yes. Even the small and helpless ones. Especially them."

Amelia cleared her throat, drawing their attention back to her. "Ethan, why don't you show Mr. North what you were working on in the loft? I'm sure he'd be interested to see it."

Ethan's face lit up with excitement. "Oh! Yes, come and see!" He turned and scampered back up the ladder, the kitten still held securely against his chest.

Owen glanced at Amelia, a silent question in his eyes. She nodded, a small, encouraging smile on her lips. "Go on. I'll be right here if you need me."

With a grateful nod, he followed Ethan up into the loft, his heart pounding with a fierce, protective love he had never known he could feel. This was his son, his own flesh and blood. What he would give to be the father the boy deserved! How had a handful of seconds overturned everything he had ever wanted or hoped for? The Army could go hang. Promotions, accolades—he wanted none of them. But to watch this small version of himself grow up... why, that would be...

Everything.

As he reached the top of the ladder, Owen found Ethan seated cross-legged on the rough wooden floor, a small carving knife in his hand. Scattered around him were bits of wood and shavings, evidence of a project in progress.

"What are you making?" he asked, settling down beside the boy.

Ethan held up a half-formed piece of wood, his brow furrowed in concentration. "It's going to be a toy for the kitten," he explained. "A little mouse she can chase and play with."

A smile tugged at his lips. "That's a wonderful idea. May I see?"

Ethan hesitated for a moment, then handed over the carving. Owen turned it over in his hands, marveling at the skill and detail that had gone into its creation.

"This is excellent work, Ethan," he said sincerely. "You have a real talent."

The boy ducked his head, a pleased flush spreading across his cheeks. "I make up stories for them when I carve them."

Owen nodded, understanding all too well the need for a creative outlet, a way to quiet the tumult of the mind. "I know what you mean. When I was your age, I used to carve little soldiers out of wood. It was my way of imagining the adventures I wanted to have."

Ethan's eyes widened, a spark of excitement flickering in their depths. "You did? Could you... could you show me how?"

"Of course. I'd be honored to share what I know with you."

And so, as the morning sun climbed higher in the sky, filtering through the cracks in the barn walls, Owen and Ethan sat side by side, their heads bent together over the small wooden figure. Owen guided the boy's hands with a gentle touch, showing him how to hold the knife just so, how to let the grain of the wood guide the blade.

They talked as they worked, their conversation flowing easily from topic to topic. Owen told stories of his childhood, of the mischief he and his friends from the village used to get up to. Ethan listened with rapt attention, his eyes shining with laughter and delight.

In turn, the boy shared his own tales—of the adventures he had with his imaginary friends, the far-off lands he visited in his dreams. North marveled at his son's vivid imagination, the boundless creativity that seemed to pour out of him like water from a spring.

As the hours passed and the kitten dozed contentedly in a patch of sunlight, Owen North felt a sense of peace, of rightness, settle over him. This was where he belonged, here with his son, sharing in the simple joys of creation and connection. For the first time in longer than he could remember, he felt a sense of purpose, of hope for a future that had once seemed lost to him.

But how the devil was he to grab hold of this life and make it his own once more when he owed his life to the crown? He had nothing... *was* nothing without his uniform. Heavens, he scarcely had enough coin to his name to pay for his fare and lodging back to London to resume his duty! How could he be anything to Amelia and his son but a burden?

But another look at Ethan's earnest blue eyes as the boy gazed up at him, and all his objections crumbled, the weight of reality shifting into some dreamscape where obligation and duty would fall away at his pleasure. There must be something... some way he could hang on to at least a small measure of this sort of heaven.

Amelia found them there some time later, the two of them so engrossed in their task that they barely noticed her approach. As she climbed the ladder to the barn loft, she heard laughter—Ethan's bright, infectious giggle mingling with a deep, rumbling chuckle that could only belong to one man.

She reached the landing and paused, her breath catching in her throat at the sight before her. Owen and Ethan sat side by side, their heads bent together over a piece of wood that Ethan was carving. Owen was gesturing animatedly, his face alight with a smile that made Amelia's heart ache with bittersweet longing.

"...and then, the evil Black Bess let out a whistle that sounded like a banshee's wail," Owen was saying, his voice low and conspiratorial. "The carriage horses froze in their traces, too terrified to move a muscle!"

Ethan giggled, his eyes wide with delight. "You're making that up!" he accused, grinning up at Owen with unabashed adoration.

Owen placed a hand over his heart, his expression one of mock solemnity. "On my honor as a soldier, I swear it's the truth."

"What happened after that?"

"Well, the noble Captain called for his best soldier, the brave lieutenant, and together, they captured the wicked highwayman, so the highways were safe for good people to travel once again."

"Did they rob from the rich and give the poor?" Ethan asked, digging his carving knife into a soft corner of the wood and then glancing back up at Owen as if every word from the man's mouth were the éclat of a prophet.

"Well, they *did* return everything that was stolen," Owen replied with a low chuckle. He looked up then, his gaze locking with Amelia's. Something flickered in his eyes—a warmth, a tenderness that made her breath hitch in her chest.

Clearing his throat, Owen stood, dusting off his trousers. "I should go," he said softly, his eyes never leaving hers. "Your mother and I have some things to discuss."

Amelia nodded mutely, not trusting her voice. She watched as Owen ruffled Ethan's hair, murmuring a goodbye before crossing to the ladder.

They descended in silence, the air between them heavy with unspoken words. When they reached the ground, Owen turned to her, his expression earnest.

"Amelia, I just want to say... Ethan is an amazing boy. You've done an incredible job raising him."

She felt a lump form in her throat, tears pricking at the corners of her eyes. "I know," she whispered, her voice rough with emotion.

For a long moment, they simply stared at each other, the years of separation and heartache stretching out between them like an uncrossable chasm.

Then, softly, Owen broke the silence. "Why didn't you tell me, Amelia? Why didn't you write, or send word through my mother?"

Amelia closed her eyes, a single tear slipping down her cheek. "Your mother knew, Owen. From the moment she saw Ethan's eyes, she knew he was yours."

Owen paled, his eyes widening with shock. "She... she knew? All this time?"

Amelia nodded, her shoulders sagging under the weight of her confession. "I begged her not to tell you. There was nothing to be done, Owen. You were in Spain when he was born, and after that..."

"She didn't know where I was," Owen finished, his voice hollow. "There was an office where she could send letters, and a handful of times, I replied, but the Army kept my location a secret, even from her."

He ran a hand over his face, his expression one of anguish. "Amelia, I... I'm so sorry. If I had known..."

"What would you have done?" she asked, her voice trembling. "What could either of us have done? We were barely more than children ourselves, Owen. And you had your duty, your service to the crown. You had no choice but to follow orders."

Owen was silent for a long moment, his eyes distant and pained. Then, softly, he spoke. "Where does this leave us, Amelia? I want to be a father to Ethan. I want... I still love you."

Amelia's heart leapt in her chest, a fierce, desperate hope blossoming to life. But even as she opened her mouth to speak, reality came crashing down around her. "We can't, Owen," she whispered, her voice thick with tears. "We're both poor, and your work... it's too dangerous. Even if we married, what kind of life could we give Ethan? The city air would be death to his lungs, and I can't risk that."

"You could stay here," Owen argued, his eyes pleading. "I could visit, take more frequent leaves..."

Amelia was already shaking her head, her heart shattering with every word. "Owen, I haven't seen you in almost six years. You cannot just... turn up and ask me to marry you!"

"But he's my son!"

She sniffed and folded her arms. "No, Owen. He's *my* son." She choked on a sudden tightness in her throat. "He's *my* whole world. And any choices I make have to be for him."

Owen's face twisted with pain, his gaze flicking to the pile of lavish gifts in the corner. "And what have I to offer you, compared to others?"

"That is not what I meant."

"Oh, I think it is," he said, his voice raw and bleeding. "I'm sorry, Amelia. Sorry I put you in this position... sorry I cannot offer what you need. I... I'm sorry for everything."

He turned to go, his shoulders hunched as if against a physical blow. Amelia reached for him, her fingers grazing his sleeve.

"Owen, wait..."

But he was already moving, his strides long and purposeful as he crossed the threshold. He paused, his hand on the doorframe, and looked back at her with eyes that swam with unshed tears.

"Goodbye, Amelia."

And then he was gone, the door swinging shut behind him with a finality that echoed in the sudden, aching silence.

Amelia sank to her knees, a sob tearing free from her throat. She pressed a hand to her mouth, her shoulders shaking with the force of her grief.

She had lost him, again. And this time, she feared, it was forever.

Chapter Fourteen

W HAT THE DEVIL HAD he been thinking, pressing for something more with Amelia? Owen swung the axe again, its sharp, rhythmic thunk splitting the crisp morning air. There was already a mountain of kindling behind him large enough to keep both his and Elliot's stoves hot for a week, but working at least gave him something to hit, some means of exhausting his frustration.

Her son, she said. Bloody right, Ethan was her son, but he was his as well, and by heaven, he would be hanged if he would just walk away and... Owen dropped the axe to look up at the sky.

What had he ever done to prove to her that she could trust him? She was right about that, at least. She had no way of knowing if he would help or harm, if he tried to wedge his way back into her life.

Sweat beaded on his brow despite the chill. What was he to do? Go back to London and forget... everything? Stay and try to convince Amelia to give him a chance—at least until he got orders to go somewhere else?

He had just set another log on the chopping block when the sound of hoofbeats shattered his focus. North looked up, his eyes narrowing as he watched a rider approach, the man's tall, broad-shouldered frame strikingly familiar.

As the horse drew nearer, North's heart leapt with a sudden, fierce joy. "Daniels!" he called out, a grin splitting his face as he dropped the axe and strode forward.

Corporal Daniels swung down from the saddle, his own smile wide and bright. "North, you old dog! Blast, but's good to see you."

They clasped hands, and North took a moment to study his comrade, taking in the younger man's strong, square jaw and the unruly thatch of blond hair that flopped over his brow. Daniels was usually a cheerful chap, but there was a line around his eyes that hadn't been there a few weeks ago.

"What the devil are you doing here?" North asked, clapping Daniels on the shoulder as he led him towards the cottage. "Not that I'm not dashed glad to see you, but I thought you were still in London with the rest of the lads."

Daniels shrugged, his smile turning a touch sheepish. "Captain Hunt got your express and send me to find you. Said you might need a hand with something, though he didn't give me much in the way of details."

North's brows shot up, a flicker of unease churning in his gut. If Hunt had sent Daniels all this way with no explanation... He pushed open the door, ushering Daniels inside. "Well, come in, come in. Let's get you settled, and then we can talk."

As Daniels shed his coat and sank into a chair by the hearth, North busied himself pouring two generous measures of whiskey. He handed one to Daniels, then settled into the opposite chair, his expression turning serious.

"So, Hunt didn't tell you anything? Just told you to come to Yorkshire?"

Daniels nodded, taking a sip of his drink. "Aye. I was hoping you might be able to shed some light on why I'm here. I assume you sent something to him?"

North leaned back, a rueful smile tugging at his lips. "Yes, I sent Hunt a message about some... unusual activities I've noticed in the village. Disappearances, strange financial transactions, that sort of thing."

Daniels' brow furrowed, his eyes sharpening with interest. "And you think it's all connected somehow?"

"I do," North confirmed, his voice grim. "But I'm deuced if I know how, or why. I was hoping Hunt might have some insight, some piece of the puzzle I'm missing."

"Well," Daniels said, setting his glass aside and leaning forward, "if the captain saw fit to send me, it means he thinks you're onto something."

"If only I knew what that was. Why can he not say?"

Daniels shrugged and shook his head. "My best guess is that he's been ordered not to put men on whatever it is, so he's just 'sending us on leave' and hoping we stumble into it by dumb luck."

North narrowed his eyes. "Another information leak at Whitehall?"

"He did not say. But no, I think it has to do with the new general who took over after Richards was disgraced. Eager to prove himself, you know, and like enough he and Hunt had differing opinions on what to do with us. With Hunt retiring, he may have had little enough pull."

"I was supposed to go to Kingston upon Hull to look into a smuggling operation," North mused.

"And I was supposed to leave Sheffield for Selby to learn all I could about... fishing." Daniels made a face. "Even *I'm* not that stupid—fishing a small river in December? Me? Hunt knows something."

"Indeed, he must. Well, then, let us think. What did he tell you about this... fishing... operation?"

"Only that I should learn how to row in an icy river."

North grunted. "How very typically cryptic of him."

"That it was. So," Daniels said, sitting back in his chair and fixing North with a keen look. "Where do we start?"

"I think we need to start with the missing prisoners," North said at last, tapping his finger against the rough-hewn surface of the table. "Find out where they were working, who they were in contact with during their time here. And then there's the bank—we need to know more about that transfer, who authorized it and where the money went. I can ask Barrow a bit more on that."

Daniels nodded, his expression pensive. "It won't be easy, getting people to talk. Folks around here seem to have a healthy respect for secrets and a deep-seated distrust of outsiders. I have already attracted glares from nearly everyone in town, and all for doing nothing more than riding up the street."

"True enough," North agreed, a hint of frustration creeping into his voice. "But we have to try. Something tells me that these disappearances, the money, it's all connected somehow."

"I think Captain Hunt thinks it is, at least. But how the bloody devil he would know about it, I've no clue."

"He's a bloodhound." North sighed, his gaze drifting toward the window, where he could see the axe he had left plunged into the stump outside. And that set his thoughts back to where they had been several moments ago, the problems of his own life. How much easier this practical situation was to apply his skills to! He had never been much good at the rest.

Daniels, sensing the dark turn of North's thoughts, leaned forward, his eyes sharp and probing. "What aren't you telling me, Lieutenant? There's more to this than just a few missing Frenchmen and some misplaced funds, isn't there?"

North hesitated. "Not to do with this, but... No, it's nothing. I... Well, Daniels, you know how it is, going back home after years away. A man finds that life..." His brow furrowed. "Life has gone on without him."

"Aye, I know that. I've avoided Sussex for just that reason."

North raised an eyebrow. "Then I shall do you the courtesy of avoiding asking about it. I will only say that I discovered a... a complication, if you will."

"Complication?" Daniels tipped back in his chair and took a drink. "Anything that will compromise our orders?"

"What orders? We are explicitly *not* under orders at the moment."

"And if you believe that, I have an invitation to a royal ball for you."

North chuckled. "Naturally. To answer your question, no. This is nothing that will compromise our orders. But it has rather entangled *me*." He stared at his mug, then shook his head. "No, never mind. There is no simple summation, so I shall spare you the details. Come, I see my neighbor's lantern lit next door. Let me introduce you, and perhaps between the two of us, we will hear sufficient details of oddities in town that we might know where to begin looking for Captain Hunt's boogeyman."

AMELIA'S BROWS FURROWED IN confusion as she opened the door to find Lord Ashwood standing on her threshold, a charming smile on his face and a basket of goods in his hands. Again? What was the man's impediment, that he kept coming back when she offered no encouragement?

"Lord Ashwood," she greeted, her tone polite but guarded. "What brings you here today?"

Ashwood's smile widened as he stepped inside, his eyes roving over the humble interior of her cottage. "I simply wanted to check on you, my dear. To ensure that you and young Ethan will have some Yuletide cheer."

Amelia bit back a sigh, gesturing for him to take a seat at the table as she busied herself preparing tea. "That is very kind of you, my lord. And I do appreciate the assistance you've provided us thus far. But I assure you, we are managing quite well on our own."

Ashwood leaned back in his chair, his expression turning thoughtful. "I must confess, I find myself quite perplexed. After our... history, I would have thought you would not trouble yourself to lie to me."

She offered a sweet smile. "I am not lying, my lord. As you see, we are managing."

"Oh, indeed. I suppose it is only my own ardent interest that draws me back here, then. I never could resist your lovely smile, Miss Grey."

She paused, her hands stilling on the teapot. "I... I would have thought you'd want to put as much distance between us as possible."

A flicker of pain crossed Ashwood's face, gone as quickly as it had come. "I will be frank. Your rejection did wound me deeply. And then after... well! Yes, I felt rightly humiliated. But my feelings for you, the connection we shared... those are not so easily forgotten."

Connection? What connection? Amelia's heart raced, a mixture of fear and confusion swirling in her gut. What game was he playing at? Surely, he couldn't claim to harbor genuine affection for her. Even when they were first engaged, he never claimed that. He had *wanted* her... but never claimed to love her. A man like Lord Garrison Ashwood did not need to tell a woman he loved her.

She turned around, studying the pot again. "My lord, surely, in five years, you could have found some prettier face to divert you."

"Alas, I have looked, but your beauty surpasses all others. I desired to approach you sooner, but you know, with your father entering his dotage, I knew it would take an almighty miracle to move you from his side. And then after his passing, I intended to give you a proper period of mourning, to allow you time to grieve and settle your affairs. But I find I cannot stay away, not when my heart yearns for you so."

A bitter laugh threatened to bubble up in Amelia's throat. More likely, she thought cynically, he had been waiting for her meager funds to run dry, for the reality of surviving her first full winter on her own to set in. But she bit her tongue, unwilling to risk provoking his anger with such an accusation.

Just then, Ethan came bounding into the room, a small wooden mouse clutched in his hand. "Look, Mama!" he chirped, his face alight with pride. "See what I made?"

Ashwood leaned forward, his eyes sparkling with interest. "Why, that's a fine toy, young man. Is it yours?"

"No, sir, I made it for my kitten. See, it's a mouse."

"I do, indeed." Ashwood inspected the toy minutely before handing it back to Ethan. "It is exceedingly well done. Did you carve it all by yourself?"

Ethan shook his head, grinning. "No, sir. The lieutenant helped me! He showed me how to use the knife properly, and how to make the tail curly."

Amelia's heart stopped, a chill washing over her at the mention of Owen's rank. She shot Ethan a warning look, but it was too late.

"A lieutenant, you say?" Ashwood's voice had gone dangerously soft, his gaze sharpening as it swung back to Amelia. "And which lieutenant might that be?"

Ethan, oblivious to the sudden tension in the room, answered brightly. "Lieutenant North, sir. He's been visiting Mama and me."

Ashwood's jaw clenched, a muscle ticking in his cheek. "I see. Thank you for telling me, Ethan. That's very helpful. Would you mind running along, lad? Perhaps your kitten is eager for her toy."

As Ethan scampered back out of the room, Amelia busied herself with the tea things, her hands shaking as she poured. "More tea, Lord Ashwood?" she asked, her voice overly bright.

But Ashwood ignored the offer, his eyes boring into her with an intensity that made her skin crawl. "Owen North," he said softly, his tone laced with a quiet menace. "I always did wonder who the boy's father was. I remember him, you know. That farm laborer with the striking blue eyes, the one who used to glare daggers at my carriage whenever I came to call. And he has come back, then?"

Amelia forced a laugh, the sound brittle and unconvincing even to her own ears. "Owen North? I hardly remember him, my lord. We ran into him by chance in the village, that's all. He means nothing to me."

Ashwood rose abruptly, his chair scraping harshly against the floor. He stalked to the door, his posture rigid with barely contained anger. Pausing on the threshold, he turned back, his eyes glittering with a cold, hard light.

"You would be wise, Amelia, to consider carefully where your loyalties lie. With handsome soldiers who would dally with your heart and then abandon you to ruin? Or with someone who has the means and the desire to provide for you and your son, to offer you a respectable future?"

He let the question hang in the air for a long, tense moment. Then, with a final, cutting look, he was gone, the door slamming shut behind him with a finality that made Amelia flinch.

She sank into a chair, her legs trembling too badly to support her. Ashwood's words echoed in her mind, the unspoken threat behind them chilling her to the bone.

What had she done, allowing Owen back into their lives? Had she inadvertently painted a target on all their backs, inviting the wrath of a powerful, vindictive man? She pressed a shaking hand to her mouth, fear and uncertainty clawing at her throat.

Ashwood controlled half the open land in the county and probably most of the businesses in town. He could have the note called on her property, work deals with other farmers not to buy her lambs and wool. But that was only in the short term. What could he do to blight Ethan's future, if he desired it? Or even Owen's?

No, that was silly. Owen was a grown man. A soldier with battle experience and enough wits to look out for himself. That was not the problem. But what would Owen do if he learned that Ashwood was threatening her? Probably something stupid... something that could get him killed, if his feelings ran away with him again. They had a way of doing that.

As the walls of the cottage seemed to close in around her, as the weight of her choices and her circumstances threatened to crush her beneath their weight, she couldn't help but wonder if perhaps, this time, she had finally run out of options.

Chapter Fifteen

"ARE YOU SURE YOU can trust this chap?" Daniels jogged to catch up with North's long strides as they rounded the garden fence between his cottage and the one next door. "A banker, you said?"

"Aye, and an honest lad. You'll see it in an instant, or I'll eat my hat."

Daniels chuckled and closed the gate as they approached the front door. "'Honest' does not always mean 'discreet,' you know."

North grunted in amusement as he raised his hand to the knocker. "I do know. But we need information, and I can think of no better place to start."

The door swung open before North had even finished knocking to reveal Thomas Barrow. The older man already had his coat and hat on, and he regarded North with squint-eyed wonder, as if marveling to find someone on his doorstep. "'Allo there, lads! I'm off to the pub. Don't wait up for me," he said with a wink, before disappearing into the night.

Elliot was just behind his father, reaching for his own hat, but he paused with a grin when he saw North and Daniels on his doorstep. "Oh, good evening, Owen. Care to join us?"

North stepped forward. "Actually, Elliot, I only wished to introduce you to... an old friend of mine. Robert Daniels, this is Elliot Barrow. He makes the finest mutton stew in these dales."

Elliot chuckled. "And I have a bit more, if you've a mind for a bite. Come in?"

North gestured for Daniels to go before him. They took the seats Elliot offered them at his kitchen table and waited for their host to join them. Elliot was prattling cheerfully about the carrots and in his root cellar trying to sprout, indecently not waiting for him to cook and eat them first, and then saying he wanted them to sample a bit of his home brew. He took a seat between them, offering them each a mug of ale, when he paused at the look on North's face.

"Something wrong, Owen?" he asked.

North cleared his throat. "Elliot, I must ask for a bit of discretion."

He lowered his mug. "Of course, of course. What can I do?"

"We were hoping you could share some information with us. About the oddities at the bank, and anything else you might know about the missing prisoners. Is there anything new?"

Elliot hesitated, his fingers tapping against his mug. "No, nothing terribly unusual. Interesting, perhaps, but not unusual."

North leaned forward. "Interesting how?"

"Oh, you know how it is, small village and all. Anything that involves London makes us all take notice."

"What about London?" Daniels asked.

"I am sure it was nothing to alarm. A solicitor came today to speak with Mr. Perkins, the bank manager. It seemed quite urgent, and while they were talking, Mr. Perkins asked me to fetch Lord Ashwood's portfolio. Probably something to do with his investments, of course, but the solicitor left directly. Did not even stop at the pub for a sup before his carriage turned back to the south road."

At the mention of Lord Ashwood's name, North's expression darkened, his jaw tightening with a flicker of anger. Daniels, noticing the change in his friend's demeanor, turned to him with a questioning look. "Why that face, North? Not a friend of yours?"

"Nor of anyone else's," Elliot put in. "Leastwise, not regular folk."

"Ah, I see how it is," Daniels said, tasting a spoonful from the bowl Elliot had placed before him. "Gets whatever he wants, does he? Always the way. Land, stock, carriages... ladies."

North remained silent; his jaw clenched tightly. Elliot met his eyes briefly, then cleared his throat. "There's, ah, there's a rumor going around. About Lord Ashwood, that is. They say he's planning to marry again."

North stiffened. "What? Who is the lady?" he asked sharply.

Elliot dipped his bread in his bowl, keeping his gaze low. "The one you, ah..." He glanced up at North, his voice taking on a strange, almost apologetic tone. "The word is, he intends to marry Miss Amelia Grey."

Daniels's eyebrows shot up, and he turned to North with a probing look. "Miss Grey? Does that name hold any significance for you, North? Judging by the way Barrow said it..."

North blinked, staring deliberately at the mug in his hands as his ears burned. After a long moment, he spoke, his voice low and rough with emotion. "I know her. Amelia Grey, that is. Yes, I know her... And her son."

Elliot's face flushed a deep red, and he scratched at his ear, suddenly finding the floor incredibly interesting. It was clear that he had put together the pieces of North's history with Amelia, and the realization had left him deeply uncomfortable.

Daniels, however, merely puckered his mouth, his expression unreadable. "Does the, ah... lady know of her impending marriage?"

North looked up swiftly, then back at the table. "I do not know."

"Hmm. Well, it bears questioning."

"Why is that?" North closed his eyes, his fist clenching on the handle of his mug. "Why would you think a poor farm maid would not leap at the chance to become lady Ashwood, mistress of a fine manor with a dozen servants at her beck and call?"

Daniels studied him, and North swallowed, daring to glance up at his comrade. Perhaps the bitterness in his tone gave too much away. Daniels was, after all, trained to sniff out anything peculiar or disingenuous.

Daniels shifted in his chair and sighed. "Well, I cannot say, North. Only that I am quite familiar with the trouble of ladies being forced by circumstances to marry where they do not desire to," he said gently. "Perhaps, while we're looking into these other matters, we ought to keep an eye out for her interests, as well."

North shook his head. "The lady declares she is capable of looking after herself." Turning back to Elliot, he cleared his throat, eager to steer the conversation back to the task at hand. "Elliot, do you think you could provide us with the names of the specific farms where the prisoners went missing? It would give us a good starting point for our investigation."

"Investigation! Why, this sounds serious, indeed. Do you think there is anything to find beyond a few loose prisoners running for the coast?"

"Perhaps. Perhaps not. But discovering the business of Frenchmen on English soil... well, it's what we do, Elliot."

A MELIA PACED THE CONFINES of her cottage, her mind whirling with the events of the past few days. Ashwood's attentions had grown increasingly bold, his gifts more extravagant with each passing day. She was walking a dangerous line, risking his wrath with every polite refusal, but what choice did she have?

Her eyes fell upon the heavy woolen cloak draped over a chair, the fine fabric mocking her with its opulence. She couldn't keep it, couldn't risk the implications of accepting such a lavish present. How could she even wear it? Everyone would talk. But how to return it without incurring Ashwood's ire?

With a heavy sigh, Amelia reached for the cloak, her fingers trembling slightly as she lifted it from the chair. She had to do something, had to find a way to extricate herself from this twisted game Ashwood seemed intent on playing.

Perhaps she could get rid of it. He *had* given it to her, had he not? It was hers to do with as she pleased. And right now, what she pleased was to no longer look at the thing. She would much rather have a little money in her pocket... money that she could put aside, in case she and Ethan... well, in case she ever found a need to leave town quickly—assuming there might be somewhere for them to go.

Today was a market day. She could take it with her and try to sell it in town, but how to keep it from being seen by Lord Ashwood? Fancy that! If he recognized his gift paraded about by Mrs. Humboldt or Mrs. Wilson, why, she would be worse off than now. But Mr. Wallis at the pub had offered to buy anything she had to sell. Indeed, a wool cloak was not precisely jam, but he *did* see nearly every face to step off the London coach, and... well, it was worth a try.

And so, that afternoon, she made her way to the pub. As she pushed open the heavy wooden door, the scent of ale and pipe smoke enveloped her, a strangely comforting aroma amidst the chaos of her thoughts. The publican looked up from the bar, his eyes widening in surprise at the sight of her.

"Mistress Grey!" he called out, a warm smile spreading across his weathered face. "What brings you here this afternoon? More jams, I take it?"

Amelia managed a weak smile in return, her arm tightening on the cloak she had buttoned inside her own coat. "Good afternoon, Mr. Wallis," she said softly, making her way to the bar. "I was hoping I might have a word with you. In private."

His brow furrowed, concern etching itself into the lines of his face. "Of course, lass. Come on back, we'll have a chat in the kitchen."

He led her through the crowded taproom, past the tables of boisterous patrons and into the relative quiet of the kitchen. Once the door had swung shut behind them, he turned to face her, his eyes searching her face for any sign of distress.

"What's troubling you, Mistress Grey?"

Amelia hesitated for a moment, the words sticking in her throat. But then, with a shaky breath, she pulled out the cloak, holding it out to him with trembling hands.

"It's Lord Ashwood," she said, her voice barely above a whisper. "He's been... persistent in his attentions. Sending gifts, making overtures. I've tried to refuse him politely, but he won't take no for an answer. I... I don't want this."

Wallis's eyes widened as he took in the exquisite fabric, the intricate embroidery that spoke of wealth and taste. "This is from him?" he asked, his voice raw with disbelief.

Amelia nodded, a lump rising in her throat. "I can't keep it, Mr. Wallis. I can't risk the implications of accepting such a lavish present. What if I were seen wearing it? He would assume things by it. But I'm afraid of what he might do if I refuse it outright. I'd rather make it go away."

The publican's face darkened, a flicker of anger sparking in his eyes. "That man's a right blackguard," he growled, his fists clenching at his sides. "Thinking he can buy whatever he wants."

"Well, he usually can. I don't know what to do," she admitted. "I cannot risk offending him, but I... I need the money. I don't want to wear this... ever."

Mr. Wallis was silent for a long moment, his gaze distant and thoughtful. Then, with a decisive nod, he reached out and took the cloak from her hands.

"Leave it with me, lass. I've got a sister in the next town over, and no doubt she's expecting something for a Christmas gift. This'll do nicely."

Amelia's shoulders sagged with relief. "Thank you!"

The publican waved off her gratitude. "Think nothing of it, Mistress Grey. I've no love for Ashwood. If he gives you any bother, I'll speak for you, and happy to do it."

Amelia felt a prickle of tears at the back of her eyes, a lump rising in her throat. But she could do no more than nod in gratitude.

Wallis turned away, reaching into a coin box to withdraw half a crown. Amelia gasped as he dropped it into her hand, her head shaking as she tried to refuse it. "This is too much," she protested.

"For this? Not in the least," he said. "It'd be worth double that in London. I've cheated you, Ma'am."

She laughed. "And yet, somehow I feel like the one who got the better end of the bargain."

"Aye, and you'd best be getting back now. The lad'll be missing his mother."

Amelia managed a small, wobbly smile. "You're right," she said, straightening her shoulders with a newfound determination. "Thank you again."

As she left the pub, the heavy coin weighing her pocket, she drank in a long sigh of the wintry air. What a relief! The cloak gone, out of her sight, and she had enough now to see her through for some time.

For a moment there—a brief one, it was true—she had thought about going to Owen for help. But what could he have done? He had been gone so long. He had no way of turning an unwanted gift from an unwelcome suitor into money that could keep food on her table. He had no sway in town, no means of diverting gossip or even pressuring Lord Ashwood into leaving her alone. And the last thing she wanted was to provoke him into confronting His Lordship and making a scene... or worse.

No, it was better this way. Discreet... finished. Resolved in the smoothest way possible.

Just as long as Lord Ashwood never expected to see her wearing that wretched cloak.

Chapter Sixteen

T HE SUN'S FIRST RAYS had just begun to paint the horizon in hues of pink and gold, warming the sheen of snow over the ground as North and Daniels approached the farmstead, their strides purposeful yet unhurried. They had taken great care in their appearance, donning the simple, worn garments of local farmhands. North's typically well-groomed hair was mussed, and Daniels had smudged a bit of dirt on his cheek for good measure.

They ought to look the part well enough. North had cut his teeth working on these farms as a lad, and Daniels used to be a blacksmith. It was not as if they were... well, Captain Hunt, with his polished ways, trying to blend in on a Yorkshire farm. He and Daniels knew what it was to labor behind a plow or build a piling out of stone. Owen cast one more glance over their attire and grunted in satisfaction.

As they neared the barn, a weathered man with a deeply lined face emerged, his suspicious gaze sweeping over the two strangers. North stepped forward, affecting a deferential tone.

"Good morning, sir," he greeted, dipping his head respectfully. "We hate to bother you so early, but we were hoping you might be able to help us."

The farmer's eyes narrowed, his hands coming to rest on his hips. "Help you with what, exactly? I don't take kindly to strangers poking around my property."

Daniels held up his hands in a placating gesture. "We don't mean any trouble, sir. We're just up from Darley, looking for work. We heard tell that some of the farms around here had lost their workers of late, and we thought maybe..." He trailed off, shrugging his shoulders innocently.

The farmer's posture stiffened, his expression turning guarded. "Not many folk look-ing for work in December. Come back in the spring."

"I know that, sir, but we've got little ones to feed," Daniels lied, stepping forward a little more. "And someone in town said you'd a guest of the crown here, feeding off your bed and board until he lighted out. We thought, sir, that mayhap you'd be a bit shorthanded without the bloke about, see."

The farmer narrowed his eyes. "I don't know anything about any 'guest of the crown,' and even if I did, I wouldn't be spreading it around to the likes of you."

North and Daniels exchanged a quick glance. "We understand, sir," North said smoothly, his tone conciliatory. "We don't mean to pry. It's just, we heard some rumors about strange goings-on, about prisoners up and vanishing in the middle of the night. We thought maybe, if we could find work on one of those farms, we might be able to keep an eye out, you know? Look out for your interests, make sure everything's on the up and up."

The farmer's eyes flashed with anger, his weathered face turning ruddy. "Are you accusing me of something, boy? I've never broken a law in my life, and I don't take kindly to insinuations otherwise."

Daniels stepped in, his tone soothing. "Not at all, sir. We're just trying to make an honest living, same as you. We don't want any trouble."

For a long, tense moment, the farmer stared at them, his gaze sharp and assessing. Then, with a grunt of disgust, he turned away. "I can't help you," he said flatly, his back to them as he strode towards the barn. "And if you know what's good for you, you'll stop asking questions and move along. There are things happening around here that are best left alone."

With that, he disappeared into the barn, the door slamming shut behind him with a resounding finality.

North and Daniels stood there for a moment, a few snowflakes furling around the fog of their breath on the air. Then, with a sigh, North turned to his companion.

"Well, that could have gone better," he murmured, keeping his voice low.

Daniels nodded, his eyes scanning the tree line. "He knows something, that's for sure. Did you see the way he reacted when we mentioned the prisoners?"

North hummed in agreement, his mind already racing ahead. "There were at least a dozen other farms that had prisoners dumped on them. Maybe one of them will be more willing to talk. And maybe we'll find some that are still put where they ought to be."

"So we can keep an eye on them," Daniels mused. "Right, then."

As they set off across the snowy fields, North couldn't shake the feeling of unease that had settled in the pit of his stomach. There was something deeply wrong here, a rot at the heart of this seemingly peaceful countryside.

And he was determined to uncover it, no matter how many farmers he offended in the process. That was what Captain Hunt wanted him to do, after all.

They spent the rest of the morning and well into the afternoon visiting farm after farm, their approach carefully tailored to each new encounter. At some, they posed as lost travelers seeking directions. At others, they claimed to be hungry men looking for work. But no matter their tactics, the result was always the same. Tight-lipped silence, wary glances, and a palpable sense of fear that hung in the air like a miasma.

It was as if the entire village was gripped by a shared terror, a dark secret that none dared speak aloud.

By the time the sun began to dip towards the horizon, casting long shadows across the land, North and Daniels were exhausted and frustrated. They had gleaned precious little information, and what they had managed to overhear only deepened the mystery. But no one seemed willing to provide concrete details, to point them in the direction of whoever might have any answers.

As they trudged back towards the village, their toes frozen in their boots and their spirits flagging, North stared at the ground and thought through one notion after another. And then, something pricked his spine, and he straightened.

"Do you know, Daniels, we may have been going about this all wrong."

"How is that, sir?"

"Well, it just occurred to me that Hunt may have given us precisely what we need. Where was it you said you were ordered to go before he sent you on 'leave' instead?"

"Selby, on the River Ouse."

"A river which flows into the Humber..." North narrowed his eyes. "And from there, joins the sea at Kingston Upon Hull."

Daniels stopped, the snow crunching under his boots. "Where does the River Ouse begin?"

"Oh, far north of here, but it flows right through the town of York, and half a dozen smaller villages. There is a bank only a couple of miles aw..." He broke off with a laugh. "Bloody hell, Daniels. That's it! They're getting out by river, in the dead of winter when no one would think to look on the water."

Daniels' handsome face split in a wide grin. "I say, sir, you probably have it. Now all we have to do is learn who's organizing the boats and paying people off. Someone is profiting handsomely off getting those folk out of the country."

"Aye. And I've a notion of where to start looking."

AMELIA TRUDGED THROUGH THE slush-drenched streets of the village, her heart heavy with worry as she clutched Ethan's hand in her own. The previous night had been another difficult one, with her son's cough worsening despite the medicine Mr. Sommers had provided. She needed to seek further help, but the options seemed frustratingly limited.

As they entered the apothecary shop, the familiar scent of herbs and medicinal concoctions enveloped them. Mr. Sommers looked up from his work, his brow furrowing with concern as he took in Amelia's troubled expression.

"Mistress Grey, what brings you here today? Is young Ethan not feeling well?"

Amelia sighed, guiding Ethan to sit on a nearby stool. "The medicine you gave us last time doesn't seem to be helping as much as we'd hoped. He had another bad spell in the night, and I just don't know what else to do."

Mr. Sommers knelt down, gently examining Ethan's breathing and pulse. After a moment, he stood, his expression grave. "I'm afraid there may not be much more we *can* do, Mistress Grey. With lungs as weak as Ethan's, the best course of action would be to move him to a warmer climate, away from the damp and chill. And, of course, away from all the animals."

Amelia's heart sank. "That's not an option for us, Mr. Sommers. Please, there must be something else you can suggest."

The apothecary rubbed his chin thoughtfully, then moved to rummage through his shelves. "Perhaps a tincture to help relax him during an attack, to prevent his lungs from seizing up quite so badly. Something with a touch of laudanum... but not too much, lest it weaken him. Let me see what I can prepare."

As Mr. Sommers worked, Amelia reached into her pocket, pulling out the half-crown she had received from selling Lord Ashwood's cloak. She pressed it into the apothecary's hand, her cheeks flushing with embarrassment.

Mr. Sommers paused, examining the coin with a curious expression before looking back at Amelia. "Forgive me for prying, Miss Grey, but is everything... as it should be? This is a rather... large denomination."

Amelia's stomach churned with guilt, realizing how it must appear. "I... I can explain. You see, I recently sold a cloak that was given to me. It was quite fine, and it fetched a good price."

The apothecary held up a hand, his eyes kind. "You owe me no explanations, Miss Grey. But I have noticed Lord Ashwood paying particular attention to you lately. If I may be so bold... do you welcome his attentions?"

Slowly, Amelia shook her head, a lump forming in her throat.

Mr. Sommers leaned in, his voice dropping to a hushed whisper. "Then you must be careful, my dear. I don't know what his lordship's intentions are, but a few months ago, I was summoned to Ashwood Manor when he sprained his ankle rather badly—a fall off his horse, nearly broke his leg, but we mended him well enough."

Amelia's eyebrow edged upward. "I had not heard of that."

"Oh, it was merely a trifle, we had him quite sound again within a few days. But when I arrived, he had been reading something with what appeared to be rather urgent interest. He set it aside while I was there, but he did not take care to conceal it at all. There was no way to avoid seeing it, I'm afraid, for I had to clear off his desk to—"

"Mr. Sommers," she sighed, "what does this have to do with me?"

"Well, it is only that the letter bore the name 'Grey'."

Amelia's brow furrowed in confusion. "'Grey,' as in my father? But he's been gone for over a year. Surely any correspondence between them would be quite old."

The apothecary shook his head. "It appeared to be a letter Lord Ashwood had just opened. I'm ashamed to admit I let my curiosity get the better of me, but I've never trusted the man. Since then, I've been paying closer attention to anything concerning you."

A chill ran down Amelia's spine, her mind reeling with the implications. She struggled to make sense of how this could relate to her current predicament, but Mr. Sommers' urgency gave her pause.

"Surely, it is nothing," she scoffed with forced lightness. "Papa wanted me to marry Ashwood, that is no secret. I am sure they had some correspondence at some point."

"This was no mere letter, Miss Grey. The wording on the top of the page... it looked for all the world like a will."

"Will! As if my father had anything to bequeath to anyone but an encumbered farm with a leaky cow shed."

He thinned his lips and shook his head. "Miss Grey, please—"

"I appreciate your concern, Mr. Sommers, truly. But I'm not sure how this bears on Ethan's health, or our situation."

The apothecary grasped her hand, his eyes pleading. "Please, Miss Grey, if you won't heed my warning, at least listen to your friend. The one in uniform, who's recently returned to the village."

Amelia felt the color drain from her face, her heart pounding in her chest. Oh, heavens! Did *everyone* know about her connection to Owen? Was it written plainly on her face, on Ethan's?

"I..." She gulped and looked away, bundling Ethan's scarf around his chin once more. "I don't know what you're talking about, sir. I... don't know why you would think any soldier would..." Her voice broke as her throat constricted.

"Miss Grey, I speak as a friend. Ashwood is not to be trifled with. You must take help where you may find it. Even if it comes from... an inconvenient source."

"No! No, I am quite well enough, and I'll thank you not to pry into my business, Mr. Sommers." She gathered her son and their belongings, desperate to escape the suddenly stifling shop. "Good day, sir."

But as she reached the door, Mr. Sommers pressed a packet of herbs into her hands. "Wait, please. Take these, for Ethan. And please, Miss Grey, take care of yourself and your boy. There be help at hand, if you will reach for it."

Amelia stared at him, the words clogged in her throat as she gaped at the old apothecary. At the man who had helped her more than anyone else in this town. What reason would he have to frighten her or lead her falsely? But that implication, that he knew of her connection to Owen... No, no, it was too much! She had to get home, away from prying eyes, where she could think a bit.

With a final, grateful nod, Amelia hurried out into the street, her mind awhirl with unanswered questions and growing fears. But she could not outrun what Sommers had said, for his words echoed in her mind all the way home.

Chapter Seventeen

THE BITTER WIND WHIPPED through North's coat as he made his way down the snow-laden path to Amelia's cottage, his mind awhirl with suspicions and unease. Lord Ashwood's sudden interest in Amelia, the missing French prisoners, the strange financial dealings at the bank—could they all be connected somehow? And if so, why?

He doubted Amelia knew much, but the question had to be asked. If for no other reason than he trusted her, and he hoped she trusted him... at least, more so than the Dales farmers seemed to trust him. At least she would not run him off with her pitchfork... hopefully. Who knew? If he were very fortunate, indeed, she might let him speak to her about more than suspicions and duty to the crown.

As he approached the gate, a flicker of movement caught his eye. There, in the yard, was Ethan, cradling his little kitten in his arms as he carried it towards the house. The boy was chattering away, spinning some fanciful tale for his furry companion, his cheeks rosy from the cold.

Owen couldn't help but smile, his heart swelling with a fierce, protective love. How was he already so smitten with a lad he had spoken with but twice? His own flesh and blood... And though he had missed so much of the boy's life already, he longed for nothing more than to be a true father to him, to guide and nurture him as he grew.

Ethan looked up, his eyes widening as he caught sight of North. "Lieutenant North! Have you come to visit Mama?"

North chuckled, ruffling the boy's hair affectionately. "I have indeed, lad. I need to speak with her about some grown-up matters. But perhaps later, you and I could continue our wood carving lessons, hmm?"

Ethan's face lit up, a grin spreading from ear to ear. "Oh, yes please! I've been practicing, I promise!"

With a final, fond pat on the boy's shoulder, North made his way to the cottage door. He raised his hand to knock, only to find Amelia already standing there, watching him with a guarded expression.

"Lieutenant North," she said, her voice carefully neutral. "To what do I owe the pleasure?"

He removed his hat, his fingers fidgeting with the brim. "I apologize for the intrusion. But I was hoping I might have a word with you, in private. There are some... concerns I need to discuss. Not of a personal nature—rather, something to do with my duty, and I believe you may be able to shed some light on the matter."

Amelia's brow furrowed, but after a moment's hesitation, she stepped aside, gesturing for him to enter. "Very well. You may as well join us for the noon meal, as I was just about to set the table."

Owen followed her inside, his eyes adjusting to the dim, cozy interior. The scent of stew simmering over the fire filled the air, mingling with the sweet, earthy aroma of the dried herbs hanging from the rafters.

As they took their seats at the rough-hewn table, Ethan bouncing eagerly beside them, Owen tried to gather his thoughts. He didn't want to frighten Amelia or make her feel as though she were being interrogated. But he needed answers, needed to know if she had seen or heard anything that might confirm his growing suspicions about Lord Ashwood's involvement in the strange goings-on in the village.

The sudden, sharp rap at the door shattered the fragile peace of the cottage, causing Amelia to start in her seat. "Oh, dash it all," she grumbled, her brow furrowing with a mix of annoyance and trepidation as she sprang up again to answer the insistent summons.

But as she pulled the door open, revealing the imposing figure of Lord Ashwood on the threshold, her expression morphed into one of outright shock and dismay.

"Miss Grey," Ashwood purred, his voice dripping with charm as he swept into an elegant bow. "I do hope I'm not interrupting anything... pressing. Oh. I... I see you already have company."

His gaze flicked meaningfully to North, who had risen from the table in a flash, his hand instinctively falling to the hilt of his sword.

"Lord Ashwood," North said, his tone carefully neutral even as his muscles tensed with readiness. "I must say, I'm surprised to see you here."

Ashwood's eyes narrowed, a jealous gleam sparking in their depths as he took in the scene before him—the cozy domestic tableau of the meal laid out, Ethan's bright, curious face peering out from behind his mother's skirts.

"I might say the same, Lieutenant," he drawled, his voice laced with a sly insinuation. "I wasn't aware that you and Miss Grey were so... closely acquainted."

North felt a hot flush of anger rise in his cheeks, his jaw clenching with the effort of maintaining his composure. Beside him, Amelia had gone pale, her hands twining anxiously with Ethan's behind her skirt.

"Miss Grey is a friend, nothing more," North said, his words clipped and precise. "But as her friend, I feel compelled to inquire as to the nature of your business here, my lord. Especially given the lady's clear disinterest in your previous overtures."

Ashwood's face darkened, a flicker of irritation breaking through his carefully cultivated facade of civility. "And what, pray tell, would you know of my overtures, Lieutenant? Or of Miss Grey's interests, for that matter?"

He took a step forward, his eyes raking over North's uniform with a dismissive sneer. "You have not been back home in a very long time, Lieutenant. Many things have changed. Perhaps you should take some time to learn the lay of the land, so to speak, before you start making baseless accusations."

North's hand tightened on his sword hilt, the leather of his gloves creaking with the force of his grip. It took every ounce of his military discipline not to draw the blade and put an end to Ashwood's smug, entitled prattling then and there. But that would only make matters worse for Amelia, to say nothing of violence in front of the child.

Instead, he drew himself up to his full height, squaring his shoulders and fixing Ashwood with a hard, unyielding stare. "I may be a stranger now to the village where I spent my youth, my lord," he said, his voice low and steady. "But I am no stranger to the ways of men like you. Men who think their wealth and status give them the right to take whatever they want, regardless of the wishes or well-being of others."

Ashwood's eyes flashed with a dangerous light, his lips twisting into a cold, mocking smile. "Be careful, Lieutenant," he said softly, each word dripping with menace. "One might think you were making threats. And that would be a grave mistake, indeed."

Amelia stepped forward then, her chin lifted and her fiery hair catching the warmth of the hearth. "I believe the Lieutenant has made himself quite clear, Lord Ashwood," she said, her voice trembling only slightly. "As have I, on numerous occasions. Your attentions are neither welcome nor desired here. I must ask you to leave, and not return."

For a moment, Ashwood simply stared at her, his expression unreadable. Then, with a huff of mirthless laughter, he sketched a mocking bow. "As you wish, Miss Grey. But mark my words, this conversation is far from over. There are matters between us that must be addressed, matters that will not be so easily brushed aside."

He turned to go, his cloak swirling around him like a dark cloud. But at the threshold, he paused, glancing back over his shoulder with a final, cutting look.

"Oh, and Lieutenant? Do give my regards to your commanding officer. I'm sure he'll be most interested to hear of your... recreational activities."

With that, he was gone, the door slamming shut behind him with a resounding finality. For a long moment, North and Amelia simply stood there, their breathing ragged and their hearts pounding in the sudden, echoing silence.

Then, slowly, North reached out, his gloved hand finding Amelia's and giving it a gentle, reassuring squeeze. "I'm sorry," he said softly. "I never meant to bring any more trouble to your door, Amelia."

She huffed and tugged her hand back from his to dust something from her cheek as she turned away. "Run along and wash up, Ethan."

The boy was still clinging to her hand, but he looked up solemnly as she gave him her directions, then glanced at North as he moved to obey. As soon as he was out of earshot, Amelia cast her eyes up to the ceiling, then turned to face him. "You do have a way of turning my life upside down, Owen North."

He stepped closer, his face as apologetic as he could make it. "I couldn't let him harass you. Forgive me. I am afraid I may have only made matters worse."

She sniffed and gave a bitter laugh. "I don't see how you could have made anything worse. He will get what he wants in the end." Amelia's eyes searched his face, a flicker of something like hope sparking in their depths. "I suppose I must thank you for your intentions, at least. No one has ever spoken up against Lord Ashwood for my sake."

"And I ought to have, years ago."

She shook her head, her face downturned. "And what would you have said? You were but a farm hand, not yet twenty years old. What could you have done against the most powerful landlord this side of the Pennines—a man with all that money and influence, and dozens of strong men in his employ? He would have had you beaten up and left in a ditch somewhere for the pleasure of it."

He drew in a sigh. "I'm not sure... something. I should have done something. Not just... left you to his mercy."

"I managed well enough. He took it like a gentleman when I refused to go through with the marriage before."

"And you think he will accept your refusal a second time?" Owen shook his head. "You told me yourself he left you alone all this while and has suddenly refocused his interest on you. There must be some reason, and he will not stop until he has what he wants."

She lifted one shoulder. "And so, what if he does? I've nothing left to resist him with, Owen. And perhaps..."

"No." He grasped her shoulders and waited for her to look up into his eyes. "Pray, do not say it. Do not be so ready to concede to that brute! You can send me away if you wish. I will respect that, and never trouble you again. But do not tell me you would accept that man simply because he backed you into a corner, refused to take no for an answer. What sort of happiness is that for you?"

Her throat worked, and a single tear hovered in the corner of her eye. Her lips parted, trembling, and she drew a breath. "Owen, it's... it's more than that. Ethan, he—"

His grip tightened on her shoulders. "What about Ethan?"

She shook her head, gulping on a convulsive sob before she found her voice again. "He's sick all winter, every year. He keeps having these spells, coughing and carrying on, unable to breathe. Mr. Sommers says the only thing to do for him is to move him somewhere warmer, but how am I to do that? I have no money, Owen! I have nowhere to go, and no way to support us even if I did manage to go anywhere."

He set his jaw grimly. "And you think Ashwood would cheerfully permit his wife to hie off to Wessex or Kent? Let you winter in Bath or Eastbourne?"

"I don't know!" She covered her face in her hands and her shoulders began to shake. "But I cannot keep turning down what chances come my way while I watch my son suffocate in this cold! What choice do I have?"

He backed away, dropping his hands from her shoulders and turning to pace before the hearth. "I would to heaven I could..." He swept a hand over his eyes. "I can offer you nothing but the strength of my arm, little as that is." Owen clenched his jaw. What good was a sword and pistol when what she really needed was a safe place for her son... *their* son? That was the one thing he owed her and could not give her. There *had* to be a way. She surely deserved that much from him, by heaven!

"Owen, I... I don't know what else to do," she whispered. "I already sold one of those outrageous gifts he gave me just to have enough money to survive the winter. I've no idea what I would have done if he had not..." She sniffed and walked toward him again, waiting for him to turn his face back to her. "Tell me you have some idea. There must be something I can do, somewhere I can go!"

He reached out, taking her hand in his own. "I wish I did. I have few enough connections of my own. I promise you will have everything I can possibly offer, but I cannot say just yet what that will be."

She chewed on her upper lip, a tear still glistening in her eye, but she was making a visible effort to steady her breathing. "I... I know. It was unfair of me to ask."

"Not unfair. Who should help you but I? And I am dashed powerless to do much. But..." He gave a slight tug to her hand, gazing earnestly down into her face as she let him pull her closer. "Truly, I did not come here today to talk about us. It is... well, it is not impossible that I may find some leverage on Lord Ashwood, something we may use to put an end to his bullying of half the county."

Her eyes cleared, and she tipped her head slightly. "What?"

"First, I need straight answers to a number of questions, and I need to know what everyone else around here has seen. They do not trust *me*, but you? You are no stranger, no threat to anyone. You can hear things I cannot."

"What are you saying, Owen?" She drew her hand back and crossed her arms over her stomach. "You want me to inform on my neighbors for you?"

"Not on them. On Ashwood. I think he may have something to do with the French captives that have gone missing of late."

She shook her head, her eyes narrowing. "How? They wandered off, Owen. They do that."

"Not in such sudden numbers. We've seen this before—enterprising traitors conspire to smuggle them out of the country in exchange for a ransom. And if they happen to be valuable prisoners, with rank or connections back in France, why, it can prove a rather lucrative operation."

Her brow furrowed. "What do you want me to do about it? Am I to walk from farm to farm, asking impertinent questions? I really would be accounted a pariah in the village!"

"No, no, nothing like that. Say you'll trust me, Amelia. Say you'll help me, and let me help you, in whatever way I can."

She hesitated for a moment, wrapping her arms more tightly around herself in a shiver. Then, with a shaky breath, she nodded. "I trust you, Owen. God help me, but I do."

Chapter Eighteen

A MELIA WALKED THROUGH THE bustling market, her basket heavy on her arm. The air was thick with the scent of roasting chestnuts and spiced cider, the sounds of laughter and haggling rising above the din of the crowd. It was the day before Christmas Eve, and the marketplace was alive with the cries of housewives and hawkers haggling over last-minute provisions for their holiday table.

But for Amelia, there was little joy to be found in the festive atmosphere. Her mind was consumed with the task Owen had set before her, the weight of the secrets she was meant to uncover sitting like a stone in her gut.

She made her way to her usual stall, setting out her wares with a practiced hand. The cream and butter, the eggs from her hens—they were humble offerings, but after selling the last of her jams, they were all she had to trade. As she arranged her goods, Amelia let her gaze wander over the other stalls, taking in the weathered faces of the farmers and the weary slump of their shoulders. These were her neighbors, her community, and they knew her. Could she manage to ask what she needed to learn without raising anyone's suspicions?

But she had made a promise to Owen, and she could not go back on her word.

Amelia could not think where to begin, but it seemed promising to strike up a conversation with the farmer to her left, a grizzled old man with a face like leather and hands gnarled from years of toil. He was here selling mutton today and turning a tidy profit for his troubles. But his back clearly pained him today, and more than once, his customers had to help him heft their purchases for examination.

"Where is your son today?" Amelia asked him at length.

He slanted her a long look. "Off tending hogs for Southerland. I'm on me own today."

"Oh, I see. I can't wait for my Ethan to grow stronger," she said, her tone carefully casual. "It would be a blessing to have an extra pair of hands around the farm."

The old man grunted, his eyes never leaving the turnips he was arranging. "Aye, a strong back is worth its weight in gold, these days."

Amelia nodded, seizing the opening. "I would have welcomed one of those French prisoners, truth be told. Though Lord knows how I would have kept him fed!" She forced a laugh, the sound brittle and false to her own ears. But it seemed to do the trick, loosening the tongues of those around her.

"You'd have been lucky to keep him at all," another farmer chimed in, his voice low and conspiratorial. "Two of my neighbors had their 'helpers' up and vanish, without so much as a by-your-leave."

Amelia's heart quickened, her fingers tightening around the edge of her stall. "Is that so? How strange."

The farmer shrugged, his eyes darting around as if checking for eavesdroppers. "Aye, strange indeed. But there's a few as still have their man."

"Oh? Only a few?" she asked lightly.

"Aye! Like Henrys, out on the edge of the moor. Still having to put up room and board for that bloody frog... For now, at least." He jerked his chin towards a figure across the marketplace, a tall, gaunt man in tattered clothes, tending to a cart laden with winter vegetables.

Amelia followed his gaze, her breath catching in her throat. The prisoner. He was right there, in plain sight. But if the pattern held, he might not be for much longer.

She forced herself to look away, to school her features into a mask of mild interest. "Well, let's hope he's still there when the owner returns. The way things have been going, I wouldn't count on it."

The farmer scoffed, shaking his head. "Oh, he'll be there. That one knows better than to run. He's got a family back home, or so I hear. Wouldn't want anything to happen to them, now, would he?"

"Less'n they be the ones what pay for his release," another added.

Amelia made herself laugh with them. "A pretty thing, that," she echoed. But a chill ran down her spine, a sickening realization dawning in the pit of her stomach. Blackmail. Coercion. Ransoms and families under threat and the horrors of war, which touched far more than the battlefield.

She was just about to press for more information, to see what else she could glean, when a shadow fell across her stall. Amelia looked up, her heart leaping into her throat as she took in the tall, broad-shouldered form of a man, his blond hair gleaming in the weak winter sunlight.

"Good day, mistress," he said, his voice warm and friendly. "I was hoping you might have some of your raspberry jam for sale. My mother is ever so fond of it."

Amelia stared at him for a long moment, her mind racing. The code. Owen had told her to expect it, had described the man who would deliver it. Corporal Daniels, his trusted friend and comrade in arms.

She swallowed hard, forcing a smile to her lips. "I'm afraid I'm all out of jam for the season, sir. But there is a fellow across the way, tending a farm cart. He might be able to help you."

Daniels' eyes met hers, a flicker of understanding passing between them. He tipped his hat, a small, almost imperceptible nod of acknowledgement. "My thanks, mistress. I'll be sure to seek him out."

And then he was gone, melting into the crowd like a ghost. Amelia watched him go, her heart pounding in her chest. She had done it. She had passed on the information, had set the wheels in motion.

But even as a sense of relief washed over her, Amelia couldn't shake the feeling of unease that had settled in her bones. And she knew, with a certainty that chilled her to her core, that this was only the beginning.

The rest of the day passed in a blur, Amelia going through the motions of haggling and trading, her mind a thousand miles away. And when at last the market began to clear, the vendors packing up their wares and the townsfolk drifting back to their homes to settle in for their Christmas celebrations, she found herself scanning the thinning crowd, searching for a glimpse of a familiar face.

But Daniels was nowhere to be seen. It was only as Amelia was making her way out of the square, her basket now laden with the fruits of her labors, that she caught a flash of movement from the corner of her eye. There, mounting a horse on the far side of the market, was a figure in plain, rough-spun clothes. A figure with broad shoulders and blond hair, his posture straight and tall in the saddle.

Daniels. Riding out of town, his gaze fixed on the distant horizon. Following the prisoner.

Amelia felt a shiver run down her spine, a sense of foreboding settling like a lead weight in her stomach. The game was afoot, the pieces set in motion. And she had played her part, had done what was asked of her.

She could only pray that Owen knew what he was doing. Sniffing around, asking too many questions... he was like to attract unwelcome attention to himself. And possibly to her.

With a final, lingering look at the empty marketplace, Amelia pulled her shawl tighter around her shoulders and turned for home. Ethan would be waiting, his bright eyes and eager questions a balm to her weary soul.

And Owen... Owen would be there too, looking after Ethan like... Well, like a father. She could not decide whether that thought was more a comfort or a challenge.

T HE COTTAGE WAS WARM and welcoming as Amelia stepped inside, the scent of Yorkshire pudding and roasted meat filling the air. Owen was there in an instant, his hands gentle as he helped her off with her cloak, his eyes searching her face for any sign of distress.

"Are you well?" he murmured, his voice low and urgent. "Did you...?"

Amelia nodded, sinking down into the chair he had drawn up for her, her legs suddenly weak and shaky. "I did. I spoke to the farmers, passed on the message to Daniels. He followed the prisoner, just as you said he would."

Owen's face broke into a smile, fierce and proud. "Thank you, Amelia. Truly. I know how difficult this must be for you, how much it goes against your nature to dissemble or hold ulterior motives." He knelt before her, taking her hands in his own, his callused fingers warm and strong against her skin.

She studied him. "Is this what you do all the time?"

His expression froze. "What do you mean?"

"I mean... you are not merely a soldier who marches into battle. You are used to this... gathering information, working in secret." She narrowed her eyes. "Who are you, Owen North? What have you become?"

His mouth worked, and he looked down at their linked hands. "I'm not sure you want to know."

"I think I *must* know."

Owen's shoulders slumped as he took a breath, then he nodded. "Just... let me see to Ethan first."

She pulled his hand before he could back away. "He's reading. He won't pay you any mind. Tell me, Owen."

She could see him swallowing, and finally, he nerved himself sufficiently to speak. "Very well. When I was in Spain, I saved the life and earned the trust of a fine soldier, who earned a promotion in rank and a special assignment for his valor. As soon as he had leave to do so, he asked for me by name, to join a clandestine unit stationed here in England. Our task was to search out French agents, and..." He closed his eyes and turned his head to the side. "Amelia, I have done things I'm not proud of."

Her mouth felt like cotton. "What kinds of things?"

Owen was silent for a moment... too long. At last, he drew a shaking breath. "Amelia, I... On our last mission, we were searching for a highwayman who played the center link in a tidy little network going all the way to Whitehall itself, and I... well, the only information we could get on his whereabouts came from barmaids."

She blinked. "You... With barmaids?" Slowly, she withdrew her hand, her sight blind as she pulled away from him and stood up to wander to the kitchen.

He exhausted a heavy sigh behind her, and she heard him getting to his feet to follow her. "Not what you think, but yes. I took advantage of their willingness, their loose tongues. Plied them with ale and coin, but..."

"But what?" She grasped the edge of the table until her knuckles were white.

"I never loved them. Not... not in that way."

She wet her lips. "*Love*, you say," she whispered. "That can mean a number of things, I suppose."

"I think you know what it means." His voice was heavy. "I could never... I could not soil the one perfect memory I had."

She whirled on him. "Owen, why are you telling me this? You..." she tried to laugh, but it didn't sound right. "You made me no vow. You owe me no loyalty."

"But I did." He eased a step closer, raising one brow as his forehead broke in anguish. "Not aloud, Heaven help me, but in my heart."

Amelia's own heart gave an odd thump, and she caught her breath. "Owen, you... you cannot mean that. Why, it... it has been nearly six years! You did not know about Ethan, and you had every reason to think I had married."

"Indeed, I had."

"Well, then, it…" She sniffed, looking down. "It makes no sense. You are lying, or you are mad. You said yourself, you… with any number of women—willing women from whom you needed information."

He wrapped his hand over hers. "And that is all I took from them. What I needed to know." He feigned a chuckle that didn't touch his eyes. "And a few drinks. I will own it, there were moments when I wanted to lose myself. To pretend it was you, with your tender arms pulling at me, your sweet lips… my head full of ale and my heart missing its favorite piece. Aye, I nearly lost myself, more than once."

Amelia was shaking her head. "I still don't understand why you're telling me all this."

"Because." He lifted her knuckles to his face, his breath tickling her fingers as his mouth hovered over them. "I want you to know that I mean what I say when I tell you that you have owned my heart since I was but a lad, and no other will ever take your place." And then, his lips gently brushed her knuckles as his eyes fixed pleadingly on hers.

"Owen," she breathed. "I don't… I cannot…"

"I know you can promise me nothing," he whispered. "You owe me nothing. But I cannot see you again, be near you again, without daring to ask for that which I do not deserve. Can you ever trust me again, Amelia?"

"It is not that. But what about…" She trailed off, unable to give voice to the fears that haunted her, the doubts that clawed at her heart.

He reached to trace her cheek with his finger. "What comes next?" he guessed.

Amelia swallowed and nodded.

Owen thinned his lips. "I don't know, love. But… I cannot bear the thought of leaving you behind again. I won't do it—I cannot, not while there is breath in me. Can you give me… even the smallest measure of hope?"

"Oh, Owen." With a smile that trembled only slightly at the edges, Amelia leaned forward, her forehead coming to rest against his. "I do love you," she whispered, her voice thick with emotion. "I always have. And I trust you, with all that I have and all that I am."

Owen's arms came around her then, pulling her close and holding her tight. He did not kiss her—the time for such passions was not now. For Ethan was but a few feet away, and too many questions remained unanswered. But a promise was made, heart to heart, in whispers that surpassed hearing or speech.

Owen North, the father of her son and the man she had loved since she first set eyes on him, would never be lost to her again.

Chapter Nineteen

O WEN PACED THE SMALL confines of his cottage, drumming his fingers on the thigh of his breeches as he moved. Earlier today, holding Amelia in his arms again... oh, heaven, it had been everything.

But what the devil was he to do now? He could not lose her again. That was the one thing he did know. But protecting her—providing for her, finding a way to keep Ethan safe and healthy, and pulling her away from Ashwood's grasp—why, that was another matter.

The best way to start was by marrying her... that much was a given, but he did not dare wait long enough to have the banns called. That was assuming she was ready to pledge herself to him, and he was not so sure she was. But three weeks' worth of public announcements would only mean three weeks that she might be vulnerable to whatever Ashwood might choose to do in retaliation for her defiance. North would not put it past the man to force himself on her, or at least create as many financial and social hardships as possible for her.

That left Gretna Green as perhaps his best option. They were not so very far from Scotland. She deserved a real wedding ceremony in a church—something she had been denied because of him. But her home parish was a risk he was not willing to take... and he had no other "home parish" to offer her. They'd have to take Ethan with them, which meant a carriage, which meant...

A knock at the door startled him from his thoughts, and he opened it for Corporal Daniels to slip inside, his face grim and his posture tense.

"What news?" Owen asked.

Daniels put off his hat and coat and sank into a chair. and crossed his boots. "I followed the prisoner, just as Miss Grey directed. Managed to strike up a conversation with a local lad who works at the same farm."

North took the opposite chair and followed suit, leaning forward in his chair and bracing his elbows on his knees. "And? What did you learn?"

"The Frenchman goes by Jean-Pierre, no surname given. But according to the boy, he claims to be someone of importance back in France. Complains to no end about being stuck here and says there's no bloody way he's waiting around until the war is over and the crown pleases to release him."

North nodded, his brow furrowed in thought. "So, it's possible he could be seeking to buy his way back home. Bribing someone to facilitate his escape."

"Well, the lad says he's never observed the man to send letters to anyone. He could be just running his mouth, claiming to be someone important to merit better treatment, or as a way of protesting being assigned to farm work."

"That is possible," North murmured. "After all, he is still here while others have managed to escape. How many others are still in the area? Have you been able to learn more about that?"

"At least three. I'll be looking into them as well. But you know, it's not the common soldiers who got sent across the Channel for the bed and board treatment. Not important enough to bother with. Neither is it the generals, for they are far *too* important."

North grunted in agreement. "Aye. Middle-ranking officers, like ourselves, perhaps. Deemed enough of an asset to Napoleon that they could not be left roaming about France loose, but not so dangerous that they were imprisoned on a hulk on the Thames."

"So, in that sense, sir, every man who escapes is a security risk. Perhaps no one man is an imminent threat, but enough of them, all returning home with a knowledge of our geography, fortifications..."

"Napoleon cannot cross the Channel," North mused. "For now, at least. But I agree, best stop the leak before it sinks the ship. We start watching the waterways. And it would not hurt to keep an eye on Ashwood, any communications coming and going from his estate. If there's a connection there, we need to find it, cut the head off the operation. Elliot's agreed to see what he can uncover at the bank."

Daniels nodded slowly. "Lad seems steady, reliable, and no admirer of Lord Ashwood, either."

"Well, he is not alone in that. You will be hard pressed to find one who is—as least, one who does not work for him."

"I see you have no fond feelings for him. Lieutenant..." Daniels cleared his throat and blinked uncomfortably. "Sir, this is not a personal vendetta, is it? Anything to do with Miss Grey?"

North thinned his lips. "I cannot deny... There is a deal of history, Daniels."

"Aye, sir. And if His Lordship has designs on a woman you fancy... All I am asking, sir, is are you sure you are thinking clearly? Anyone could be profiting from the smuggling of prisoners; it need not be the most obvious. There is not some jealousy clouding your judgment?"

"I know very well what you are asking, and the answer is no, I am not approaching this from a position of cold detachment, but neither am I a fool or vindictive just for the pleasure of it. If Miss Grey..." He swallowed. "If she welcomed his attentions, I would step away."

"Would you, sir?"

North glared at the younger officer. "I did once before, though it tore the heart out of me. And so help me, I would do it again, if it was what she wanted, but it is not. For the lady's sake alone, Daniels, I would seek a way to check his plans, but with everything else—

his sudden interest in Miss Grey after all these years, the timing of it all—it's too coincidental."

Daniels regarded him carefully, his expression one of understanding tinged with concern. "I know you care for them, sir. But we have to be strategic about this. The captain did not send us up here to stop some rich blighter from pursuing a farm maid. We can't let our emotions cloud our judgment."

North sighed, some of the tension draining from his shoulders. "You're right, of course. It's just... the thought of any harm coming to them, it's more than I can bear."

"We won't let that happen," Daniels assured him. "We'll keep Miss Grey and the boy safe, sir."

North met his friend's gaze, a flicker of gratitude warming his chest. "Thank you, Daniels."

Daniels waved off the thanks, a small smile tugging at his lips. "Think nothing of it. So, how do we watch the river without drawing too much attention to ourselves?"

North heaved to his feet and began pacing again. "The same way we always do. Find someone who is already there and learn what they know."

THEY RECONVENED AT THE cottage the next evening, after a long day of scouting along the river and gathering information from local contacts. "Not much luck to the north-west," he said as he unwrapped two pork pies he had bought from the market and set them on plates. "Anything to the south-east?"

Daniels nodded, his eyes fixed on the plate before him. "Aye. Some."

"What's the matter, Daniels? I hope you did not stumble upon something else we must now unravel?"

Daniels shifted in his seat, a slight flush creeping up his neck. "No, sir. And I did learn some useful information."

"Excellent." North produced two mugs of beer and sat down opposite the corporal. "What did you learn?"

Daniels bit off some of the pork pie and chewed. He waited until he had swallowed before speaking. "There was a boat two days ago, with one pilot and the hold covered with a tarpaulin. No sign of any fishing, and he was not merely crossing but clearly traveling downriver. She said it was an odd time of year for that sort of thing."

North raised a brow. "'She?'"

Daniels shifted uncomfortably. "A fisherman's daughter I met in the alehouse. A... very friendly sort."

A smirk tugged at the corner of North's mouth. "Ah, I see. Finally learning to woo the ladies, are you?" he teased lightly.

But as soon as the words left his lips, Daniels' expression darkened, his discomfort becoming more pronounced. North immediately regretted his jest and fell silent, waiting for his friend to speak.

"It's not like that, sir," Daniels said quietly, his eyes downcast. "I despise playing on a lady's sympathies, charming her with drinks and compliments and making her think I fancy her, when all I want is information. It feels... dishonorable."

North nodded. "It does, that."

They sat in silence for a moment, the weight of their duties and the sacrifices they'd made hanging heavy in the air. "Sometimes," North began, his voice low and contemplative, "it seems our country demands everything of us. Our loyalty, our lives, even our very sense of self."

Daniels met his gaze, a flicker of recognition in his eyes. "Aye, sir. It's right despicable." He sniffed as his fingers broke into another piece of the crusty bread, and his big feet shifted under the table. "I still do it, because the captain said so."

"He is no longer our captain," North reminded him. "We're to have a new chap—we probably already do."

"Unless it's yourself, sir." Daniels looked up with a thin smile. "That's what Hunt was pressing for."

North leaned back in his chair, his brow furrowed in thought. "And now, I cannot say that I want it. You're right, Daniels. It is... dreadful, the things we've done for king and country. I've had to face up to some of them. But recall, if you will, the lives we have saved by skirting the bounds of decency at times."

"Aye, sir." Daniels nodded heavily, not looking up. "I try to tell myself that. I'll never be able to look anyone else in the eye, but..." He shrugged. "Well, now, there aren't many left for me to face up to, anyway."

"Daniels, are you fit for duty?"

The corporal's eyes flashed up to him at last. "Yes, sir. Why would I not be?"

"Because you've the look of a man who wants out."

Daniels scuffed his boots on the floorboards again. "It's not that, sir. I know my duty, and I know what I signed on for. What we do is more than just running about with swords and pistols. I just..."

"You've been so focused on serving the Crown that you forgot why you were doing it in the first place."

Daniels blinked and nodded. "Although, I know why. I think of the 'why' every day. I just can't get round the how, and it's like I've lost a bit of the who." His mouth worked, and he took a swig of the beer North had given him. "When I signed up, I figured I'd be sent for the grunt work. Big hands like mine, and all. Thought I'd be shoeing for the cavalry. Not..." His face wrinkled and he lifted his mug again.

"Not lying for a living." North's gaze grew unfocused.

"Something like that." Daniels forced a smile. "But serving under the captain, now, that was an honor, and no mistake. I just don't know if I'm the man to keep on, without…" He shrugged. "You know. No disrespect, sir."

"None taken." North paused. "And I am quite in line with your way of thinking. We are good at what we do, Daniels, and if might please the army to leave us there for a good long while. But I've a mind to find a way out. I cannot keep on with that if I…" He shook his head and gestured with the last bite of his pork pie. "Well. I might need to change some things."

Daniels regarded him carefully, his expression a mix of admiration and something akin to longing. "You're lucky, sir," he said heavily. "You've found the one thing that's more important to you than duty." He hesitated, as if weighing his next words. "But for me… what I want, I cannot have. So, all I have is duty."

North felt a pang of sympathy for his friend, a curiosity about the hidden depths he'd just glimpsed. He had always wondered if Daniels had a secret sweetheart, someone he loved but could not be with. But he knew it was not his place to pry, to ask questions that might cause more pain than comfort.

Instead, he cleared his throat, steering the conversation back to the task at hand. "You did well today, Daniels. The information you gathered will be invaluable."

Daniels straightened in his chair, his expression clearing as he focused on their mission once more. "Thank you, sir. What's our next move?"

"I want to survey Ashwood Manor," North replied, his tone growing serious. "We need to learn the layout, the routines of the household. Find the best vantage points for surveillance."

Daniels nodded, rising to his feet. "I'll make the necessary arrangements, sir. We can begin at first light."

Chapter Twenty

A MELIA AND ETHAN TREKKED along the snow-laden path that wound from her neighbor's farm back to her quaint cottage nestled in the hills. The Hampton family were her closest neighbors, so she and Ethan had dropped in with a basket of what gifts she could put together for them—some of which, if she were honest, had come from the trove delivered by Lord Ashwood. In return, they were marching home with a basket of hand pies, Parkin, cheese, and curd tarts. They would have a merry evening, she and Ethan, and tomorrow, Owen had promised to come share a Christmas meal with them. The thought made her feet light as they trudged through the snow.

"Fancy a little song, Ethan?" she asked. "It will make the walk home pass by in a mere moment. Let me see..." She frowned for a moment as a faint melody danced through her mind. "Oh, yes, I remember how it goes. 'God rest ye merry, gentlemen...'" With a soft smile, Amelia sang the familiar strains, her voice mingling with Ethan's cheerful laughter.

She stole a glance at him, his cheeks flushed with excitement as he tried to mimic the tune. He was off-key and short of breath, but he was smiling. And for the first time in a very long while, so was she. Because tomorrow... tomorrow was going to be a Christmas worth remembering.

Pausing for a moment, Amelia knelt beside Ethan, her gloved hands adjusting the scarf snugly wrapped around his neck. "Feeling warm enough, sweetheart?"

Ethan beamed up at her, his breath forming wisps in the frosty air. "Yes, Mama. Will L'tenant North come tomorrow?"

She smiled at the way Ethan said "Lieutenant" around the gap in his front teeth. "He promised he would, yes. Do you like him, then?"

Ethan nodded enthusiastically. "He's nice to me."

Amelia stroked her son's cold cheek. "I believe he is very fond of you already. Come, let us hurry home before you freeze to death." She rose to her feet, scanning the slope ahead through the gathering darkness of a winter's afternoon. Around the next bend in the path, through the veil of falling snow, she could just make out the flicker of lamplight emanating from her cottage windows. Another half hour of walking, at least. She should not have stayed so long talking to Mrs. Hampton, because it would be well past dark when they made it to their door.

The tranquil silence enveloped them, broken only by the soft crunch of their footsteps in the snow. No sound of hooves or wheels disturbed the peaceful serenity, for in these hills, the snow muffled all but the gentlest of sounds.

That was, until a muffled jingle from behind shattered the tranquility of the wintry scene. Amelia's heart skipped a beat as she glanced over her shoulder and caught sight of the approaching sleigh, its elegant frame adorned with the crest of Lord Ashwood. He closed in on her swiftly, and the horses whinnied softly as they came to a halt beside her, their breath forming clouds of steam in the frosty air.

"Mistress Grey! What a pleasant surprise. And young Master Ethan, too. You both look chilled to the bone. Please, allow me to offer you a ride home."

Amelia hesitated, her grip tightening on Ethan's hand. The last time she had accepted a ride from Ashwood, it had left her feeling unsettled and trapped. She had no desire to repeat the experience.

"Thank you, my lord, but we're quite all right, and we have not far to go. The walk will do us good."

Ashwood's smile faltered, a flicker of annoyance passing over his features. "I must insist, Mistress Grey. The weather is turning, and I would be remiss in my duties as a gentleman if I allowed you to continue on foot."

There was an edge to his voice, a subtle warning that made Amelia's stomach clench with unease. Reluctantly, she allowed him to help her and Ethan into the sleigh, settling her basket on her lap and spreading her cloak onto the plush velvet seat with a sense of trepidation.

As the sleigh lurched forward, Ashwood leaned back, studying Amelia with a calculating gaze. "I must say, I've been quite concerned about you, my dear. The talk in the village... well, it's not kind to a woman in your position."

Amelia stiffened, her arms instinctively tightening around Ethan. "I'm not sure I know what you mean, my lord."

"Come now, Amelia. Let's not play games. We both know that young Ethan here bears a striking resemblance to a certain lieutenant. It's only natural that people would... talk, and they have begun to do so."

Amelia felt the blood drain from her face, her heart pounding in her chest. How did everyone seem to know? She had been so careful, so guarded with her secrets.

"I... I don't..."

Ashwood held up a hand, silencing her. "There's no need to explain, my dear. I understand perfectly. A young woman, alone in the world, falling prey to the charms of a handsome soldier. It's a tale as old as time."

He leaned forward, his eyes glinting with a predatory light. "But you must understand, Amelia, that such indiscretions have consequences. For you, for your son... and for Lieutenant North."

Amelia's eyes widened, fear and anger warring in her chest. "What do you mean? What have you done?"

"Done? Why, nothing, but I do mean to look out for your best interests. Your father would have hoped for nothing less from an old friend."

"My interests are my own to look after, thank you very much."

Lord Ashwood leaned forward. "Then I suggest you practice a little more care before ruining yourself and your son's future. I've no wish to harm you, Miss Grey, but I can and will make life very difficult for a man like North, if he decides to press in where he is not wanted. His career, his future... all could be destroyed with a few well-placed words."

Amelia's jaw dropped. "How dare—"

He sat back, his tone turning conversational. "Of course, it doesn't have to be that way. If you were to accept my proposal, to become my wife... well, I could ensure that North's prospects remain bright. I could even see to it that Ethan is provided for, given every opportunity to thrive."

Amelia's mind raced, her throat tight with unshed tears. The thought of marrying Ashwood, of tying herself to him for the rest of her days... it was unbearable. But the alternative, the threat to Owen and Ethan's future...

"You would blackmail me into marriage?" she whispered, her voice trembling. "You would use my child, the man I... you would use them as pawns in your game?"

Ashwood's eyes narrowed, his hand coming to rest on her knee in a gesture that made her skin crawl. "Blackmail is such an ugly word, my dear. I prefer to think of it as... an arrangement. One that benefits us all."

"But why? What could I possibly have that you could want?"

He frowned. "I should think that would be quite obvious."

Amelia clenched her fists, darting a glance at Ethan, who was hunkering lower in the sleigh, visibly upset by their arguing. "I'm afraid it is not. You are not without alternatives, my lord."

"That is where you are mistaken." The sleigh slowed to a halt outside Amelia's cottage, and Ashwood offered to hand her out. "Think carefully, Miss Grey. You have a choice to make. A choice that will determine the course of not just your life, but the lives of those you hold most dear."

With that, he sat back, his expression once again pleasant and benign. "Good day, Mistress Grey. I look forward to hearing your decision."

Amelia stumbled from the sleigh, her legs weak and shaking. She clutched Ethan to her side, watching Lord Ashwood pull away, the horses' hooves kicking up a spray of mud and snow.

Her mind whirled with the implications of Ashwood's words, with the terrible choice that lay before her. To marry a man she despised, to condemn herself to a life of misery and every sort of control... or to risk the ruin of the man she loved and the future of her child.

B LAST IT ALL. CHRISTMAS Eve, and this was how they were obliged to spend it!

North and Daniels had been surveilling Ashwood Manor from various vantage points throughout the day, the bitter cold seeping into their bones as they huddled in the dense tree line surrounding the estate. As the sun began to set, they reconvened at their designated meeting spot, their breaths clouding in the frigid air.

"I don't think we're going to find anything else today," Daniels said, rubbing his hands together for warmth. "It's been quiet as a tomb since this morning."

North nodded, his jaw clenched against the chill. "Agreed. And as much as I hate to admit it, we may need to consider watching the house tomorrow as well."

Daniels raised an eyebrow. "On Christmas Day? What would the old cad be about on the holy day? Besides, I thought you had plans with Miss Grey and young Ethan."

A flicker of warmth passed through North at the mention of Amelia and his son, a momentary respite from the cold and the tension of their mission. "I do," he said softly. "And I intend to keep them. But if Ashwood is up to something, we can't afford to let our guard down, even for a day."

Daniels sighed, his breath puffing out in a cloud of white. "I suppose you're right. Elliot and his father invited us to share a meal with them, but duty comes first."

North clapped a hand on his friend's shoulder, a silent acknowledgment of the sacrifice they were both making. "We'll make it up to them, Daniels. Once this is all over, we'll—"

He broke off, his eyes narrowing as a flurry of movement caught his attention. A sleigh, jingling up the drive of the house. "That's Ashwood," North murmured. "Where the devil has he been, so late? I doubt that was a pleasure drive."

"And alone, too," Daniels mused. "Not even a coachman to drive him."

As they watched, Ashwood halted before the house and handed the horse off to a coachman, but before he allowed the animal and sleigh to be led away, he bent over to pull a bundle out from under the seat.

"Look," North hissed, pointing towards the man. "He's carrying something."

Daniels squinted, trying to make out the details in the gathering gloom. "A sack of some kind. A bundle of clothing, perhaps?"

Ashwood hailed another man and passed off the bundle after a moment of quiet conversation. Instruction or orders, something of that nature. A moment later, they parted, with Ashwood turning for the door of the manor and the other splitting off in the opposite direction.

"He's heading for the stables," North said.

They watched as the figure disappeared into the outbuilding, only to emerge moments later leading a horse. With a swift, practiced motion, the man mounted the beast and set off at a brisk trot through the snow, the sack secured behind the saddle.

"Follow him," North said, already moving towards their own hidden mounts. "But keep your distance. We don't want to spook him."

They rode out, keeping to the shadows and maintaining a careful space between themselves and their quarry. The man led them away from the manor, down winding country lanes and across frost-covered fields.

Just as North was beginning to fear they would lose him in the darkness, the rider came to a stop at the edge of a small, dense copse of trees. Dismounting, he retrieved the sack and disappeared into the woods, the horse left to steam and stamp in the cold.

North and Daniels exchanged a glance, a silent communication passing between them. Quietly, they slipped from their own saddles and crept forward, every sense straining for any sign of their target. They followed the man through the snow, their footsteps muffled by the soft, white blanket that covered the ground. The bitter cold nipped at their faces, but they pressed on, determined to uncover the secrets that lay hidden in the depths of the forest.

For what seemed like another mile, they tracked their quarry, staying just far enough behind to avoid detection. The man moved with purpose, his strides long and quick through the snow drifts, as if he were on a mission of great importance.

At last, he came to a halt in a small clearing, the trees pressing in close around him like silent sentinels. North and Daniels crouched low, their breaths frosting in the air as they watched the man reach into the sack and withdraw a small, tightly-wrapped parcel.

Another figure emerged from the shadows, his face obscured by a heavy scarf and a low-pulled hat. The two men exchanged a few brief words, their voices too low to carry on the wind, and then the parcel changed hands.

As quickly as he had appeared, the second man vanished back into the trees, his footsteps crunching softly in the snow as he hurried away. North and Daniels exchanged a glance, their eyes meeting in a moment of silent communication.

With a nod, they rose from their hiding place and began to follow the new trail, their own steps careful and deliberate to avoid leaving any trace of their passage. The path led them deeper into the woods, away from the main roads and the usual traffic of the countryside.

After a few minutes of careful tracking, they found themselves on the banks of a secluded stretch of the river, the water dark and still beneath the thin layer of ice that coated its surface. And there, half-hidden among the reeds and the overhanging branches, was a small boat, its hull scraped and battered from long use.

North approached cautiously, his hand resting on the hilt of his sword. As he drew closer, he could see the signs of recent activity—footprints in the snow, a length of rope coiled neatly on the bench, a scattering of provisions tucked beneath the seats.

"This is it," he murmured, his voice low and tense. "This is where they're planning to smuggle out the next group of prisoners."

Daniels nodded, his eyes scanning the surrounding woods with a wary gaze. "We'll need to keep watch, to make sure we intercept them before they can make their escape."

North agreed, his mind already racing with plans and possibilities. They would need to be careful, to avoid tipping their hand too soon. But with a little luck and a lot of persistence, they might just be able to put an end to this operation once and for all.

As they made their way back through the forest, the moonlight filtering through the bare branches overhead, North felt a flicker of hope kindle in his chest. They were close.

Too close to take their leisure now... Christmas or not.

Chapter Twenty-One

A MELIA STOOD AT THE frosty window, her eyes scanning the snow-covered path
that led to her cottage. The winter sun hung low in the sky, casting a pale, watery
light over the landscape, but still, there was no sign of Owen.

Her heart clenched with a mixture of worry and disappointment. He had promised to
be here, to share a Christmas meal with her and Ethan. But the hours had ticked by, and
now the daylight was fading, and she couldn't help but fear the worst. Had something
happened to him? Or had Lord Ashwood made good on his threats, had he found a way
to drive Owen away from her once and for all?

The memory of her encounter with Ashwood the day before sent a shiver down her
spine, a cold, creeping dread that seemed to sink into her very bones. The way he had
looked at her, the thinly veiled menace in his words... it had shaken her to her core, had
left her feeling vulnerable and exposed in a way she had never experienced before.

And now, with Owen's absence, those fears seemed to take on a new, terrifying shape.
Because if Ashwood could get to him, if he could use his influence and his power to tear
them apart...

Amelia closed her eyes, fighting back the sting of tears. She couldn't bear the thought
of losing Owen, not now, not when she had only just found him again. He and her son
were the only bright spots in her life, the only hope she had for a future that wasn't mired
in hardship and struggle.

Behind her, Ethan chattered happily to himself as he played with his carved wood-
en soldiers, blissfully unaware of the turmoil that raged in his mother's heart. Amelia
watched him for a moment, her love for him a fierce, protective thing that seemed to fill

her entire being. She would do anything for him—anything to keep him safe, to give him the life he deserved. Even if it meant sacrificing her own happiness, her own chance at love.

With a sigh, Amelia turned back to the window, her forehead resting against the cool glass. The minutes ticked by with agonizing slowness, each one feeling like an eternity. And then, just as she was about to give up hope, just as the last of her faith began to crumble... the door burst open, and there he was.

Owen stood on the threshold, his arms laden with parcels and his face ruddy from the cold. He looked exhausted, his eyes shadowed and his hair disheveled, but when he saw her, his whole countenance seemed to light up, a smile breaking across his face like the sun emerging from behind a cloud.

"Amelia," he breathed, his voice rough with emotion. "I'm so sorry I'm late. I got held up with... well, with something important. But I'm here now."

Amelia stared at him for a long moment, her heart pounding in her chest. And then, before she even realized what she was doing, she was flying across the room, her arms wrapping around him in a fierce, desperate embrace.

Owen staggered back a step, clearly caught off guard by the intensity of her greeting. But then his own arms came up to encircle her, the parcels falling forgotten to the floor as he held her close.

"What's this?" he murmured, his breath warm against her ear. "It's alright, love. I'm here. I'm not going anywhere."

Amelia clung to him, her face buried in the rough wool of his coat. She couldn't speak, couldn't find the words to express the depth of her relief, the sheer, over-whelming joy of having him here, solid and real in her arms.

But somehow, he seemed to understand. His hand came up to cradle the back of her head, his fingers tangling gently in her hair. "I'm sorry," he said again, his voice low and fervent. "I never meant to worry you."

Amelia pulled back, swiping at her eyes with the back of her hand. "I thought... I thought perhaps Lord Ashwood had..." She trailed off, unable to give voice to the fears that had haunted her. But Owen's expression darkened, his jaw clenching with a quiet fury.

"Ashwood," he growled, the name like a curse on his lips. "I won't let him hurt you, Amelia. I won't let him come between us. Not again."

She nodded, a small, watery smile tugging at her lips. "I know. I do. I just... I can't help but worry."

Owen's gaze softened, his hand coming up to cup her cheek. "I know, love. And I'm sorry for that. But I promise you, it will take a deal more than Ashwood's ire to drive me away. I will do everything in my power to keep you and Ethan safe."

Amelia leaned into his touch, her eyes fluttering closed for a brief, blissful moment. But then Ethan's excited voice broke through the quiet, his small form barreling towards them with all the energy of a miniature whirlwind.

"L'tenant North!" he cried, his face alight with joy. "You came! And you brought presents!"

Owen laughed, scooping the boy up into his arms and spinning him around. "I did indeed, my lad. And I think there might just be something special in there for you." He set Ethan down gently, then bent to retrieve the scattered parcels. Amelia watched as he handed them to her one by one, his expression almost shy.

"I know it's not much," he said, his cheeks flushing beneath his stubble of a beard. "But I wanted to bring you something, to show you how much I... how much you both mean to me."

Amelia felt her heart swell with emotion, her throat tightening with unshed tears. "Owen, you didn't have to do this. Your being here, that's more than enough."

But he just shook his head, a small, crooked smile tugging at his lips. "I wanted to. Please, just open them."

And so, she did, her hands trembling slightly as she untied the twine and peeled back the brown paper. Inside, she found a treasure trove of small, precious things—a single teapot of fine bone China that used to grace Mrs. North's table, the delicate teacups nestled in a bed of straw. A bolt of soft, warm wool, the rich green hue reminding her of the rolling hills in springtime. And at the very bottom, a small, carved wooden figure, its paint faded and chipped but still recognizable as a gallant soldier atop a rearing steed.

"That was mine," Owen said softly, his eyes distant with memory. "My father made it for me, before I was even born. I thought perhaps Ethan might like to have it, to play with and cherish as I once did."

Ethan's eyes went wide, his small hands reaching out to take the toy with a reverence that made Amelia's heart ache. "For me?" he whispered, his voice filled with wonder.

Owen nodded, ruffling the boy's hair affectionately. "For you, my boy. May it bring you as much joy as it brought me."

Amelia watched as Ethan clutched the soldier to his chest, his face alight with a happiness that she had rarely seen. And in that moment, she felt a rush of love for the man beside her, a fierce, overwhelming gratitude for the way he had brought light and laughter back into their lives.

But even as she basked in the warmth of the moment, even as she let herself be swept up in the joy of having Owen here, with them, where he belonged… she couldn't quite shake the sense of unease that lingered in the back of her mind, the fear that whispered that this happiness was all too fragile, all too fleeting.

And when Owen turned to her, his eyes shining with a hopeful, questioning light, she felt her resolve crumble, the tears she had been holding back spilling down her cheeks in a hot, unstoppable flood.

"Amelia?" he asked, his brow furrowing with concern. "Love, what is it? What's wrong?"

She shook her head, unable to speak past the lump in her throat. But Owen was persistent, his hands gentle as he took her by the shoulders and turned her to face him.

"Please," he said softly, his thumb brushing away a stray tear. "Talk to me. Let me help."

And so, with a shuddering breath, Amelia told him everything. About Ashwood's visit, about his threats and the sickening insinuations. About the fear that had taken root in her heart, the certainty that the lord would stop at nothing to get what he wanted… even if it meant destroying the man she loved.

"I'm so afraid, Owen," she whispered, her voice breaking on a sob. "Afraid of what he might do, of how far he might go. I can't bear the thought of anything happening to you, not because of me."

Owen's jaw clenched, his eyes flashing with a fury that made her heart stop. But when he spoke, his voice was soft, almost tender. "Amelia, listen to me. You don't have to be afraid, not anymore. Daniels and I, we've been watching Ashwood. We're sure he's involved in something, something big. The smuggling of those French prisoners… we're gathering proof that he might be the one behind it all."

Amelia's eyes widened, her heart stuttering in her chest. "But… but why? What could he possibly have to gain from such a thing?"

Owen shook his head, his expression grim. "Money, power, influence… who knows? But what I do know is that we're close, Amelia. Close to exposing him for the snake he is. And when we do…"

He trailed off, his hand coming up to cradle her cheek. "When we do, he won't be able to hurt you, or anyone else, ever again. I swear it."

Amelia leaned into his touch, her eyes fluttering closed. She wanted so badly to believe him, to trust in the strength and the surety of his words. But the fear still lingered, a cold, creeping thing that wound its way around her heart and squeezed tight.

"But what if he finds out?" she whispered, her voice trembling. "What if he realizes what you're doing, and he tries to stop you? Owen, he has so much power, so much influence. I'm afraid of what he might do, of how far he might go to protect himself."

Owen's expression softened, his thumb tracing the delicate line of her jaw. "I know, love. And that's why... that's why I think it might be best if you and Ethan went away for a while. Just until this is all over, until Ashwood is dealt with, and we can be sure you're safe."

Amelia's eyes flew open, her heart clenching with a sudden, sharp panic. "Leave? But... but where would we go? And what about the farm, the animals? I can't just abandon them, Owen. They need me."

He nodded, his gaze steady and reassuring. "I know they do. And I would never ask you to neglect them, not for anything. But I was thinking... what if we hired someone to look after things for a while? Just until you can come back, until it's safe for you to be here again."

Amelia hesitated, her mind racing with the implications of his words. The thought of leaving, of entrusting her beloved farm to someone else... it went against every instinct she had, every fiber of her being that had fought so hard to build this life for herself and her son.

But she also knew that Owen was right. As long as Ashwood was out there, as long as he held the power to hurt them... she and Ethan would never truly be safe.

"Very well," she said at last, her voice barely above a whisper. "We'll go. But... but where, Owen? Where can we possibly hide that he won't find us? It is not as if I have relatives in another town."

Owen's brow furrowed in thought, his mind clearly racing with possibilities. But then, like a flash of lightning, the answer came to her.

"Mr. Sommers," she said, her eyes widening with realization. "The apothecary. He's always been kind to us, always looked out for Ethan and me. And since his wife passed, he has that big old house in the village, with plenty of room for us to stay."

Owen's face broke into a grin, his eyes shining with pride and admiration. "Hiding in plain sight. Ashwood would never think to look for you there, and even if he did, you would not be alone up here in the middle of the Dales, with no one to hear you calling for help. It is an improvement, at least."

Amelia felt a rush of relief, a flicker of hope kindling in her chest. It wasn't a perfect solution. There were still so many unknowns. But like Owen had said, it *was* a start. "Owen," she whispered, "I... I don't know what I would have done if you had not come back... Thank you. For... for trying to help, for being so kind to Ethan..."

He shook his head, his hand coming up to tangle gently in her hair. "You don't have to thank me, Amelia. Not for this, not for anything. I love you. I've always loved you. And I will spend the rest of my life proving that to you, if you'll let me."

Her breath caught in her throat, her heart pounding so hard she was sure he must be able to hear it. "Owen, I... do you mean...?"

He smiled, his eyes crinkling at the corners in that way she loved so much. "I do. Amelia, I want to marry you. I want to build a life with you, a family. I want to be there for you and Ethan, always. If you'll have me."

For a moment, Amelia couldn't speak, couldn't breathe past the sudden, overwhelming swell of emotion that rose up to choke her. She had dreamed of this moment, had imagined it in a thousand different ways over the long, lonely years. But never, not in her wildest fantasies, had she dared to hope that it might one day come true.

"Owen," she managed at last, her voice trembling with joy and disbelief. "Are you... are you sure? Is this really what you want? Not just to protect us, but...?"

"But because I love you," he finished, his voice low and fervent. "Because I have always loved you, and I will never stop loving you, not for as long as I live. This is my second chance, Amelia. Our second chance. And I am not going to waste it, not for anything in the world."

Amelia felt a smile break across her face, a joy so bright and fierce that it seemed to fill her entire being. And then, before she could second-guess herself, before she could let the doubts and the fears creep back in... she leaned forward and kissed him, her lips soft and warm against his own.

Owen made a small, surprised sound in the back of his throat, but then his arms were coming around her, pulling her close as he deepened the kiss. And for a long, blissful moment, there was nothing else in the world but him, but the taste of him and the feel of him, solid and real and here, with her, where he belonged.

They broke apart, breathing hard and grinning like fools. And then they were laughing, the sound bright and joyful in the quiet of the cottage.

"I love you," Amelia whispered, her forehead resting against his. "I love you so much, Owen North. And yes, yes, I will marry you. Today, tomorrow, whenever you want. I am yours, now and always."

Owen's smile was brighter than the sun, his eyes shining with a happiness that took her breath away. "And I am yours, Amelia Grey. Forever and always, until the end of my days."

They kissed again, slow and sweet, savoring the feeling of finally, finally being exactly where they were meant to be. And when Ethan came barreling over, his small arms wrapping around them both in a fierce, joyful hug... This, right here, was what heaven must feel like.

"Merry Christmas, Owen," she whispered, her heart so full she thought it might burst. "And thank you, for the best gift I could ever have asked for."

Owen smiled, his hand coming up to cradle her cheek. "Merry Christmas, my love. And here's to many, many more."

Chapter Twenty-Two

A MELIA FOLLOWED OWEN'S SHADOWY figure, with Ethan riding piggyback on his shoulders as they hurried through the deserted streets of the village, the pre-dawn darkness cloaking their movements like a protective shroud. They had to come early, to be secretive. Owen had slept a few precious hours on the floor, guarding her front door while she and Ethan had tried to rest, but by three in the morning, he had roused them to make the journey into town before anyone was on the roads. And with the fresh snow falling in heavy clumps, their most recent tracks would soon blend in with the indistinct divots from all their previous passings.

They reached the apothecary's door just as the first hints of dawn began to paint the sky in hues of pink and gold. Owen set Ethan on his feet and stepped forward, his hand raised to knock, but before his knuckles could make contact, the door swung open, revealing a disheveled and slightly bewildered Mr. Sommers.

"Miss Grey?" he said, his brow furrowing in confusion. "Master Ethan? What brings you here at this hour? Is the lad unwell?"

But then his gaze fell on Owen, standing tall and imposing behind them, and his eyes widened, his posture straightening almost unconsciously. "Lieutenant North, sir. Forgive me, I didn't see you there. Is something amiss?"

Amelia felt her cheeks flush, her tongue suddenly thick and clumsy in her mouth. How could she explain the situation, the danger that had driven her to seek refuge almost in the middle of the night? But before she could stumble through an explanation, Owen stepped forward, his voice calm and assured.

"Mr. Sommers, I apologize for the intrusion at such an early hour. But I'm afraid Miss Grey is in need of a safe place to stay, somewhere she can remain unobserved for a few days. I was hoping you might be able to provide that sanctuary."

Sommers' expression cleared, a look of understanding dawning on his face. "Of course, of course. Come in, please. I'm glad you thought of me." He ushered them inside, the warmth of the house enveloping them. But even as Amelia felt herself begin to relax, she couldn't help but notice the way Ethan clung to her hand, his small face pinched with anxiety.

"Mama," he whispered, his voice trembling slightly. "Where are we? I want to go home."

Amelia's heart clenched, her throat tightening with emotion. "It's alright, my love," she murmured, kneeling down to look him in the eye. "We're just going to stay with Mr. Sommers for a little while, like an adventure. Won't that be fun?"

But even as she spoke the words, she could see the fear in Ethan's eyes, the uncertainty that made his breathing quicken and his chest heave.

"Here, lad," Sommers said gently, "Let me fix you a steaming mug of something to will help calm your nerves, settle your breathing. I have in my pantry a special blend, just for brave boys like you."

Ethan looked up at the apothecary, his eyes wide and trusting. "For me?" he asked, his voice small.

Sommers smiled, pressing the mug into his hands. "For you, Master Ethan. And for your mother as well, if she'd like."

He glanced up at Amelia, his expression warm and inviting. "Lieutenant North? Will you join us?"

But Owen was already shaking his head, his posture stiff and formal. "Thank you, Mr. Sommers, but I'm afraid I have matters to attend to. Time is of the essence, and I cannot delay."

He turned to go, but Sommers stepped forward, his hand outstretched as if to stop him. "Lieutenant, wait. There's something I need to..."

But then he glanced at Amelia and Ethan, his expression suddenly uncertain. "No, never mind. It can wait. But please, sir... be careful. The roads are treacherous this time of year, and the weather can turn on a moment's notice."

North nodded, his gaze softening slightly as he looked at the old apothecary. "I will, Mr. Sommers. And thank you for welcoming Miss Grey and her son."

He turned to Amelia then, his eyes locking with hers in a moment of silent communication. "I'll return as soon as I can," he said quietly. "Until then... stay safe. Stay hidden. I'll take care of the rest."

Amelia nodded, her throat too tight to speak. She watched as he strode out the door, his tall, broad-shouldered form disappearing into the early morning mist.

"Hmmf. Extraordinary!" Sommers breathed as Owen went out.

"Truly, Mr. Sommers, I am sorry. The lieutenant has reasons to believe—"

"I know exactly what he believes." Sommers gently took her by the elbow and led her to a seat. "And I'm blessed glad of it. About time someone took note of things, I say."

Amelia tipped her head in confusion. "I beg your pardon, Mr. Sommers, but... what do you know?"

"Oh, nothing terribly helpful, I shouldn't think. Nothing that cannot wait until we have you both settled. Come then. I've got a spare room upstairs, with a nice cozy bed and plenty of blankets. I'd warrant the lad there is wrung out."

Amelia turned to him, her eyes stinging with sudden tears. "Mr. Sommers, I... I don't know how to thank you. I know this must be a terrible imposition..."

But the old apothecary waved away her protests, his smile warm and genuine. "Nonsense, my dear. You could not have done better than to come to me. In truth, I'm glad of the company. Christmas was a lonely affair this year, with my dear wife gone and my children grown and scattered to the winds. Now, are you more tired or hungry? I've got some fresh eggs in the larder, and a bit of fresh bread that's just begging to be toasted and slathered with butter."

Ethan perked up at the mention of food, his eyes brightening with interest. "With jam, too?" he asked, his voice hopeful.

Sommers chuckled, ruffling the boy's hair with a fond touch. "With jam, too, Master Ethan. Made by the finest jam-maker this side of the Pennines."

As Amelia followed the apothecary into the kitchen, Ethan's hand clasped tightly in her own, she felt a sense of peace settle over her, a calm that she hadn't known in longer than she could remember. Here, in this warm, cozy house, with the scent of tea and toast filling the air and the kindness of a true friend surrounding her like a protective cloak... she felt safe.

If only she could be sure that Owen was not marching into danger on her behalf.

THE BITTER CHILL OF the winter night seeped into North's bones as he crouched in the shadows, his eyes fixed on the grand facade of Ashwood Manor. For three days, he had kept a relentless vigil, watching and waiting for any sign of the lord's activities. Daniels, on the other hand, had been watching the river, and at their last conversation some hours earlier, there had been no movements of the boat or provisions.

Tonight, Ashwood's estate was a blaze of light and noise, carriages pulling up to the front entrance in a steady stream. North's jaw clenched as he watched the guests arrive, their laughter and chatter carrying on the frigid air. "Deuce take it," he muttered, his breath clouding in the darkness. "How am I to make sense of this chaos? Any one of those guests could be complicit or innocent."

He strained his eyes, trying to make out faces, to place names to the shadowy figures that flitted past the windows. But it was futile, a needle in a veritable haystack of silk and lace and glittering jewels.

As the hours ticked by, North's frustration grew, his muscles aching from the cold and the strain of his unrelenting focus. He watched as the party began to wind down, as the carriages departed one by one, until at last, the manor stood silent and dark once more.

With a heavy sigh, he pushed himself to his feet, his joints protesting the sudden movement. He had learned nothing, gained no new insight into Ashwood's dealings. It was a bitter pill to swallow, a night wasted in fruitless surveillance.

Wearily, North made his way back to his cottage in town, his mind still churning with unanswered questions and nagging doubts. As he pushed open the door, he was surprised to find Daniels sprawled in a chair by the fire, his head lolling against his chest in slumber.

At the sound of North's entrance, the corporal jerked awake, his hand flying to the pistol at his hip. "Who goes there?" he demanded, his voice rough with sleep.

"At ease, Daniels," North said, a wry smile tugging at his lips despite his exhaustion. "It's just me."

Daniels relaxed, rubbing a hand over his face as he straightened in his seat. "Apologies, sir. I must have drifted off."

North waved away the apology, sinking into the chair opposite his friend. "It's no matter. I'm glad you're here, actually. I've had a devil of a night, watching Ashwood's blasted party. A fat lot of good it did me."

Daniels leaned forward, his brow furrowed. "A party, you say? Seems a strange thing, for a man under suspicion of treason."

North snorted, shaking his head. "Indeed. But what better than a large yuletide party to cover his tracks? A smokescreen, to divert attention from his true dealings. I may have let a dozen traitors slip away in their carriages tonight, or there might not have been so much as a card cheat among them." He sighed, pinching the bridge of his nose between his fingers. "I feel like I'm chasing shadows, Daniels. Always one step behind."

Daniels was silent for a moment, a strange expression on his face. Then, slowly, a grin began to spread across his features. "Well, sir, I might just have some news that will put a spring back in your step."

North sat up straighter. "What is it? What have you learned?"

"I was in the village to the southeast, following up on a lead from the fisherman's daughter. She got word to me that a boat was making its way down the river. They'd slipped right past my nose, used another boat, and I nearly missed it."

North's eyes widened, his exhaustion forgotten in the surge of excitement that rushed through him. "Another boat? Did you intercept it?"

Daniels nodded, his grin widening. "I did, sir. Rode ahead and commandeered another vessel, then forced the blighters ashore at pistol-point. And what do you think I found under the tarpaulin?"

"A boat full of frogs," North breathed, hardly daring to hope. "Jean-Pierre among them."

"The very same," Daniels confirmed, his voice ringing with triumph. "I turned the lot of them over to the local militia, but not before I got some very interesting information out of our dear boat captain."

North leaned forward, his elbows on his knees. "What did he say? Did he implicate Ashwood?"

"Not directly," Daniels admitted. "But he had papers on him, documents that bore Ashwood's seal. It's not a smoking gun, but it's a start."

North felt a rush of pride, a fierce, exultant joy that made his heart sing. "Daniels, you magnificent scoundrel. You've cracked this thing wide open."

The corporal ducked his head, a pleased flush staining his cheeks. "I don't know about that, sir. But it's a step in the right direction, to be sure."

North clapped him on the shoulder, his grip firm and reassuring. "A dashed big step, Corporal. This is the break we've been waiting for."

He sat back, his mind racing with the implications of Daniels' discovery. "Did the pilot say anything else? How long before Ashwood will learn about the interception?"

Daniels shook his head. "Well, again, he never named any names, but he claimed that his contact had already been paid, that he'd washed his hands of the whole affair. Seems our lord isn't one to get his own hands dirty."

North nodded, his jaw tight. "No, he wouldn't be. Too much risk, too much chance of being caught out."

Daniels leaned back in his chair, his expression thoughtful. "What now, sir? Do we bring the evidence against Ashwood to the authorities?"

North hesitated, his mind whirring with possibilities. "Not yet," he said at last. "We need more, something ironclad that even Ashwood's allies can't ignore. Did you speak to Elliot Barrow, by any chance? If Ashwood has been paid, perhaps it passed through the bank."

Daniels nodded. "I did, sir. Didn't let on any specifics, just casual conversation, but he had nothing new to report. No unusual transactions, no suspicious activity since that one transfer of funds."

North sighed, running a hand through his hair. "Dash it all. I was hoping he might have uncovered something more. But no matter. I'll send word to the captain that you made a catch."

He stood, his exhaustion forgotten in the surge of renewed purpose that filled him. "I need to speak to Amelia, to let her know what we've discovered. She deserves to know that we're making progress, that there's hope for an end to this nightmare."

Daniels rose as well, a yawn stretching his features. "Of course, sir. But might I suggest we both get some rest first? It's been a long night, and we'll need our wits about us."

North hesitated, torn between his desire to see Amelia and the knowledge that Daniels was right. "Very well," he said at last, his shoulders slumping. And so, with a final, weary nod, the two men made their way to their respective beds, the weight of the day's revelations and the promise of the morrow heavy on their minds.

As North lay in the darkness, his eyes fixed on the ceiling above, he couldn't help but feel a flicker of hope, a glimmer of light amidst the shadows that had threatened to consume them all. They were close, so close to proving Lord Ashwood was a traitor to the crown. And when they did... when they finally brought the blackguard to justice...

North's lips curved in a grim, determined smile. Oh, what a reckoning that would be.

Chapter Twenty-Three

A MELIA SAT BY THE window of the small, cozy room, her eyes fixed on the bustling street below. The apothecary's shop was a hive of activity, with customers coming and going in a steady stream, but up here, in the quiet sanctuary of Mr. Sommers' private quarters, she felt a world away from the chaos and the noise.

It had been four days since she and Ethan had taken refuge here, four days of hiding and waiting and trying not to let the fear and the uncertainty consume her. Owen had been adamant that they stay out of sight, that they remain hidden until he and Daniels could gather the evidence they needed to bring Lord Ashwood to justice.

But the waiting was taking its toll, the hours stretching out in an endless, monotonous blur. Amelia felt like a caged animal, pacing the confines of her small room and trying not to let her mind wander to dark, frightening places.

A soft knock at the door startled her from her thoughts, and she turned to see Mr. Sommers standing on the threshold, a folded piece of paper in his hand.

"Miss Grey," he said, his voice low and gentle. "A note for you, from Lieutenant North. He asked young Mr. Barrow to deliver it this morning."

Amelia's heart leapt in her chest, a sudden, fierce hope blossoming to life. She crossed the room in two quick strides, her hand trembling slightly as she took the note from the apothecary's outstretched fingers. "Thank you, Mr. Sommers," she said. "Oh, did he tell you anything?"

"Probably no more than is in that note. I'll leave you alone, then."

"No, wait." She held a hand up. "Please. It may concern you, too. I.. I mean, after all, we did impose on you..."

Mr. Sommers stopped, then with a slight hesitation, settled himself on a threadbare sofa. "It might at that. And it is no imposition, Miss Grey."

She smiled as a lump rose in her throat, her fingers already unfolding the note with a desperate, hungry urgency. She read the words silently, then summarized the note aloud, her voice trembling slightly as she spoke.

"He says they... they have gone to speak with the colonel of the militia, to see what more could be learned of the men the corporal captured. Owen... Lieutenant North believes they have more evidence now. Not enough to openly accurse Lord Ashwood of treason, but they have arrested some of his fellows, and soon, Ashwood is bound to learn of it..." She looked up, her eyes wide and fearful. "He's worried about Ethan and me, Mr. Sommers. He thinks Ashwood might try to hurt us, to use us as leverage once he feels sufficiently threatened."

The apothecary was silent for a long moment, his face creased with a troubled frown. He turned away, his gaze drifting to the window as he paced the length of the small room.

Amelia watched him, a flicker of unease stirring in her gut. "Mr. Sommers? Is something amiss? Have you... have you heard something in town?"

The old man started, as if he had forgotten she was there. He turned back to her, his expression carefully neutral. "No, no, Miss Grey. All is well. I just... I was lost in thought, that's all."

But there was something in his voice, a hesitation that made Amelia's stomach drop. She took a step closer, her eyes searching his face.

"Mr. Sommers, please. If there's something I should know, something that could help keep Ethan and me safe... you must tell me."

The apothecary sighed, his shoulders slumping as if under a great weight. He moved to the chair by the fire, sinking down into it with a weariness that seemed to seep into his very bones.

"I didn't want to interfere," he said softly. "I know that some things are best left unspoken, best kept hidden from prying eyes and wagging tongues. But Miss Grey... Amelia... there's something you should know."

Amelia felt a chill run down her spine, a sense of foreboding that made her stomach clench with dread. She sat down across from him, her hands clasped tightly in her lap. "What is it, Mr. Sommers?"

The old man took a deep breath, his eyes fixed on the flickering flames of the fire. "It's about Lieutenant North's mother," he said at last, his voice rough with emotion. "She...

she confessed something to me, just before the fever took her. Something that I've kept secret, out of respect for her memory and for your privacy."

Amelia's heart stopped, her breath catching in her throat. "What... what did she tell you?"

Mr. Sommers looked up, his gaze meeting hers with a steady, unflinching intensity. "She told me that Lieutenant North is Ethan's father."

Amelia felt the blood drain from her face, a wave of shame and embarrassment washing over her like a cold, bitter tide. She looked away, her cheeks burning with the heat of her humiliation.

"I... I know what you must think of me, Mr. Sommers. A fallen woman, a sinner who brought shame upon herself and her family. But I swear to you, I never meant for it to happen. Owen and I... It was just supposed to be a goodbye, but..."

The apothecary reached out, his hand coming to rest on her knee in a gesture of comfort and support. "Miss Grey, please. You don't have to explain yourself to me. I'm an old man, and I've seen more of life than most. Matters of reputation, of propriety... they mean little to me now."

He leaned forward, his expression earnest and sincere. "What matters to me is the safety and well-being of you and your son. And that's why... that's why I've been so concerned about Lord Ashwood's intentions towards you, even months ago, before he started trying to gain your attention."

Amelia frowned, confusion and unease warring in her gut. "What do you mean, Mr. Sommers?"

The old man sighed, his fingers drumming a nervous staccato on the arm of his chair. "It was back in the autumn," he said at last, his voice low and troubled. "Lord Ashwood came into the shop, asking about conditions that cause weak lungs. He wanted to know what time of year would be the hardest, the most desperate... which medicines helped, what didn't, and whether some could even save a life."

Amelia's mouth felt like cotton, and a sudden, terrible suspicion took root in her mind. "Did he... did he say who the patient was? Was it someone in his household?"

Mr. Sommers shook his head, his expression grim. "No, he never gave me a name. But he kept pressing for more information, more details about the symptoms and the treatments. I tried to pry, to get him to tell me more about the specific circumstances, but he was evasive, almost... almost suspicious."

He looked up, his eyes locking with Amelia's in a moment of terrible understanding. "I told him I could not possibly give an answer without examining the patient, or at least hearing the symptoms. So, by way of learning something from me, he said, 'Oh, you know, like that young Grey boy's condition, I suppose.' As if he knew... as if he had been watching Ethan, studying him."

Amelia felt a wave of nausea wash over her, a sickening sense of violation that made her skin crawl. She pressed a hand to her mouth, her eyes wide and horrified.

"But why?" she whispered, her voice trembling with fear and confusion. "Why would he be interested in Ethan's condition? What possible reason could he have for wanting to know about my son's health?"

Mr. Sommers shook his head, his expression troubled and uncertain. "I don't know, Miss Grey. I've been asking myself that same question for months now. But after hearing the rumors about Lord Ashwood's plans to marry again, and knowing what I know about your history with him... I couldn't help but worry that he might have some ulterior motive, some reason for wanting to get close to you and your boy."

A chill ran through her, a sense of dread that settled in the pit of her stomach like a leaden weight. She thought of all the times lately Ashwood had tried to insinuate himself into her life, all the gifts and the flattery and the not-so-subtle hints about marriage and respectability. And how all those had begun to mount up in the dead of winter, when her finances and Ethan's condition were at their most fragile.

Had it all been a ploy, a calculated move to gain access to her through her son? To use Ethan's condition as some sort of leverage, some twisted bargaining chip in his games of power and control?

The thought made her feel sick, made her want to gather Ethan in her arms and run, run as far and as fast as she could until they were safe, until they were free from the shadow of Ashwood's obsession.

"I didn't mean to frighten anyone," Sommers went on. "I thought, surely, I was being a silly old fool, but then when Ashwood came into my shop again to buy nearly all the medicine I had, I asked about a bit. No one at Ashwood Manor has weak lungs—at least not that I can learn of. And so, I..." He cleared his throat and his eyes dropped. "Well, I feel I ought to speak to the lieutenant, but I am glad. Terribly glad that you have some manner of help, ma'am."

"Mr. Sommers," she said, her voice steady and sure despite the tremor of emotion that ran through it. "The lieutenant is not the only one to help me. I want to thank you, from the bottom of my heart, for everything you've done for us. For taking us in, for keeping our secrets, and for being a true friend when we needed one most."

The old apothecary smiled, his eyes crinkling at the corners. "It's been my honor, Miss Grey. Truly."

OWEN STOOD RAMROD STRAIGHT, his hands clasped behind his back as he and Daniels listened intently to the colonel's account. The private room in the militia barracks was spare and utilitarian, much like the man himself. Colonel Westbrook was lean and tall, and suffered not a whit of insouciance in his presence.

"Have you learned anything about how these French prisoners managed to secure funds from their homeland to orchestrate their own escape?" Owen asked. "They had to have had someone who could send word on their behalf."

The colonel nodded, his weathered face grim. "Aye, that's the long and short of it. Each man told a similar tale—they were approached with an offer to carry a message back to France. If they could procure payment from their families or connections back home, they were promised a means of escape."

Daniels glanced at North. "And did they say who made this offer? Who was pulling the strings behind this operation?"

The colonel shook his head, frustration evident in the set of his jaw. "No names were given, more's the pity. Either they truly didn't know, or they're more loyal to their mysterious benefactor than they are to their own skin."

"Doubtful. Our suspect is no fool." North paced the length of the room, his mind racing. "But they all ended up with the funds, correct? Enough to secure passage downriver to Kingston upon Hull, and from there to Guernsey?"

"Aye, that's the way of it. A tidy sum, too—more than most mid-grade officers could hope to raise on their own."

Daniels let out a low whistle, his eyes widening. "Just how much are we talking about, sir?"

"Five hundred pounds seems about the usual."

The figure that made North's blood run cold. He exchanged a look with Daniels, seeing his own shock and disbelief mirrored in the other man's face. "That's a king's ransom,"

North muttered, his mind reeling with the implications. "And you said there were several prisoners who had managed to secure such funds?"

"Half a dozen. And those are just the ones Corporal Daniels here managed to intercept. Who knows how many more slipped through our fingers?"

North resumed his pacing, his boot heels clicking against the worn floorboards. "And the money itself? Did any of the prisoners say how it was conveyed to them?"

"No specifics, I'm afraid. But from what we could gather, it seems the funds were funneled through a London bank before making their way north."

Daniels sat up straighter, his eyes narrowing. "A London bank, you say? That's a new wrinkle."

North nodded, his mind already racing ahead. "Indeed. And one that bears further investigation." He turned to the colonel, his expression grave. "Sir, I must thank you for sharing your information with us. We shall return to our duty and report anything we discover that might be helpful."

Colonel Westbrook inclined his head. "Think nothing of it, Lieutenant. We hope to return the favor."

As they took their leave, North's thoughts were a whirlwind of speculation and suspicion. He and Daniels walked in silence for a time, each lost in their own musings. Finally, Daniels broke the quiet. "What do you make of it, sir? This business with the bank, and the funds being sent from France?"

North shook his head, his jaw clenched tight. "I don't know, Daniels. We need to find a definitive link to Ashwood. I say we go back to Elliot Barrow, see if he can poke around a bit more."

"But the way it sounds, Ashwood might be being protected by the bank manager himself. Suppose Barrow tips his hand, maybe even loses his position?"

North growled as his toes scuffed a little in the snow. "He will have to decide if it's a risk he can take. I hope to heaven he does."

Chapter Twenty-Four

"ARE YOU SURE ABOUT asking Barrow, sir?"

Owen buried his hands in his pockets and hunched his shoulders against the chill. "He is free to decline."

"But you know he will not. You are asking him to do something that could very well put him out of work, or even land him in gaol."

"Come, come, Daniels, surely Barrow knows how to be discreet. It is not as if the lad will be required to harm anyone."

"All the same, sir, I preferred it when we could look our quarry eye to eye, squaring off like men. Not shadows and subterfuge, making others do our work for us."

Despite himself, a wry smile tugged at North's mouth. "Perhaps you will get your wish. But for the moment, I am afraid we shall have to depend on a little help from willing parties."

North raised his hand and rapped sharply on the weathered wood of the door. A moment later, it swung open to reveal Elliot's curious face, his brow furrowed in concern at the sight of his unexpected visitors.

"Lieutenant North, Corporal Daniels," he greeted in surprise. "What brings you to my door at this late hour?"

North stepped forward, his expression grave. "Elliot, I am afraid I have a rather great request. May we come in?"

The banker hesitated for a moment, his gaze darting between the two men. But seeing the urgency in their eyes, the solemn set of their jaws, he nodded and stepped aside, ushering them into the warmth of his home.

"Is your father here?" Owen asked as Elliot invited them to sit.

"Oh, no, never when his mates are at the pub. I shan't be seeing him for a few hours yet."

"I'm surprised you are not there yourself," Daniels commented.

Elliot grinned bashfully. "Well, ah... as a matter of fact, I have just come from calling on Miss Baker."

North and Daniels exchanged a look. Somehow, it made what they were about to ask of Elliot worse, to consider that a lady's hopes might be dashed if the young man were caught in some disgrace. But there was no help for it—Elliot was their best place to start, and, as Owen had said, the lad could always say no.

As they settled themselves around the small table, North leaned forward, his voice low. "Elliot, we've just come from a meeting with the colonel of the militia. He had some rather disturbing information about the escaped French prisoners. They were all ransomed, and the funds paid to someone local, we believe. We would like to follow the trail back to the source, but that means we need to track down the funds used to secure their passage."

Elliot's eyes widened, his fingers tightening around the mug he had poured for himself. "Funds? From where?"

Daniels cleared his throat, his gaze flickering to North before settling on the banker. "From France, it would seem. Most likely funneled through a London bank before making their way north."

Elliot's brow furrowed. "You think Lord Ashwood is involved."

North nodded, his jaw clenched tight. "We are certain of it. But we need proof, Elliot. We need to trace the flow of these funds, to see if they passed through your bank in any way. But... there is a risk to yourself, which you know better than I."

The banker was silent for a long moment, his gaze distant and thoughtful. Finally, he spoke, his words measured and careful. "I understand the gravity of what you're asking, Lieutenant. And I want to help, truly I do. But I'm not sure what I can do. The inner workings of London banks are a mystery to me, and even if I could find something, the risk..."

"We appreciate the risk, Elliot. And believe me, we would not ask if we had any other choice. But you're our best hope of getting to the bottom of this quickly."

Daniels leaned forward, his expression earnest. "Perhaps we do not have to ask you to do anything that would compromise your position. Just to keep your eyes and ears open, to let us know if anything unusual crosses your desk."

Elliot was silent for a long moment, his gaze fixed on the swirling depths of his tea. "That hardly answers the need, Corporal. For me to find anything of value to you, I'd have to go digging for it."

Owen thinned his lips. "That you would. Do you have access to such information?"

"That is just the thing. The most private files are kept locked whenever the manager is out. Aye, I can get a key, but not without raising suspicions."

"Have you ever had cause to do that in the past?"

"Yes. The publican, Wallis, he took out a loan year before last to mend his roof, and he had to make a payment. I suppose I could..."

"Is Mr. Wallis a man to be trusted?"

Elliot nodded. "I believe so, sir."

North smiled. "Then I believe I will pay him a little visit to see if he is able to make another payment, sometime when your manager is out."

"He takes tea every afternoon at two." Elliot's mouth crunched into a frown, and he was nodding slowly. "Very well. I'll do it."

THE FOLLOWING EVENING FOUND North and Daniels once again at Elliot Barrow's door, and the neighbor let them in quickly. "What did you find?" Owen asked, his voice low and urgent as they settled themselves in the banker's small sitting room.

Elliot was silent for a moment, his gaze distant and thoughtful. Finally, he spoke, his words measured and careful.

"I'm not entirely sure what to make of it, Lieutenant. But there was something... odd, in Lord Ashwood's file."

North leaned forward, his heart hammering in his chest. "Odd how?"

Elliot's brow furrowed, his fingers drumming a nervous staccato on the arm of his chair. "Well, you remember that large transfer we discussed? The one that had no proper name attached to the account?"

North nodded. "Aye. What of it?"

"It's gone. I checked the file again today, while the manager was out for his afternoon tea. And there was no record of it, no trace that it had ever existed."

North exchanged a glance with Daniels. "Odd."

"But that's not all," Elliot continued, his voice dropping to a whisper. "There was something else in the file, something that caught my eye. A copy of a will, naming the former Lord Danbury Ashwood as executor—moreover, it claimed he was a brother to the deceased."

North's brow furrowed, his mind racing with the implications. "What would that be doing in Garrison Ashwood's bank file?"

Elliot shook his head, his expression troubled. "I don't know. But I thought it was strange, so I took a closer look. And what I saw... well, it raised more questions than it answered."

Daniels leaned forward, his eyes narrowing. "What did you find?"

The banker took a deep breath, his gaze flickering between the two men as he drew out a piece of paper. "I wrote it down, see? The will was in the name of Clarence Merriweather. And there was a note attached, stating that Merriweather had been declared deceased earlier this summer."

"Deceased? How?"

Elliot shrugged, his expression helpless. "I don't know. The note didn't say, but I imagine he must have been rather older, being Lord Ashwood's uncle. It was all very strange, very... unsettling. Why would that be with Lord Ashwood's financial documents?"

North was silent for a long moment, his mind churning with the implications of Elliot's discovery. It made no sense, this business with the will and the mysterious brother. What could it possibly have to do with the missing funds, the escaped prisoners? "If it was an uncle, I presume Ashwood is the heir."

"No, another was named as the heir. A woman's name, oddly enough—Rose Merriweather. Does the name mean anything to you, sir?"

"Not a thing. You do not know, either?"

"I'm sorry, sir, but no. I could ask around—"

"Do not do that," North interrupted him. "It may well be nothing, but if you suddenly start asking about a name that is found only on a document you were not supposed to see, it will bring suspicion on you."

Elliot nodded jerkily. "Just so, sir. You can keep my note, but I put everything back just as I found it," Elliot said, his voice trembling slightly. "Before the manager returned. But Lieutenant, I... I don't know what to do now. "

North reached out, his hand coming to rest on the banker's shoulder in a gesture of reassurance. "You did well, Elliot. And you were right to bring this to us. But I need you to promise me something."

Elliot looked up, his eyes wide and uncertain. "Anything, Lieutenant."

"Promise me that you won't expose yourself any further. That you'll let us handle this from here on out. I won't have you putting yourself at risk, not for this."

Elliot Barrow hesitated for a moment, his gaze searching North's face. "I promise. But Lieutenant, what will you do now? How will you find the truth?"

"I don't know," he admitted. "But I'll be sending word to the captain. Thank you, Elliot."

AMELIA STOOD AT THE stove, stirring a pot of hearty vegetable stew, the aroma of herbs and spices wafting through the cozy kitchen of Mr. Sommers' house. She had insisted on helping with the cooking, desperate to find some way to make herself useful, to repay the kindness of the elderly apothecary who had taken them in without question.

But even as she focused on the task at hand, her mind was a whirlwind of worries and fears, of doubts that gnawed at her like hungry rats. How long could they stay here, hidden away from the world? How long before they were discovered, and what would Ashwood do when he discovered that she'd hidden from him?

And what of Owen? What of the brave, stubborn man who had risked everything to keep them safe? Amelia's heart clenched at the thought of him out there alone, facing unknown dangers while she remained tucked away, unable to do anything to help.

A tug at her skirts drew her attention, and she looked down to see Ethan's wide, pleading eyes staring up at her. "Mama," he said, his voice small and plaintive. "Can we go outside? Please? Just for a little while?"

Amelia felt a pang of guilt, a sharp ache in her chest at the sight of her son's restless, yearning expression. She knew how hard this was for him, to be cooped up in a strange house, away from the farm and the animals he loved so dearly.

"Oh, my darling," she murmured, setting down her spoon and kneeling to gather him into her arms. "I know how much you miss home, how much you want to be outside in the sunshine. But we must be careful, we must stay where it's safe."

Ethan's lower lip trembled, his eyes filling with tears. "But Mama, what about Bessie? What about my kitten? Who will take care of them while we're gone?"

Amelia's heart broke at the tremor in his voice, the genuine concern that radiated from his small frame. "Lieutenant North made sure they're looked after," she assured him, running a soothing hand through his hair. "He promised he would, remember?"

Ethan buried his face into her sleeve, sniffling a little. "He said he would come back."

Amelia brushed his hair off his forehead and kissed it. "Yes, he did, and he will keep that promise, too. Ethan, I must ask you something very serious. Do you like Lieutenant North?"

He nodded against her shoulder and turned his face a little so he could smash the back of his hand against his nose to scratch it. "He's my friend."

"He... He would like very much to be more than your friend, Ethan. How would you like to have him for your papa?"

Ethan pulled his head away from her shoulder and blinked at her. His mouth popped open a little, and he made another swipe at his runny nose. "A papa?" he whispered. "Like grandpapa was your papa?"

"Yes, like that. The lieutenant has asked me to marry him. Would you like to call him Papa forever?"

A wide smile blossomed on Ethan's mouth, and his eyes lit up like the silvery winter sky. "He won't get mad?"

"Never. It would please him very much to hear you say it, I am sure. So, what do you think?"

"Can I call him Papa next time he comes? Or do you have to get married first?"

Amelia chuckled. "I think you can call him that as soon as you like. He would be pleased above all things."

Ethan leaped from her arms, crowing in delight. "I'm going to finish carving the soldier and show it to him!"

"Oh, Ethan, not in the house! You will get shavings everywhere."

"Can't I go outside here, Mama? Just in the chicken coop behind the house? I promise I'll be good, I won't wander off."

Amelia hesitated, torn between her desire to keep Ethan happy and her fear of exposing them to any unnecessary risk. She knew the garden was secluded, surrounded by high walls that would shield them from prying eyes. And the fresh air would do Ethan good, would help to ease the restlessness that seemed to consume him more and more with each passing day.

Gently, she took his face in her hands. "Let me think about it," she said softly, her voice tender but firm. "I need to make sure it's safe, that we won't be seen."

Ethan nodded, his eyes shining with a tentative hope. "I'll be careful, Mama. I promise. And I just want to see the chickens, that's all, and do my carving in the barn like I did with Papa."

Amelia's heart clenched at the earnestness in his voice, the simple, innocent request that meant so much to her little boy. She knew how much he loved animals, how much joy and comfort he found in their presence. And it was sweet how he already thought of Owen as his papa, the man who helped him carve his toy soldier in the warm comforts of the barn loft. After all the upheaval and uncertainty of the past few weeks, didn't he deserve a small moment of happiness, of normalcy?

She was just opening her mouth to reply when the sound of footsteps echoed from the hallway, and Mr. Sommers appeared in the doorway, his face creased with a warm, gentle smile. "Something smells delicious," he said, inhaling deeply as he made his way to the table. "You're spoiling me, Mistress Grey, with all this wonderful cooking."

Amelia felt a flush of pleasure at the compliment, a small spark of pride that momentarily chased away the shadows of her worry. "It's the least I can do," she demurred, turning back to the stove to give the stew a final stir. "After all you've done for us, all the kindness you've shown."

Mr. Sommers waved away her gratitude with a dismissive gesture, his eyes twinkling with a mischievous light. "Nonsense. You and young Ethan are a breath of fresh air in this old house. I should be thanking you for bringing some life and laughter back into these dusty rooms."

As he settled himself at the table, his gaze fell on Ethan, and his expression softened with a mixture of concern and understanding. "And how are you faring today, my boy? Feeling a bit cooped up, are we?"

Ethan nodded, his small face scrunching with a look of such hopeful entreaty that Amelia's heart nearly shattered in her chest. "Yes, sir. I was just asking Mama if we could go outside for a little while, just in the garden. I promise I'll be good; I won't cause any trouble."

Mr. Sommers' eyes met Amelia's over the top of Ethan's head, a silent question passing between them. She hesitated for a moment, her gaze flickering to the window, to the sunlit expanse of the garden beyond.

"Oh, the garden," Sommers mused. "A capital idea. Good for a lad of your age, getting out of the house. And a nice, quiet little place it is back there."

Amelia studied him, the hint of encouragement in the apothecary's voice. Then, almost without conscious thought, she found herself nodding, a small, tentative smile tugging at the corners of her mouth. "I suppose a few minutes couldn't hurt. As long as we're careful, as long as we stay out of sight."

Ethan's face lit up with a joy so bright, so incandescent, that it seemed to chase away all the shadows and doubts that had plagued Amelia's mind. He threw his arms around her waist, hugging her tight as he bounced on the balls of his feet. "Thank you, Mama!" he cried, his voice ringing with a happiness that made Amelia's heart swell with love and pride. "Thank you, thank you, thank you! I promise I'll stay with the chickens!"

Amelia brushed a kiss against his forehead, her heart swelling with a love so fierce, so all-consuming, that it stole the very breath from her lungs. "I know you will, my darling. You're such a good boy, such a brave and clever lad."

She straightened up, turning to Mr. Sommers with a grateful smile. "Thank you for understanding," she said softly, her voice thick with emotion. "I know it's a risk, letting him outside. But he's been so cooped up, so restless."

The apothecary nodded, his eyes sparkling with a warm, paternal light. "Of course, my dear. And you're right, a bit of sunshine and fresh air is just what the doctor ordered. It might help to clear his lungs, to ease that little wheeze he's been having."

Amelia's heart clenched at the mention of Ethan's lungs, at the reminder of the fragility that lurked beneath his bright, indomitable spirit. She had been listening to his breathing all morning, her ears straining for any hint of the telltale rattle that signaled a worsening of his condition.

But there had been nothing for the last few days, no recent sign of the illness that had plagued him for so long. And as she watched him now, his small hand clasped tightly in her own as they made their way to the back door, she felt a flicker of hope, a tiny, tentative spark that perhaps, just perhaps, they had turned a corner.

Chapter Twenty-Five

NORTH PACED INSIDE THE cottage, his mind churning with the weight of the task before him. The evidence he had gathered, the scraps and fragments of truth that pointed to Lord Ashwood's treachery, weighed heavily upon his shoulders. He knew, with a bone-deep certainty, that Ashwood was profiting off betraying his own country.

But knowing and proving were two very different things.

North ran a hand through his hair, his frustration mounting with each passing moment. Plenty of people in that village had seen the man's true face, had glimpsed the rot that festered beneath the veneer of respectability and charm. But none of what anyone could say would hold up in a court of Ashwood's peers. How to prove it? How to tear away the mask and expose the viper beneath?

At least Amelia was close. He could go to her, touch his forehead to hers and squeeze her shoulders and let whatever inspiration she had to offer pour into him. He had not dared to visit her, not wishing to call attention to Sommers' house just now. But surely, in the middle of winter, enough people had worked up a cough that a call on the village herbalist was not so unheard of.

So it was that half an hour later, North found himself standing before Sommers' door, his hand poised to knock. With a deep breath, North rapped his knuckles against the weathered wood, his heart pounding in his chest as he waited for the old man to answer.

"Lieutenant North," Sommers said, his eyes widening in surprise as he ushered the soldier inside. "Something urgent to bring you here at this late hour?"

North hesitated, the words sticking in his throat. He had come this far on instinct and desperation, but now, faced with the apothecary's piercing gaze, he found himself at a loss.

"I... I came to see Miss Grey," he said at last.

"Ah, naturally. I believe she is helping young Ethan to bed. Lad had a most excellent afternoon, playing in the chicken coop, but it was a bit dusty, you know, so she thought a bath was in order. Would you like a drink while you wait?"

Owen's eyes drifted up the stairs as he only partially heard Sommers' words. "Oh. Yes, of course."

Sommers led the way into his little sitting room, clinking glasses as he found them on the shelf. "Please, make yourself comfortable. There is something I had meant to tell you, Lieutenant, and I ought to out with it now, while I've a chance." He turned around, his face pinched into an uncomfortable grimace. "You see, I was the one who sent the letter to you."

Owen blinked. The letter? Why, he had nearly forgot all about it in these last days. "You..." He tilted his head, the words running on without form in his mind. "The letter about my mother?"

Sommers screwed up his mouth and passed Owen a glass of spirits. "Not exactly. If you recall, the letter said, 'your family...' not your mother, God rest her soul."

Owen's stomach dropped, and the glass in his nerveless fingers nearly did, as well. "My..."

"I am sorry, Lieutenant. Yes, I knew. Your mother, you see—I was tending her when she took ill with that fever, and she, ah..." He cleared his throat. "She thought someone in town ought to know, if she was no longer here..."

"She told you about Amelia and Ethan," Owen whispered.

"Not to bring shame upon anyone," Sommers said hurriedly. "But so that there might be another to look out for them, and... well, with the way Ashwood began behaving these last few months, I am rather glad she told me." He offered an apologetic smile. "As well as passed on the only direction she had for you."

Owen shook his head in disbelief. "Blast it, Sommers, but I thought that whole thing was a cruel hoax at best! Or at worst, some scheme to terrorize me into action, for what cause I knew not. You really took that on, sending that off on the chance I might see it, just to protect Amelia and Ethan?"

Sommer shrugged. "Of course, I did not know you would get it. Your mother said you had not written in an age, and she only knew you were alive because she kept getting the pay you sent to her."

Owen blinked. "My pay... why, by Jove, what happened to it this past year? Someone must have been collecting it, for I'd never any notice..."

"That was your mother again, Lieutenant. She tried to have it diverted to Miss Grey, but without notifying you. I cannot know why she would not wish for that, but I do not think Miss Grey was ever notified, either. All I know is that your mother sent some letter to the effect, and I am sure someone, somewhere, is trying to verify it."

"How can they, without first having confirmation from me?"

"That, I cannot speak to. Your mother did say you were so seldom within reach of any correspondence at all. I thought it miracle enough that you got my letter and could come when you did."

Owen's shoulders sagged, and his gaze grew unfocused for a moment. "So am I." He drew a long breath, letting it out in shaky relief. "I will speak to the war office about the pay, but all this does answer one question for me—something that has been troubling me from the first. I shan't have to press a blade to your throat to force an answer out of you about your intentions in sending that letter."

Sommers chuckled. "I am an old man, Lieutenant. I'm afraid you would not even need a blade."

"I was only in jest." Owen drew a sip of the ale Sommers had offered, then looked back at the older man in thought. "I say, perhaps you might know the answer to another riddle that is puzzling me."

Sommers' brow furrowed, his expression growing serious. "Go on, Lieutenant. I'm listening."

And so, North began to speak. He told of the smuggling operation, of the French prisoners and the missing funds. He spoke of Lord Ashwood's shadowy dealings, of the whispers of treason and betrayal that seemed to dog the nobleman's every step. Perhaps the apothecary had seen more that he had not mentioned, for many men saw things that they did not account as important until asked to reexamine them.

And then, almost as an afterthought, he mentioned the will. He said nothing of where it was discovered, but he did ask, rather urgently, if Sommers recognized the names Clarence and Rose Mayweather.

"Clarence Merriweather?" he repeated. "I had almost forgotten that name, had buried it so deep that I thought it lost forever."

North leaned forward, his heart pounding in his chest. "You knew him? The Danbury Ashwood's brother?"

Sommers nodded, his eyes distant. "I did. Grew up at Ashwood Manor, he did, but as the younger brother, he struck out to shift for himself. Word was that he took the settlement that he inherited from his mother and got into some line of business, although I'm not entirely sure what. Word was, he was wealthier than his brother at one point, but," he laughed, "that may all be just hearsay."

"And have you any memory of this Rose Merriweather? Apparently, the paperwork said she was his daughter."

"Oh, no idea. Like as not, the man married some London lass, and his daughter is still there."

North grunted in frustration. "Like as not."

"Well, you did not come here to sit with an old man. Let me see if Miss Grey is free to speak with you. Another drink while you wait, Lieutenant?"

Owen raised his glass. "No, thank you."

AMELIA KNELT BESIDE THE old copper tub, her sleeves rolled up to her elbows as she gently poured warm water over Ethan's sudsy head. The boy giggled and splashed, sending a spray of bubbles and water droplets flying through the air.

"Hold still, my little rascal," Amelia chided, a smile tugging at the corners of her mouth. "Or you'll be going to bed with chicken feathers in your hair."

Ethan grinned up at her, his eyes sparkling with mischief. "But Mama, the chickens like it when I play with them! They told me so! I was not done playing."

"I'm sure they do, my darling. But even chickens need their rest, and so do little boys."

She reached for a towel, wrapping it snugly around Ethan's wriggling form as she lifted him from the tub. The warmth of the fire, crackling merrily in the hearth, chased away the chill of the evening air as she rubbed him dry and helped him into his nightshirt.

Just as she was tucking him into bed, a soft knock sounded at the door. Mr. Sommers poked his head in, his face etched with a strange mixture of excitement and trepidation.

"Forgive the intrusion, Mistress Grey, but Lieutenant North is downstairs, and he's asking to see you."

Amelia's heart leapt in her chest, a sudden, fierce joy surging through her at the mention of Owen's name. It had been days since she had seen him, days since he had risked exposure and watched all night to bring her and Ethan to safety. The thought of being near him again, of losing herself in the steadfast warmth of his gaze, was almost more than she could bear.

She rose to her feet, her hands trembling slightly as she smoothed the wrinkles from her skirts. But before she could take a step towards the door, Ethan's small hand shot out, grasping at her wrist with a surprising strength.

"Wait, Mama," he said, his brow furrowed with a sudden, anxious concern. "I forgot to feed the cat."

Amelia paused, her head tilting to one side as she regarded her son with a puzzled frown. "The cat? What cat, my love? I thought you were playing with the chickens."

Ethan shook his head, his eyes wide and earnest. "No, Mama. Well, yes, I was playing with the chickens. But there's a cat, too. She lives in the straw, in the corner of the coop. And I think..." He lowered his voice to a conspiratorial whisper. "I think she's going to have kittens soon."

Despite the urgency of Owen's summons, despite the desperate longing that pulled at her heart, Amelia felt a smile tug at her lips. Of course, Ethan would find a way to befriend every creature, great and small, that crossed his path. It was one of the things she loved most about him, one of the qualities that made him so utterly, unmistakably, his father's son.

"Very well," she said, pressing a kiss to his forehead. "But you must promise me you'll come straight back to bed afterwards. No dallying, no adventures. Understood?"

Ethan nodded solemnly; his small face set with a look of grave responsibility. "I promise, Mama. I just want to make sure she has some warm milk before it gets cold outside. So, she and her babies will be cozy and happy."

Mr. Sommers, who had been watching the exchange with a look of fond amusement, stepped forward, his hand coming to rest on Ethan's shoulder.

"Let me take care of the milk, lad," he said, his voice warm with affection. "You just worry about getting yourself settled for the night. I'll make sure your furry friend is well taken care of."

Ethan beamed up at him. "Can I carry it to her? Please?"

Amelia looked down into that face that she had never been able to resist and sighed. "Oh, very well, but no getting dirty again, or chilling yourself until you start coughing."

"Thank you, Mama."

With a final, reassuring squeeze of her son's hand, Amelia followed Mr. Sommers out of the room, her heart pounding in her chest as she descended the narrow staircase. And there, waiting for her at the bottom, his face haggard with exhaustion but his eyes shining for her, was Owen.

"Amelia," he breathed, his voice raw as he gathered her into his arms. "By heaven, I've missed you."

She clung to him, her face buried in the solid warmth of his chest as the tears she had been holding back for so long finally spilled over. "Owen," she whispered, her voice muffled by the fabric of his coat. "I've been so worried for you. Are you sure you should be here now?"

He pulled back, his hands coming up to cradle her face as he looked deep into her eyes. "I know, love. I was careful—no one followed me, but I had to see you. How is Ethan?"

She tipped her head back over her shoulder. "Trying to take care of all the animals in town. His cough is better... I hate to say it, but I wonder if being away from the cold barn and hay and all that has helped him."

"Very possibly." Owen tucked a lock of her hair behind her ear. "And you?"

She smiled and pressed a kiss to his chin. "Perfectly well. Where is Corporal Daniels? Did he not come with you?"

Owen shook his head and let his hand slip down to hers, leading her to a chair. "No, he stayed behind, talking to our friend Elliot Barrow. Still trying to piece together... well, a number of things."

"Such as?" She slid into the chair beside his. "More escapes?"

"No, not that. A strange document... Tell me, you do not happen to recognize the name Merriweather, do you? I do not know why you would, but—"

Amelia felt the breath leave her lungs in a rush, her knees turning to water. It was a very good thing she was seated. "R-Rose... Merriweather?"

Owen's expression sharpened. "The very one. Who is she?"

Amelia bit her lips together. "Who *was* she, do you mean? She... she was my mother."

Chapter Twenty-Six

THE ROOM SEEMED TO spin around Amelia as she listened to Owen's report, her heart pounding in her chest with a sickening mixture of fear and rage.

"My mother... was an heiress?" she murmured. "No, that cannot be right! She was a poor farmer's wife, of no importance to anyone save Father and me."

Owen shook his head, his face grave and his eyes filled with a quiet, burning intensity. "I'm afraid it's not that simple, Amelia. The documents Elliot found, the will he saw... it tells a different story. Your mother, Rose... she was the daughter of Clarence Merriweather, the brother of the former Lord Ashwood. The father of the man who now holds that title, Garrison Ashwood."

The air left her lungs in a rush, her mind spinning with the implications of his words. Her mother, the granddaughter of a nobleman? The cousin of the man who had been trying to marry her against her will for years?

"No," she whispered, her voice barely audible over the pounding of her own heart. "No, that can't be. It doesn't make any sense."

She looked to Mr. Sommers, her eyes pleading for some kind of explanation, some way to make sense of the impossible truth that had been laid before her. But the old apothecary merely shook his head.

"Barrow wrote all the names down from the will," Owen continued. "Clarence Merriweather passed away just six months ago, and in his will, he named your mother as his sole heir. The rightful inheritor of his estate and fortune."

Amelia felt a wave of dizziness wash over her, her knees buckling beneath her as she sank into a nearby chair. This couldn't be happening. It had to be some kind of mistake, some cruel trick of fate that sought to upend everything she had ever known.

"But why..." she whispered, her voice cracking with emotion. "No, no, this cannot be. My mother had no fortune! If she did, why was she married to a humble Dales farmer without a penny to his name? And another thing makes no sense—why would Garrison Ashwood's uncle not bear the same name? If he and Danbury Ashwood were brothers, if they came from the same paternal line..."

"I believe I do recall something of that..." Sommers' brow wrinkled as his eyes squinted in thought. "Some sort of a rift between them, years ago when Clarence left for London. It must have been something significant, to make him turn his back on his own blood like that."

"Or perhaps his own blood disowned him," Owen suggested. "You did say that Merriweather struck up some sort of business... no idea what it was?"

"No, but it must have been rather lucrative, for Garrison Ashwood to be trying to grasp whatever fortune there is now to claim."

Amelia's stomach clenched. "Fortune... Is there really a fortune?" she whispered.

"I do not know the details," Owen confessed. "We are not privy to them, but if your mother was Merriweather's only heir, and you are her closest relative, then... the inheritance would be yours, Amelia."

Amelia closed her eyes, her mind reeling with the implications of it all. Her mother, the daughter of a man who had renounced his own family. A man who had left his ancestral home and taken on a new name, a new identity... and who had, apparently, fathered a child that no one around here had ever known about, then named her as his only heir.

It didn't make sense. None of it made sense. And yet, as she sat there, her heart pounding and her mind spinning, a tiny flicker of memory began to stir in the depths of her consciousness.

A box of letters, hidden away in the attic of her childhood home. A box that her mother had kept locked and hidden, that her father had forbidden her to touch on pain of punishment. She had never understood why, had never been able to fathom what secrets those faded pages might hold.

But now, with the truth of her mother's identity laid bare before her... she knew. She knew that those letters held the key, the missing piece of the puzzle that would make sense of it all.

"There was a box," she said softly, her voice barely above a whisper. "A box of letters that my mother used to keep in the attic. I never looked for them, never tried to find them... because my father forbade it, and I was too afraid to disobey."

She looked up at Owen, her eyes bright with a sudden, desperate hope. "But if there's a chance that those letters could tell us something, could give us some clue about my mother's past... then we have to find them. We have to know the truth."

Owen nodded. "Tell me where to look, Amelia. I'll ride up to the farm first thing in the morning, I'll turn that attic upside down until I find them."

Amelia felt a rush of gratitude, a swell of love so fierce it nearly took her breath away. Owen, her steadfast guardian, her unwavering protector... he would stop at nothing to help her. And by some miracle, this man was back in her life, after she had thought him lost forever.

But before she could speak, before she could utter a word of thanks or comfort... a sound shattered the room, a sound that turned her blood to ice in her veins.

A cough, harsh and ragged, echoing from the garden beyond. *Oh, Ethan!* He had never come inside after feeding that ridiculous cat! He was going to be coughing again all night and might possibly take a serious chill.

She leapt to her feet, her heart pounding as she raced to the window, her eyes scanning the shadowed hedgerows for any sign of her son. Probably still in the chicken coop with that cat.

She gathered her skirts, lifting them above the wet of the melting snow on the stoop, readying herself to cross the little garden area... and that was when she saw it. A figure, cloaked in black, lurking at the edge of the garden. A figure that moved with a predatory grace, a sinister purpose that made her blood run cold.

She opened her mouth to scream, to cry out a warning... but it was too late. The figure lunged for the chicken coop, a sharp, piercing cry shattering the night air as it wrapped its arms around a small, struggling form and dragged it into the shadows.

Ethan.

"*No!*" Amelia's world shattered, her heart splintering into a thousand jagged pieces as she hurled herself towards the door, Owen's shouts of alarm and Mr. Sommers' cries of dismay ringing in her ears. She burst out into the garden, her feet flying over the uneven ground as she raced towards the spot where her son, her heart, her very reason for living, had disappeared through a rough-cut break in the hedge.

But there was nothing, no sign of the cloaked figure or the precious child it had stolen. Only the eerie stillness of the night, the mocking whisper of the wind as it stirred the leaves of the trees above.

"Ethan!" she screamed, her voice raw and ragged with terror. "Ethan, where are you?"

Behind her, she could hear Owen's pounding footsteps, the rasp of his breath as he shouted orders to Mr. Sommers. But all she could focus on was her own frantic heartbeat, the desperate, clawing need to find her son and bring him back to safety.

She scoured the garden, tearing through the bushes and hedgerows with a manic intensity. But there was nothing, no trace of Ethan or his abductor.

Until, at last, she found it.

A scrap of fabric snagged on a thorn at the edge of the garden. A scrap of fabric that she recognized, with a sickening lurch of dread, as belonging to her son's nightshirt.

She sank to her knees, a sob tearing from her throat as she clutched the scrap to her chest. Ethan, her sweet, innocent boy... he was gone, torn from her arms by a monster in the night.

And as Owen's arms wrapped around her, as he pulled her close and whispered words of comfort and reassurance, even as his hand dropped to his side to pull out his weapon.

OWEN'S HEART POUNDED IN his chest as he raced through the snowy streets of the village, his breath coming in ragged gasps and his mind consumed with a single, desperate thought: *Ethan*. His son, the boy who had come to mean more to him than life itself, was in danger, and every second that passed was a second too long.

Beside him, Daniels matched his pace, his face set with grim determination as they followed the distant sound of Ethan's cries. Owen had stopped on the road just long enough to bang on Elliot's door and summon his comrade, and they were off again, following the footprints in the snow. Ethan's coughing echoed ahead of them through the night, each ragged hack like a knife to Owen's heart.

"Hold on, Ethan," he growled as he pushed himself a little harder. "We're coming for you, lad. Just hold on."

As they reached the edge of the village, Owen skidded to a halt, his eyes widening with horror at the sight that greeted them. There, struggling in the grip of a cloaked figure, was Ethan, his small face streaked with tears and his eyes wide with terror.

"Papa!" he cried. "Papa, help me!"

Papa... a word he had never in his life thought to hear. Owen's heart shattered, a rage unlike anything he had ever known surging through his veins. With a roar of fury, he lunged forward, his hand reaching for his sword...

But it was too late. In a single, fluid motion, the figure hoisted Ethan onto a waiting horse, the boy's cries of fear and pain rending the night air like a physical blow.

"No!" Owen shouted, his voice raw and ragged with desperation. "Ethan, no!"

He ran, his boots pounding against the frozen ground as he chased after the horse, Daniels close at his heels. But the beast was fast, its hooves kicking up a spray of snow as it fled into the darkness, bearing its precious cargo away from the safety of home and family.

Owen's lungs burned, his muscles screaming with the strain of the pursuit. As they reached the outskirts of the village, Owen's keen eyes caught sight of a livery stable, its doors yawning open in the darkness. Without a second thought, he veered towards it, his hand already reaching for the nearest horse.

"We'll never catch them on foot," he shouted to Daniels, his voice barely audible over the pounding of his own heart. "Mount up, man. We'll run those bastards down if it's the last thing we do."

Daniels nodded, his jaw clenched with determination as he swung himself onto the bare back of a second horse. No saddles or bits, only leather halters for tack—well, they had ridden with worse odds. They urged their mounts forward, the beasts plunging over snowy roads as they gave chase.

The night air whipped at Owen's face, the cold biting into his skin like a thousand needles. But he barely felt it, his entire being consumed by the need to reach his son, to bring him back to safety. They followed the tracks left by the kidnapper's horse, the hoofprints stark and unmistakable against the pristine snow. Owen's heart pounded with each stride, his mind racing with the possibilities of what might lie ahead.

And then, just as he was beginning to despair, just as the tracks seemed to vanish into the darkness, blending with the flattened prints of a dozen others... he saw it. A carriage, its lanterns glowing like twin stars in the night. And there, being dragged from the back of the horse and thrust towards the waiting vehicle, was Ethan.

"Papa!" the boy cried, his voice thin and reedy with exhaustion and fear. "Papa, help me!"

Owen urged his horse forward, his eyes narrowed as he gave a thunderous bellow to the skies. "Let him go!" But as he drew closer, as the carriage came into sharper focus... his blood ran cold, a sickening realization washing over him like a tidal wave.

For there, seated in the plush interior of the carriage, a smug smile playing at the corners of his mouth... was Lord Garrison Ashwood himself.

"Owen, my boy!" he called, his voice dripping with false joviality. "What a pleasant surprise. I was just taking young Master Grey out for a bit of air. The poor lad seemed quite overwrought, you see. Needed a calming influence."

Owen's vision swam with rage, his hand tightening on the reins until his knuckles turned white. "Ashwood!" he snarled, his voice low and deadly. "Release the boy. Now!"

But Ashwood merely laughed and raised a pistol... then pointed it at Ethan's head. "I think not, Lieutenant. If Miss Grey wants him back, you can tell her she will know where to find me."

Owen surged forward, but Daniels' grip on his shoulder checked him. "You would threaten a child?" he thundered.

"I care nothing for the child. In fact, he is rather in my way, but his mother? Now that is a different story. I need her, and her alone. And you, Lieutenant..." Ashwood pulled back the hammer on his pistol. "You have meddled where you do not belong." Ashwood bit his lip and gave a sharp whistle, and a footman closed the door of his carriage. "Do not follow, Lieutenant!" he warned. "These roads do have so many nasty bumps!"

Owen was already breaking free of Daniels' grip to charge after them, but before he could even lash at the horse's lead rope, the carriage door slammed shut, the horses lurching forward as the driver cracked his whip.

"Ethan!" Owen cried, spurring his own mount forward in a desperate attempt to give chase. But it was too late. The carriage was already disappearing into the night, bearing his son, his heart, his very reason for living, away from him.

"Stop, sir!" Daniels caught up and tried to jerk back on his "borrowed" horse's halter. "We can't risk it, sir! He might shoot the lad!"

But North slashed at his friend's hand and tugged the rope free. "Do you think it will be better if we let him go, do as he pleases? Should we let him hunker down at his estate, where we have to break through a wall of his men to get to him?"

Daniels shook his head. "He said the boy is useless to him, sir. That means he'll kill him if we get too close."

"So what?" North raged. "You think I should bring Amelia to him? Let him use her son to threaten her?"

Daniels's mouth worked, but after a second, he shook his head and set his teeth. "What do you want to do, sir?"

"I want to get my son back!"

Daniels blinked and sucked in a breath. And Owen's face blistered hot with the realization of what he'd blurted aloud. The thing had been a nebulous understanding between them, perhaps. Surely, Daniels had to suspect... but to confess it, so loudly...

"Daniels, I—"

"No, sir, you're right." Daniels nodded and turned his mount's head with the single lead rope. "We can't afford to let Ashwood get back to the manor, and surely, we can outrun that carriage."

Owen nodded, his jaw clenched so tightly he thought it might crack. He closed his eyes, the image of Ethan's terrified face burning behind his lids like a brand as terror slipped down his face in an icy cascade of tears.

"A hero," Ethan had called him once. He could only pray that the boy had not misjudged him.

Chapter Twenty-Seven

"**E**THAN!"

Amelia stumbled through the snow-covered streets, her heart pounding in her chest as she fought to keep pace with the rapidly disappearing hoofprints. The icy wind whipped at her face, stinging her eyes and stealing the breath from her lungs, but she barely felt it, her entire being consumed by a single, desperate thought: Ethan, her precious boy was in danger, and she had no way to reach him.

Behind her, she could hear Mr. Sommers' voice, his cries of concern and alarm nearly lost over her own shouts. "Miss Grey!" he called, his footsteps crunching in the snow as he tried to catch up to her. "Miss Grey, please, you must come back inside! You'll catch your death out here!"

But Amelia couldn't stop, couldn't turn back. Not when her son needed her, not when every second that passed was another second he was in the clutches of a madman. "I can't!" she cried, her voice raw and ragged with desperation. "I have to find him, Mr. Sommers! I have to bring him home!"

Tears streamed down her face, freezing on her cheeks as she ran, her skirts tangling around her legs and her lungs burning with the effort. She knew it was futile, knew that she could never hope to catch up to them on foot. She couldn't even see Owen any longer, and as much faith as she had that he would do whatever it took to reach Ethan, she knew the kidnapper had a head start on him. Even Owen might not be able to reach him...

But she couldn't bear the thought of doing nothing, of standing by while her child was torn away from her. And so, she ran—no coat, no hat, and poor Mr. Sommers huffing after her in the night air.

And then, just as she was about to collapse from exhaustion, she heard it: the sound of hoofbeats, the jingle of bits and the low, urgent murmur of men's voices. Her head snapped up, her eyes widening as she saw a group of cavalry officers trotting into town, their uniforms crisp and their mounts prancing with barely restrained energy.

"Help!" she cried, waving her arms frantically as she stumbled towards them. "Please, you must help me!"

The lead officer, a tall, imposing figure on a massive black horse, raised a gloved hand, bringing the group to a halt. The beast snorted and pawed at the ground, its eyes rolling and its nostrils flaring as if it could sense the urgency of the situation.

"Captain Nicholas Hunt of His Majesty's light cavalry, at your service, madam." He gestured to the man beside him, a grizzled, stern-faced gentleman in the uniform of the local militia. "And this is Colonel Westbrook. What's the trouble, madam?" the captain asked, his voice deep and commanding as he swung down from the saddle.

Amelia nearly collapsed with relief, her hands shaking as she grasped at his arm. "My son," she gasped, her words tumbling out in a desperate rush. "He's been taken, kidnapped—I know not why! Lieutenant North went after him, but I fear... I fear they may be in grave danger."

At the mention of Lieutenant North's name, the officer's eyes narrowed, his hand instinctively reaching for the pistol at his hip. "Lieutenant North, you say? Which way did he go?"

Amelia pointed a trembling finger up the road, her heart hammering in her chest. "That way, sir. Please, you must hurry. My boy, my Ethan... he's all I have in this world."

The officer nodded curtly, his jaw clenching with determination. "We shall do everything in our power to bring your son back to you."

"Please," Amelia whispered, her voice breaking on a sob. "Please, bring him home to me."

Captain Hunt swung back into the saddle, his black horse dancing beneath him as if eager to be off. "We'll find him, madam. You have my word."

With a nod to his men, he wheeled his mount around, the group falling into formation behind him as they thundered off into the night. The sound of their hoofbeats echoed through the streets, a promise of hope and deliverance that made Amelia's heart soar even as fresh tears spilled down her cheeks.

"Miss Grey," Mr. Sommers said softly, his hand coming to rest on her shoulder. "Come, let us get you inside. You're chilled to the bone, and there's nothing more you can do out here."

Amelia hesitated, her gaze fixed on the point where the cavalry had disappeared into the darkness. She wanted to follow them, to be there when they found Ethan, to hold him in her arms and never let go. But she knew that Mr. Sommers was right, that she would only be a hindrance to the rescue effort.

"You're right," she whispered, her voice thick with tears. "I just... Oh, what shall I do if anything happens to him?"

The old apothecary nodded, his voice filled with sympathy. "I know, my dear. But you must have faith. Lieutenant North and Captain Hunt will stop at nothing to bring him back to you. They are men of honor, men who know the value of a child's life."

As he led her back towards the house, Amelia saw a paper fluttering in the frame of the door. It was wedged between two boards, clearly stuck there on purpose. She stepped up and grabbed it before Sommers had even noticed it, and her fingers were tearing it open as they rushed back into the.

"What now?" Sommers asked. He guided her to a chair by the hearth and stirred the fire into a roaring blaze. "Open it, Miss Grey."

With shaking hands, she flattened the scrap of paper. The words written on it struck her like a punch to the stomach, stealing away her breath and crushing her momentary elation.

"I told you to call off the lieutenant," she read aloud, her voice cracking. "He has interfered where he does not belong, and I am forced to act to preserve my interests. You will come alone to the old forester's cabin at the edge of the estate at midnight. It is you I want, not the boy. Tell no one, for I do have my pistol and I should hate for him to be harmed in an accident."

"Dear God in Heaven," Sommers breathed. "What manner of monster is this?"

Amelia crumpled the note, her breath coming fast and sharp. The fear was a living thing, clawing at her throat, but beneath it, a feverish determination took hold. "A monster I intend to face, Mr. Sommers. For Ethan's sake."

"Miss Grey, no!" Sommers reached for her as she bolted from the chair, but she evaded his grasp. "You cannot go alone. It's madness, pure and simple."

"What choice do I have?" Tears blurred her vision as she snatched her cloak from its peg. "I have already sent the militia after them! If I don't go, if I don't stop the others, he'll kill Ethan!"

"And if you do go? What then? He says he wants *you*, Miss. You are no fool. You must know what he means by it!" The old man's voice shook, but whether from cold or fear, she couldn't say.

"Shall I just do nothing? I have to try." In her mind, Ethan's cherubic face swam, his guileless eyes and ready laughter. Her son, her heart. "Tell Captain Hunt... tell Owen... I'm sorry. And if I... if I don't make it back..."

Sommers grasped her shoulders, his grip surprisingly strong. "Don't talk like that, Miss Grey. The lieutenant—"

"You mustn't let him follow me! If he comes back... Please, Mr. Sommers. I cannot lose them both!"

The apothecary blinked, then his hand fell away, and he swallowed, his face pale. "God speed, Miss Grey."

"**B**LAST IT, YOU WORTHLESS nag, move!" Owen urged his mount forward, his heart pounding in time with the horse's reluctant hooves as they thundered through the snowy landscape. He'd tied the lead rope in a loop from one side of the horse's halter to the other, giving him at least some measure of control over their direction, but the fact was that the horse was far from a gallant charger.

Beside him, Corporal Daniels was having similar problems, his jaw clenched and his knuckles white as he gripped the horse's mane. The animals beneath them were ill-suited for the task at hand, their coats thick and shaggy with winter growth, their backs bare of saddle or bridle. North and Daniels were both experienced in fighting horseback under the most abysmal conditions, but riding unwilling nags with hardly any means of compelling them forward was costing them precious time.

"We need a plan," North shouted over the wind, his voice rough with exertion and barely contained rage. "We can't just charge in blind, not with Ethan's life at stake."

Daniels nodded, his brow furrowed in thought. "The road ahead narrows, sir. If we can get ahead of the carriage, find a place to cut them off..."

"Cut them off? We would need faster horses for that!"

North's mind raced, his tactical instincts warring with the desperate, clawing need to reach his son. Daniels was right, they needed to be one step ahead of Ashwood if they wanted any hope of gaining the advantage. But the thought of Ethan, scared and alone and possibly even fighting to breathe as Ashwood carried him off, made his blood boil and his vision turn red until he could hardly think straight.

"There's a bend, about a mile ahead," he said at last, his voice tight with barely contained fury. "Deuce take me if I know how we're going to do it, but if we can get there first, find a way to block the road…"

But even as the words left his lips, he felt his horse falter beneath him, the animal's stride hitching as it plunged its feet into the snow to turn back towards the warmth and safety of the stable. North cursed, his hands tightening on the makeshift reins as he fought to keep the beast on course.

"Wretched beast!" he growled, his frustration and fear boiling over. "We'll never make it at this rate. These horses are worse than useless!"

Daniels opened his mouth to respond, but his words were lost in the sudden thunder of hoofbeats that echoed from behind them. Owen twisted on the horse's back, his eyes widening as he saw a group of mounted soldiers galloping towards them, their red uniforms crisp and their weapons gleaming in the moonlight.

At their head rode a figure that made North's heart leap with a sudden, fierce hope. *Captain Hunt!* The sight of him, his face set with grim determination and his black mare surging beneath him like a force of nature, was like a breath of fresh air.

"Captain!" he cried, his voice cracking with relief as the cavalry drew alongside them. "Bloody hell, I never thought I'd be glad to see that black beast of yours!"

The captain drew rein and patted his horse's neck. "I'm sure she's glad to see you, too, Lieutenant."

"Sir, how did you…?"

"A woman, Lieutenant. We came to learn more of these prisoners you collared, and a woman met us in the street. She told us you had gone after a kidnapped child. What the hell is going on here?"

"It's my son, sir. Ethan. Lord Ashwood, he… he took him. And he's the one behind the prisoner smuggling, too."

Hunt's jaw clenched, his hand tightening on the reins of his mount. The black monster beneath him snorted and danced, her eyes rolling and her nostrils flaring as if she could sense the urgency of the moment. "Your son?" he repeated, his voice low and dangerous. "And you're certain it's Ashwood?"

North nodded, his heart hammering in his chest. "Yes, sir. He was there, in the carriage. He had a gun on Ethan, said that if Miss Grey wanted him back, she had to come to him."

Hunt's eyes narrowed, a cold fury settling over his features like a mask. Owen had only seen his captain like this once before—when he heard that his Bess had been taken captive. "The blackguard," he growled, his hand brandishing his pistol. "We'll get the boy back, North. I swear it."

He turned to the men behind him. "Colonel Westbrook, will you and your men follow Lieutenant North's lead? I believe the lieutenant's quarry and yours are one and the same."

The militia officer nodded, his face grim and his hand resting on the hilt of his sword. "Certainly, Captain. My lads have been itching for some action."

Hunt turned back to North, his eyes softening for a moment with a deep, abiding sympathy. "We'll get him back, Owen," he said quietly, using North's given name for the first time in their long acquaintance. "I promise you, we'll bring your boy home safe."

"Sir, we cannot just rush in pell-mell. Ashwood has the advantage of us, and he won't hesitate to use it. He wants Amelia—his mother."

Hunt's brows arched. "Then we will have to make sure he doesn't get her."

With a nod to his men, the captain spurred his horse forward, the cavalry falling into formation behind him as they thundered down the road. North and Daniels followed close on their heels, their own mounts plunging beneath them with renewed willingness, for it meant joining company with the other horses.

The road narrowed ahead, the trees pressing in close on either side like silent sentinels. North could see the bend that he had spoken of, the place where they might have a chance to cut off the carriage and force a confrontation. But as they drew closer, he saw that the way was already blocked, a fallen tree stretched across the path like a barricade.

"Blast," he growled, his heart sinking as he realized the implications of the obstacle. "They must have known we were coming. They're trying to funnel us towards the manor, to trap us on their own ground."

Hunt's face was grim, his eyes narrowed as he surveyed the scene. "Then we'll just have to be smarter than them, won't we, lads? Colonel, take your men and circle around to the east. Try to find a way to flank them, to come at them from behind."

Westbrook nodded, his hand already raised to signal his troops. "With pleasure, Captain. We'll give the blighters a taste of their own medicine."

As the militia peeled off, disappearing into the shadows of the trees, Hunt turned back to North and Daniels, his expression fierce and determined. "We'll keep going straight on, boys. If Ashwood wants a fight, then by God, we'll give him one he won't soon forget."

North felt a surge of adrenaline course through his veins, a reckless, raging need to confront the man who had dared to threaten his child. He knew that it was a risk, that they were walking into a trap with their eyes wide open. But he also knew that he would gladly lay down his life to save his son, to bring Ethan back to the warmth and safety of home.

With a nod to his commander, he urged his horse forward, the animal's hooves kicking up a spray of snow as they leapt over the fallen tree and plunged onwards towards the manor.

Chapter Twenty-Eight

AMELIA'S HEART THUNDERED IN her ears as she rode through the snow-covered woods, the old horse beneath her plodding steadily despite the uneven terrain. Mr. Sommers had been so kind—he had tried everything he could to talk her out of this, but failing that, he had bundled her up in warm clothes and promised her that his horse would take care of her. She could still feel the warmth of his embrace, the gentle reassurance in his voice as he helped her into the saddle.

But now, alone in the darkness, with only the moon to guide her, Amelia felt the full weight of her fear and desperation pressing down upon her. Ethan, her precious boy, was out there somewhere, in the clutches of a madman. And despite all the gallant men who had set out after him in the dark, she was the only one who could bring him back to safety.

She followed the tracks of the militia in the snow, the hoofprints stark and clear against the pristine white. She could see where they had split off, some horses veering to the east while others rode straight on towards the manor. A flicker of hope kindled in her chest at the thought of Owen and his men, of the cavalry riding to her son's rescue.

But there was that note, the chilling words it contained about any efforts to summon help. Ashwood had been clear in his instructions—she was to come alone, to tell no one of her destination. If she disobeyed, if she brought others with her... Ethan's blood would be on her hands.

A shudder ran through her, a sickening sense of dread that made her stomach churn and her hands tremble on the reins. She couldn't risk it, couldn't gamble with her son's life. And so, with a heavy heart and a whispered prayer on her lips, she turned her horse towards the third path, the one that led deep into the woods surrounding Ashwood Manor.

The trees pressed in close around her, their branches reaching out like grasping fingers in the darkness. The snow was deeper here, untouched by hoof or boot, and Amelia felt a flicker of unease at the realization. How had Ashwood gotten Ethan to the gamekeeper's cottage, if not by this route? He must have gone to the manor first, circled back through the woods to avoid detection. Or he was not really there at all, which meant... what?

The thought made her blood run cold, her mind racing with the possibilities of what the lord might have in store for her. This was all some kind of trap, a twisted game meant to lure her away from the safety of Owen's protection, and here she was, walking right into it.

As she rode deeper into the woods, the sounds of the outside world began to fade away, swallowed up by the eerie stillness of the forest. But then, just as the silence was beginning to press in on her from all sides, she heard it—the distant snorting of horses, the low murmur of men's voices carrying on the wind.

Owen. He was out there somewhere, leading the charge to rescue their son. Amelia's heart leapt in her chest, a sudden, desperate longing filling her at the thought of him. She wanted to call out to him, to let him know that she was there, that she was fighting just as hard as he was to bring Ethan home.

But she couldn't, not without risking everything. If Ashwood heard her, if he realized that she had disobeyed his orders... She shuddered to think what he might do, the terrible price that Ethan might pay for her recklessness.

And so, she rode on in silence, her eyes straining to pick out the path ahead in the dim, silvery light of the moon. The gamekeeper's cottage loomed ahead, a dark, hulking shape against the backdrop of the forest. Amelia's heart pounded in her chest as she drew closer, her breath coming in shallow, rapid gasps that clouded the air before her face.

There was no window, at least none facing her. No way to know if a lantern burned inside, no way of seeing if Ethan really was in there... or who else might be. Amelia slipped off the horse and stood frozen, her hand still outstretched, her heart pounding so hard she thought it might burst from her chest. Every instinct, every fiber of her being screamed at her to run, to flee this place of danger and death and never look back.

But she couldn't, not without Ethan. With a trembling hand, she pushed open the door, the hinges creaking in protest as she stepped over the threshold. The room beyond was dark, lit only by the faint, flickering glow of a single candle. Shadows danced on the walls, long and distorted, like the twisted figments of a nightmare.

"Ethan?" she called. "Ethan, sweetheart, are you here?"

A figure separated itself from the shadows—Lord Ashwood, his mouth puckered as if he found the whole thing amusing. "Miss Grey, how good of you to join me."

"Where is my son?" Amelia demanded, her hands balling into fists at her sides.

"Your son is safe, for now." He tipped his head, arching a nonchalant brow. "But his continued well-being depends on your compliance."

"What do you want from me?"

Ashwood stepped closer, his eyes glinting in the candlelight. "I think you know, Miss Grey."

He reached for her, trying to pull her into a kiss, but Amelia shoved him away, her heart racing with fear and revulsion. "Don't touch me!"

Ashwood's face darkened. "You forget yourself, Miss Grey. You're already ruined. Why fight the inevitable?"

Amelia struggled as he grabbed her, his strength overpowering her. They grappled, a violent tangle of limbs, until Ashwood pinned her to the ground, twisting her arm behind her back. Pain lanced through her, and she cried out, tears streaming down her face. "Stop! You're hurting me!"

"It doesn't have to hurt," he rasped, his breath hot on her neck. "I would treat you kindly, if you would permit it. But you had to defy me, and now I cannot trust you."

"You can trust me!" She hissed in pain as he twisted her arm harder.

"The time is past for that. You still fancy that lieutenant will save you. Will he still want you after I have had my way with you? That was why you sent *me* away before, was it not? You were carrying *his* bastard—aye, the apple does not fall far from the tree in your family."

She jerked, trying to angle her other elbow upward into his stomach, but he had her pinned too tightly to get any leverage. "I don't know what you're talking about!" she growled through gritted teeth.

He lifted his weight from behind her just enough to slam her against the floor again until her cheek exploded in pain, and she cried out. "Don't play the fool with me. I've been patient enough with you. You were promised to *me*, and I will have my due!"

He started ruffling her skirt, fumbling with the cloth, and Amelia bucked against him again, trying with the last of her strength to fight him off, but her twisted arm made it almost impossible to move at all.

But then, her fingers brushed against something cold and hard at Ashwood's waist—his pistol. Desperate, she worked her fingers behind her back, feeling for the trigger. She wasn't even sure where the thing was pointed—only that, by the angle of her hand, it was not pointed directly at her. She stretched her hand and held her breath as her finger moved.

The shot rang out, the bullet tearing harmlessly between Ashwood's legs, but it was enough to startle him backward. Amelia scrambled to her feet, the pistol clutched in her shaking hands. "Don't move!" she warned, aiming the barrel at his chest. "This is a double trigger. I still have one shot left."

Ashwood froze, his eyes widening with surprise and a flicker of fear. "You wouldn't dare."

"Try me," Amelia spat. "Now, talk. Why are you so insistent on marrying me?"

Slowly he edged his hands away from his body, holding them out in a gesture of truce. "Why, for my inheritance, of course. Or should I say, *your* inheritance?"

Amelia squinted, and when she did, she realized the hammer on the second trigger was not back. Grimacing, she pulled it back and waved the pistol again at Ashwood. "What are you talking about?"

His lip curled and he let out a hiss, no doubt peeved with himself for missing the opportunity to grab the pistol from her before she had armed it properly. "Your grandfather, Clarence Merriweather. My uncle. He was your mother's father."

Amelia flinched at the name, confusion swirling through her. So... Owen *was* right... but it still made no sense, and she dared not let on that she had heard of this before. "You're lying. My mother was a poor farmer's daughter."

Ashwood scoffed. "Is that what she told you? No, your mother was cast off by her father for having a child out of wedlock. Married off to the first farmer who would take her."

"No," Amelia whispered, her blood running cold. "That's not true."

"Oh, but it is," Ashwood purred. "Why else do you think your 'father' never let you court any of the local lads? He knew who your mother was, knew you might inherit. He hoped to profit from it."

Amelia's hand shook, the pistol wavering. "But why marry me? You had the title! Your father was the elder brother, with the fortune and the land—everything! What could the younger brother even have to pass on?"

He scoffed, his hands lowering, until she pointed the pistol more intently at his heart, causing him to sober a little. "Clarence Merriweather had no lands. But he did have a profitable... business venture. One that I took over at his passing."

She arched her brows and pressed closer, raising the pistol's point to his face. "Then take it and go. What do you need me for?"

Ashwood's face twisted with rage. "Because that old bastard Clarence cut me out of the will. Signed everything over to you, his 'precious' granddaughter whom he never set eyes on, purely from spite."

Amelia's eyes narrowed, and her hand shook on the pistol. If this was true... if *she* was an heiress to some nameless fortune, then that meant that even if she married, her husband would ultimately not control it. Not indefinitely. It would pass to...

"Ethan," she whispered. "Where is he? What have you done with him?"

Chapter Twenty-Nine

NORTH CREPT THROUGH THE shadows surrounding Ashwood Manor, his heart pounding with a mixture of fear and determination. Beside him, Daniels and a handful of militia officers moved with silent precision, their weapons at the ready as they closed in on the watchmen patrolling the grounds.

With a series of swift, brutal movements, they neutralized the sentries, gagging them and binding them to the trees that dotted the perimeter. North's blood sang with the thrill of the fight, his mind focused on a single, all-consuming goal: Ethan.

As the last watchman slumped unconscious, North turned to Daniels, his sword glinting in the moonlight. "Report back to Captain Hunt and the colonel. Tell them the perimeter is secure, but we haven't spotted Ethan inside yet."

Daniels nodded, melting back into the shadows as North approached one of the bound watchmen, his jaw clenched with barely contained rage. He ripped the gag from the man's mouth, his voice low and dangerous. "The boy. Where is he?"

The watchman's eyes widened with fear, his breath coming in ragged gasps. "Upstairs," he stammered. "Under guard. They'll shoot him if you break through the door."

North's vision flashed red, his hand fisting in the man's collar as he slammed him back against the tree trunk. "A small boy, held under guard? Why? What threat could a child possibly pose?"

The watchman shook his head frantically, his words tumbling out in a terrified rush. "Not the boy. It's who they knew would come for him."

North's grip tightened, his heart pounding in his ears. "Explain. Now."

"Ashwood's business," the watchman babbled. "Someone compromised it. He's taking measures, ensuring he'll be left alone in the future."

A sickening realization washed over him, his stomach twisting with dread. So, Ashwood had found out about his interference, the prisoners they had tracked down and captured. The how of it did not matter—what mattered was that Ashwood would never have gone after Ethan if he did not know of Owen's involvement. He was using a child to threaten the man... not as the decorated lieutenant of His Majesty's Army, but as a father.

It was personal.

He released the watchman, his hands shaking with a mixture of fear and fury as he turned to Captain Hunt, who had materialized silently at his side. "Sir, I request permission to take the house alone. By stealth. I can't risk Ethan—"

Hunt's hand clamped down on his shoulder, his grip firm and grounding. "Easy, North. You're too seasoned to let your feelings cloud your judgment."

But Owen was in no mood for sense, and he shook off his captain's grip. "Is that what you thought when you stormed that inn? When they shot you down in the road because you went off on some fool madman's rampage?"

Hunt turned him around, making Owen stare him in the face. "No, it is not. I helped no one by my tirade, and I nearly got myself killed."

"And if faced with that same circumstance, knowing only what you knew in that moment, tell me you would not do it again!" Owen seethed.

Captain Hunt's jaw twitched, and he blinked. "I might."

Owen straightened, staring Hunt in the eye. "Then I request permission to take the house! Sir."

Hunt pressed his mouth into a thin line. "We have the militia."

"Aye, all barely trained, callow fools!"

"North, listen to yourself! Those aren't the new recruits. I asked the colonel to bring his best. Westbrook didn't have to come at all! He outranks me, but he's been waiting to crack this open for months."

Owen paused to gape at his captain. "Westbrook? That's how you knew?"

"He made a report some while back, claiming prisoners were escaping downriver, and it was ignored. I only learned of it when I was getting my papers from Richards' old documents. Quite the accident, I think, for when I asked about it, I was told to leave it alone. All Westbrook needed was a spark to blow it open, something his superiors could no longer ignore."

"A bloody spark!" Owen pointed toward the house. "My *son* is in there with a pistol to his head! You would blow up a powder keg just to take down Ashwood, and devil take that innocent boy!"

"Calm yourself, North. I intend no such thing. We'll get your boy back, but we do it together, and you *will* follow orders."

Owen forced himself to breathe, to unclench his fists and offer a shaky nod, even as fury exploded in his head and blasted his vision. "Very well, sir. What is the plan?"

NORTH CREPT ALONG THE portico, his heart pounding and his breath coming in shallow, controlled bursts. The information from the captured watchman had been clear: Ethan was being held in this room, guarded by one of Ashwood's men. The curtains drawn over the windows prevented any glimpse inside, though. No way to verify if the man had been lying, or if Ethan had been moved in the last few minutes.

He pressed his back against the wall, signaling to the other soldiers to take their positions. Some would enter through the house, moving quietly to avoid detection, while North would breach the room through the window. They had to time it perfectly.

Below, he heard an occasional whispered command, but most of the sounds on the air were of wind and creaking trees under the weight of snow. He held his breath, his eyes on the edge of the tree where one red-coated junior officer stood poised to give him the signal when the others had slipped inside.

As he waited, every muscle tense with anticipation, North strained his ears for any sound from within. And then, he heard it: Ethan's cough, a terrible, hacking fit that seemed to go on forever. North's heart clenched, his hands tightening on his weapons. The cough was more than just a tickle in Ethan's throat—it was a deep, heaving cough, with scarcely a breath between each bark. The poor lad was probably doubled over and unable to even move under such a vicious attack from his lungs.

Owen tensed. Surely, the others must be inside by now! He was certain of the room, was ready to burst through the window the instant he got the signal. Meanwhile, he inched closer to the window, and as he approached, he found a split, a narrow gap between the curtains. Owen angled his head to peer through, but saw nothing at first. Ethan was still coughing... a little to the right. Owen moved a little to the left, working to get a better view of the other side of the room...

And there was the guard, his back to the window, and his hand... something in his hand... pointed at the floor. Owen moved his head up a little, his breathing tight as he tried to see the floor. There, finally, he could see his son, curled in on himself as the coughing fit wracked his small frame.

The guard finally moved just a little, shaking his head as he paced around Ethan while the boy coughed. "Keep it down, brat! You want to bring the whole house down on us?"

But Ethan's coughing only intensified, each ragged hack tearing at North's heart. He inched closer to the window, peering through the narrow gap between the curtains.

The guard's patience was wearing thin. With a growl of frustration, he stuffed his pistol into his coat and crossed the room, his heavy boots thudding against the floorboards. North watched, his muscles coiled with tension, as the man grabbed a pitcher from the washstand, filling a glass with water.

Owen glanced desperately at the woods and realized with an instant of self-loathing that the young man had been waving frantically, trying to give him the signal while he was distracted. Owen waved back and set his jaw grimly. This was it.

As the guard's back turned, Owen sprang into action. He leapt forward, shattering the window with a single, powerful blow. Glass rained down around him as he vaulted into the room, his sword already drawn and ready.

The guard whirled, dropping the glass with a crash as he fumbled for his weapon. But North was faster, his blade slicing through the air with deadly precision. The man barely had time to cry out before the sword found its mark, burying itself deep in his chest.

As the guard crumpled to the floor, North was already moving, dropping to his knees beside Ethan's trembling form. "Ethan," he breathed, his voice cracking with emotion as he gathered the boy into his arms. "I've got you. You're safe now."

Ethan clung to him, his small hands fisting in North's coat as he buried his face in his father's shoulder as he coughed. Owen picked him up, wrapping Ethan's arms around his neck as he carried him to the water basin and poured him a drink of water. He coaxed Ethan to drink it, slowly, and after a moment, the deep chest-rending coughs faded for a few seconds.

"Papa," he sobbed, his voice muffled and weak. "I knew you'd come. I knew you'd find me."

North held him close, his eyes burning with unshed tears as he rocked his son gently. *Papa...* "Always," he whispered fiercely. "I will always find you, Ethan."

The sound of footsteps and muffled shouts from below told him that the other soldiers had breached the house, securing the lower floors. But North barely registered the noise, his entire focus on the precious boy in his arms.

He pulled back slightly, his hands running over Ethan's face and body, checking for any signs of injury. "Are you hurt? Did they..." He swallowed hard, unable to finish the thought.

Ethan shook his head, his eyes wide and haunted. "No, Papa. They didn't hurt me. But I was so scared. I thought... I thought I'd never see you again!"

North's heart shattered, the broken pieces lodging in his throat. "Oh, Ethan," he murmured, pulling the boy back into his embrace. "I'm so sorry. I'm so sorry you had to go through this. But it's over now."

"Where's Mama?"

Owen stroked his son's head. "She is safe with Mr. Sommers. As soon as it is clear below, we will—"

The door pounded open, revealing Hunt, with Daniels towering behind his shoulder. Owen hefted Ethan in his arms to show them that the boy was safe, and the captain's eyes slipped over the fallen form of the guard behind him.

"You killed him?" the captain asked.

"He was holding a gun to a child's head," Owen retorted. "Tell me why I should have spared him."

Hunt hesitated, then nodded. "Very well. The house is clear, and the colonel and his men are waiting for us downstairs."

Owen set Ethan on his feet and found a blanket from the bed to wrap around him. "And Ashwood?"

Hunt and Daniels exchanged a glance and shook their heads. "I thought he would be in here with the boy."

Owen narrowed his eyes. "No. But he must be here somewhere. It was he who had Ethan in the carriage."

Ethan buried his face against Owen's sleeve to fight back a cough, then tugged on Owen's hand. "That man left. He—" another cough "—said he was going to meet my mama."

A chill shivered down Owen's spine. "He said what?" He whirled on the captain. "Where is he?"

Hunt's hand went back to his sword. "Question the men below, Daniels! North, let me take the boy."

Hand off his son? Owen's arms tightened and he instinctively shook his head. But if Ashwood meant to go for Amelia... He had to at least question Ashwood's men, find out the truth to make sure she was safe, and that meant trusting Ethan to Captain Hunt.

He dropped to his knees, cupping Ethan's face in his hands. "Listen to me, son," he said, his voice low and urgent. "I need to go find your mother, to make sure she's safe. But I'm going to leave you with Captain Hunt. He'll keep you safe until I get back."

Ethan's lower lip trembled, his eyes filling with fresh tears as he hid another cough in the crook of his arm. "But Papa..."

"I know," Owen soothed, brushing a strand of hair back from the boy's forehead. "I know you're scared. But I need you to be brave for me, just a little while longer. Can you do that?"

Ethan sniffed, his small shoulders squaring with a determination that made Owen's heart swell with pride. "Yes, Papa," he whispered. "I'll be brave. I promise."

North pressed a kiss to his son's brow, his eyes closing briefly against the sting of tears. "That's my boy," he murmured. "That's my brave, strong boy."

From below, he could hear shouts and the clanking of swords sweeping free of their scabbards as Daniels went from man to captured man, questioning each about the where-abouts of their employer. Owen bundled Ethan into his arms again and carried him down the stairs, Hunt trailing after them until they reached the bottom.

"Any word, Daniels?" Hunt demanded.

Daniels looked back at them, his pistol still leveled at one man's face. Across the room, the colonel and one of his officers had apparently questioning two others, and they met Daniels' glance with nods of agreement. "The woodsman's cottage," Daniels replied. "Same report from all three of these cowards. This one here is the blighter who tacked the note for Miss Grey to the apothecary's door. Do you think she saw it and took the bait, sir?"

North squeezed Ethan's shoulder, drawing his son a little closer. "She would. I'm certain of it. Where is this cottage?"

"A mile east of here, deep in the forest. You'll see Ashwood's tracks in the snow. They say it's isolated, easy to defend. The perfect place for an ambush."

Owen blinked, his decision made before he had even drawn breath. "I'm going. Captain?" He nudged Ethan a little closer to his commanding officer, watching that man's face for the permission he needed to take off in pursuit.

"What are you looking at me for? I'm not your commanding officer anymore," Hunt said, even as he reached a hand to place on Ethan's shoulder.

Owen tilted his head with a question. "I thought... No, never mind. I'm going, then."

"Preston, Galloway, and Marshall, go with the Lieutenant," the colonel ordered. "Lord Ashwood is wanted by the crown for questioning."

Owen nodded his thanks to the colonel and dropped to one knee to kiss his son's cheek. "I'll bring back your mama, Ethan." With a final, lingering look, he rose to his feet, entrusting Ethan to Hunt's waiting arms with a look of naked agony. "He's my whole life, sir."

Hunt nodded, pulling Ethan close to his side. "Understood, Lieutenant. Take my horse. I know you have no fond feelings for her, but she's faster than anything else in these woods. She'll get you there. And keep your wits about you."

Chapter Thirty

"**D**ON'T COME ANY CLOSER!"

The pistol in Amelia's hand trembled slightly as she kept it trained on Lord Ashwood's chest. The air in the cabin was thick with tension, the only sound the scuffling of his boots across the floor and the ragged pounding of her own pulse in her ears.

Ashwood circled her slowly, his eyes glinting in the light of the single candle. Not enough light to blind him, even if she could maneuver him so the glare was in his eyes… She swallowed and cast a quick glance behind her to make sure she wasn't being forced into a corner.

"Come now, Amelia," he purred, his voice soft and coaxing. "Surely you don't mean to shoot me. Not when I hold the key to your son's safety, to your own future?"

Amelia swallowed hard, her finger tightening on the trigger. "Stay back," she warned, her voice shaking despite her best efforts to keep it steady. "I won't hesitate to use this if you come any closer."

Ashwood chuckled. "You are already hesitating. You could have shot me a dozen times by now, but yet, you waver. What do you hope to accomplish here? You're trapped, with nowhere to run and no one to turn to."

"Owen North will come," Amelia said, her chin lifting in defiance.

The lord's smile turned to a snort of derision. "Will he, now? And what makes you so sure of that? For all you know, he's already dead, cut down by my men as he tried to storm the manor."

Amelia's heart clenched, a wave of icy fear washing over her. No. It couldn't be true. Owen was too clever, too skilled to fall into Ashwood's trap. He would find a way to save Ethan, to come for her.

Besides, Ashwood didn't know about Captain Hunt and the militia she'd sent after Owen. Surely, with all those experienced officers, even the defenses of Ashwood Manor would fall.

But... Well, it was true that she could not know that. And every minute she let Ashwood keep circling her was another minute for him to study her, try to find a weakness or a distraction to break her focus. What *was* her end plan? Even if she broke and ran, he would catch her before she had gone ten paces.

She had tried numerous times to angle her steps to carry her closer to the door as he maneuvered around her, but he kept blocking every effort. Indeed, she was the one who held the pistol, but short of actually pulling the trigger, she had no idea how to use it to better effect than she was already. And if she fired and missed again, well, there would be her last hope vanished.

A strange whistling sound shattered the tense silence. Amelia's hand wavered faintly, but she tightened her grip, refusing to let her eyes wander from Ashwood's face. It was a trick of some kind...

Except, he had heard it, too, and was glancing nervously toward the door. There was no other sound to follow it, but it had caught him off guard for an instant. Amelia decided to press her advantage, taking a wide step to the right and trying to force him back.

And then, in a burst of splintering wood and flying debris, Owen was there, crashing through the door with his sword drawn and murder in his eyes.

"Amelia!" he cried.

For a moment, Amelia felt a surge of pure, blinding relief, a joy so acute it brought tears to her eyes. She broke focus, her attention diverted to the man she loved. But then, in a flash of movement too quick to follow, Ashwood was behind her, his arm locked around her throat and the pistol wrenched from her grasp.

"Not another step, Lieutenant," he snarled, the barrel of the gun pressed hard against Amelia's temple.

Owen froze, his sword lowering fractionally as he took in the scene before him. Amelia could see the calculations racing behind his eyes, the desperate search for a way to turn the tables, to gain the upper hand.

"Let her go, Ashwood," he said, his voice low and dangerous. "This is between you and me. Leave Amelia out of it."

The lord laughed, a harsh, grating sound that made Amelia's skin crawl. "Gladly. Shall I shoot her now, then?"

Owen flinched, surging forward, and Amelia jerked against Ashwood's arm. "He can't shoot me, Owen!" she cried. "So long as Ethan is safe, he needs me to claim the inheritance!"

Owen's eyes met hers—met hers, and answered the question she had left hanging in her outburst. Ethan... was he safe? And by the little curl beside Owen's mouth, she had her answer. She could breathe again.

Owen's gaze returned to Ashwood's. "Well, then, my lord, we are at an impasse. You need Miss Grey, so you cannot shoot her. But the instant your hand wavers to turn toward me, I will have you. What shall it be? *What shall it be, Ashwood?*"

Lord Ashwood tightened his grip on her throat, his breath hot and fetid against her ear. "All I need is her hand in marriage. I care not if she lingers and dies in a few days from a festering shot wound. But before that, I'll make her watch while I put a bullet in her lover's head."

Amelia's eyes were trained on Owen's. What could she do? Ashwood was too strong for her to struggle and free herself. She could drop her weight against his arm, like Ethan did when he didn't want to be picked up for bed. It might work...

But even as she twisted her hands against his, trying to find a weak point, Ashwood whirled her away—the gun still pointed at her for the split second it took for him to face her about. And by the time her back was to Owen, Ashwood had taken advantage of that split second of indecision, where Owen had no clear shot, to whip the pistol around.

Amelia saw only a blur. Ashwood's free hand was at her throat, digging into the cords of her neck to maximize the pain of his one-handed grip and weaken her from lack of air, while his other hand twisted round, his head turning to aim...

But Owen was already moving, lunging forward with a roar of fury and desperation. Ashwood reacted instinctively, his finger tightening on the trigger even as a cry tore from Amelia's throat.

The shot rang out like a clap of thunder, the acrid scent of gunpowder filling the air. Amelia screamed, a sound of pure, animal anguish as she watched Owen stagger back, his hand clutching at his shoulder as he fell to his knees.

"No!" she shrieked, wrenching free of Ashwood's grasp and flinging herself towards Owen's prone form. She covered him with her body, her tears falling hot and fast as she cradled his head in her lap.

"Owen," she sobbed, her fingers stroking his face, his hair. "Please, God, no. Don't leave me. Don't you dare leave me."

Red bloomed through Owen's shirt, and he grasped her hand with a grimace. Oh, where was his pistol? Dropped to the floor behind him, and she could not possibly reach it. Nor did she even care, for without him...

"It's not in your heart," she kept murmuring. "The shot went high... Keep breathing... Owen!"

Behind her, Ashwood chuckled. "How touching," he sneered as he walked around Owen's body to pick up his loaded pistol. "But I'm afraid your lover's sacrifice was for nothing, my dear. I told you he was not worthy of you."

But before he could raise his hand, the sound of a cocking pistol made him freeze, his eyes widening with sudden, terrified realization.

"I don't think so, my lord," Corporal Daniels said, his voice cold and hard as he stepped into the room, his pistol leveled at Ashwood's heart and his sword gleaming in his other hand. His order was backed up by two militia officers rushing in to flank him, both with weapons drawn.

"Drop the gun and step away from Miss Grey. Or I'll send you to hell myself."

Chapter Thirty-One

THE PAIN WAS A searing, white-hot agony that lanced through his shoulder with every ragged breath. Owen gritted his teeth against it, his vision swimming as he struggled to make sense of the chaos erupting around him.

Daniels and the militia officers had burst in behind him, their weapons drawn, and their faces set with grim determination. Through the haze of pain, he could hear the clatter of steel, the shouts of men as they subdued Lord Ashwood and wrestled him into submission.

And then Amelia was there again, her face pale and her eyes wide with fear as she hovered over him, her hands fluttering helplessly over his wounded shoulder.

"Owen," she choked out, her voice breaking on a sob. "Oh, heavens, Owen. What have you done?"

He tried to smile, to reassure her that all would be well, but the effort turned into a grimace as another wave of agony crashed over him. "Had to," he managed, his words slurring slightly. "Couldn't let him hurt you."

Daniels appeared at his side, his face tight with concern as he surveyed the damage. "You bloody fool," he growled, even as his hands moved with careful efficiency to staunch the flow of blood. "What were you thinking, charging in like that? You should have waited for us!"

North shook his head, immediately regretting the motion as the room spun sickeningly around him. "Hunt's horse," he mumbled, his tongue feeling thick and clumsy in his mouth. "Black Bess. She wouldn't be held back. Got here first, saw Amelia with the gun. Seemed as good a time as any."

Daniels snorted, his eyes rolling heavenward. "Aye, and a fine mess you've made of it, too. You'll be lucky if you don't bleed out before we can get that ball out of your shoulder."

He turned to one of the militiamen, his voice sharp with command. "Fetch a stretcher, man. We need to get him back to the village, to the apothecary."

But Owen was already struggling to sit up, his good arm braced against the floor as he fought to clear his head. "No," he gritted out, his jaw clenched with determination. "No stretcher. I can ride."

Amelia made a small, distressed sound, her hand coming to rest on his uninjured shoulder. "Owen, no. You're too badly hurt. You need to rest, to let us care for you."

He turned to her, his heart clenching at the fear and anguish written across her beloved face. "I'll be all right, love," he said softly, mustering a smile that felt more like a grimace. "I've had worse."

With a grunt of effort, he levered himself to his feet, swaying slightly as the blood rushed from his head. Daniels was there in an instant, his arm coming around North's waist to steady him. "Easy there, Lieutenant," he murmured, his voice gruff but not unkind. "Let's get you back to the village in one piece, aye?"

North nodded, his vision graying at the edges as he fought to remain conscious. He took a step forward, leaning heavily on Daniels as Amelia hovered anxiously at his other side.

"Mr. Sommers," he said, his words coming in short, panting gasps as they made their slow, painful way out of the cabin. "Do you think he'd mind another house-guest? I doubt he has any experience digging balls out of wounds."

Amelia made a choked, tearful sound that might have been a laugh. "I'm sure he does, Owen. He's seen his fair share of hunting accidents and brawls over the years."

Owen tried to grin, but it came out as more of a pained grimace. "Good. Don't let me pass out, Amelia."

"Owen, you should lie back for a moment. You've lost a lot of blood, and—"

"Not from that. From Hunt's horse. I was right to be terrified of her. Did you hear that scream she does?" He shuddered. "Downright unnatural. Don't put me back on her."

Amelia looked helplessly to Daniels. "He's not making any sense. Is it shock?"

Daniels hefted Owen's shoulder up a little more, trying to take on more of his weight. "Could be, but you haven't met that horse, ma'am. We all said she was a demon. Have a care, Lieutenant! You're going down again! Maybe we should do as the lady says and lay you back."

"No, no, on my feet," Owen slurred. "Wouldn't want to faint at the sight of a little blood. Ethan would never let me hear the end of it."

His knees buckled then, a wave of dizziness and nausea crashing over him with brutal force. He would have fallen, but for Daniels' strong grip and Amelia's slender arms coming around him, bearing him up.

"Owen!" she cried, her voice thick with tears. "Stay with me, my love. Please, you must stay awake."

He wanted to reassure her, to tell her that all would be well, that he would never leave her side again. But the darkness was rising up to claim him, the pain and the blood loss dragging him down into a whirling, silent abyss.

The last thing he heard, before the shadows swallowed him whole, was Amelia's voice, pleading and fervent in his ear. "Fight, Owen! Stay awake, my love, and come back to us."

"Amelia," he whispered, as the world fell away, and the shadows closed in. "My Amelia."

And then he knew no more.

THE WARMTH OF THE fire crackling in the hearth did little to chase away the chill that had settled deep in Amelia's bones. It was mid-morning of the next day as she sat in Mr. Sommers' parlor, Ethan nestled in her lap, his small body a comforting weight against her own. But even the solid, reassuring presence of her son could not ease the fear and worry that gnawed at her heart.

Upstairs, Owen lay unconscious, his shoulder swathed in bandages and his face pale and drawn. The apothecary had worked tirelessly to extract the ball, to clean and stitch the wound with careful, steady hands. But the danger was far from over, the risk of infection and fever a constant, looming threat.

Captain Hunt sat across from her, his handsome, scarred face softened by the flickering firelight. He had been regaling Ethan with tales of Owen's bravery, his voice low and soothing as he spun stories of heroism and sacrifice.

"Did you know, young Master Ethan, that your father once saved my life?" he asked, his eyes twinkling with a fond, faraway look.

Ethan's eyes widened, his small hands clutching tighter at the wooden toy soldier he held. "He did?"

Hunt nodded, leaning forward in his chair as if imparting a great secret. "Indeed, he did. It was in Spain, during a particularly nasty skirmish. My horse was shot out from under me, and I took a piece of shrapnel to the face. Thought I'd lost my eye, and my life along with it."

Amelia felt a shiver run down her spine, her heart clenching at the thought of Owen in such peril. But Hunt's voice was steady, his tone almost reverent as he continued.

"But your father, he didn't hesitate. He charged right into the thick of it, heedless of the danger to himself. Got me to safety, and then went back for a dozen more men. Called them to better ground, organized a defense that saved countless lives that day."

Ethan's face was alight with wonder, his eyes shining with a fierce, proud love. "I want to be a soldier like Papa when I grow up," he declared, his chin lifting with a determined set. "I want to be brave and strong, just like him."

Hunt chuckled, reaching out to ruffle the boy's hair with a gentle hand. "There are many noble things a man can be, young Ethan. A soldier is one of them, aye. But a man who loves and cares for his family, who puts their needs above his own? That's a fine thing, too. Perhaps the finest of all."

Amelia felt a lump rise in her throat, her eyes stinging with sudden, unshed tears. Somehow, she had managed to find a man who was noble in both ways—the soldier who saved lives in battle... and the father who came back for his son and the woman he loved.

The sound of footsteps on the stairs drew their attention, and Amelia's heart leaped into her throat as Mr. Sommers appeared in the doorway, his face lined with exhaustion but his eyes bright with relief.

"He's resting comfortably," the apothecary said, his voice soft and reassuring. "The wound is clean, and there's no sign of infection. With luck and care, he should be waking soon."

A wave of relief washed over her, so powerful it nearly took her breath away. She hugged Ethan close, pressing a fervent kiss to the top of his head as she whispered a silent, grateful prayer. "Thank you, Mr. Sommers!"

Captain Hunt rose to his feet, his eyes meeting Amelia's with a look of understanding and shared joy. "I should take my leave of him," he said, his voice gruff but not unkind. "My own family is waiting for me, and I've tarried here long enough."

He paused, his gaze flickering to the stairs with a hint of wistfulness. "This was to be my last mission, you see. I'm turning the regiment over to North, if he wants it. There's a promotion waiting for him in London, a chance to serve in a different way. But... he will have to decide if that's what he wants."

Amelia's heart stuttered, a flicker of hope and trepidation warring in her breast. A promotion, a new life for Owen in the city... it was everything he had ever dreamed of, the chance to make a name for himself and serve his country with honor. But... would there be a place for her and Ethan there, in London? The smoky, busy city was no place for a boy with Ethan's lungs.

She swallowed hard, forcing a smile to her lips as she met Hunt's gaze. "Thank you, Captain," she said softly. "For everything you've done, for the sacrifices you've made. Owen is lucky to have served under a man like you."

Hunt inclined his head, a flicker of understanding passing between them. "The honor was mine, Mistress Grey. Your Owen is a fine man, a true hero in every sense of the word. I'll miss him sorely, but I know he'll do great things, whatever path he chooses."

With a final, fond glance at Ethan, the captain made his way up the stairs to bid his lieutenant farewell, his steps heavy but his shoulders straight and proud. Amelia watched him go, her heart aching with a bittersweet mix of gratitude and loss.

With a trembling hand, Amelia brushed a stray curl from Ethan's brow, her heart swelling with a fierce, protective love. "Come, my darling," she murmured, rising to her feet with her son cradled close. "Let's go and see your Papa."

AMELIA SAT BESIDE OWEN's bed, her fingers absently leafing through the stack of papers Elliot Barrow had delivered just an hour earlier. The young banker had taken it upon himself to report the bank manager's suspicious activities to the militia, resulting in the man's arrest pending a trial. As the assistant manager, Barrow had deemed it appropriate to bring Amelia all the documents pertaining to the inheritance left to her by Clarence Merriweather.

As she pored over the papers, her eyes widened at the staggering sum that would now be hers—over fifty thousand pounds! It was an amount she had never even dreamed of anyone possessing, let alone *her*. The sheer magnitude of the wealth made it difficult for her to even comprehend, much less plan for. A part of her wondered if the funds would be seized, considering the dubious nature of Merriweather's business dealings.

Ashwood had not explicitly said as much, but it seemed logical that Merriweather had been the one to trade in illegal smuggling, and that was the "business" Ashwood had taken over. She tried not to get her hopes up but couldn't help indulging in a little fantasy of being able to afford a move to a warmer climate for Ethan's health, perhaps a peaceful coastal town in Kent.

Lost in her thoughts, Amelia failed to notice Owen's eyes fluttering open. It wasn't until she glanced up from the documents that she found him smiling at her, his gaze filled with adoration.

"How long have you been awake?" she asked, a soft smile playing on her lips.

"Long enough to watch the most beautiful woman in the world sitting beside my bed," he replied, his voice still thick with sleep but laced with undeniable affection.

Amelia reached for his hand, bringing it to her lips for a tender kiss. "And how are you feeling, my love?"

Owen grimaced slightly as he shifted in the bed, but his smile never wavered. "Never been better," he assured her.

She raised an eyebrow, a playful accusation in her tone. "You're lying."

"I'm in earnest," he insisted, his eyes locking with hers. "This is the best moment of my life, waking up to you."

A blush crept up Amelia's cheeks as she savored his words. Owen, seemingly emboldened by her reaction, continued, "So, is that idea of getting married still on the table?"

Leaning in close, Amelia captured his lips in a sweet, lingering kiss. As she pulled back, she whispered, "Do you really think I'm going to let you get away again?"

"I was hoping not," he chuckled softly, "but it wouldn't matter. All the king's men couldn't drag me away now."

Amelia laughed, the sound like music to Owen's ears. She sat back, her hand gently caressing his face as a more serious expression settled on her features. "Speaking of the king's men, they may indeed come to drag you away."

Owen's brow furrowed in confusion, prompting Amelia to explain what Captain Hunt had told her about a promotion waiting for him in London. A shadow passed over

Owen's face as he firmly stated, "I won't accept it. I'm going to find a way to get out of the army."

"You might at least hear them out. The captain did not give any specifics, but there was a bit of a twinkle in his eye when he mentioned that promotion. I think he already knows what you're thinking, and maybe he also knows something about where they've a mind to assign you."

"Hmm." Owen scratched his chin. "I'll have to go to London anyway, if I mean to sell out. I've served my obligations, but I'll confess, I'd make a lousy butcher or baker. And please don't ask me to shear sheep for a living."

She chuckled. "I have some thoughts about that. Perhaps there's a way for you to do what you do best while still being with your family. At least see what the army might offer you."

Owen brought her hand to his lips, pressing a fervent kiss to her knuckles. "I promise to consider taking the king's marching orders once more," he conceded, "but the first thing I'm going to do is march you to the altar, like I should have done six years ago."

With a jaunty salute and a heartfelt laugh, Amelia leaned forward, resting her head on his uninjured shoulder. "Owen North, I've loved you all my life," she murmured, her voice thick with emotion, "and God willing, I will love you for the rest of yours, too."

Epilogue

Portsmouth, September 1811

T HE SALTY SEA BREEZE danced through the open window of Captain Owen North's study, carrying with it the distant cries of gulls and the gentle lapping of waves against the shore. He stood at his desk, his hands braced against the weathered wood as he pored over the latest intelligence reports from the continent.

A year had passed since that fateful day when he had faced down Lord Ashwood and won not only his son's freedom but the heart of the woman he loved. In that time, much had changed, yet the core of his existence remained blessedly unaltered.

He was still a soldier, still bound by duty and honor to serve his country. But now, his battlefield was the bustling port town of Portsmouth, his mission to coordinate the flow of information and resources between Wellington's men and the powers that be in London.

It was a role that suited him well, one that made use of his keen mind and hard-won experience while sparing him the physical toll of frontline combat. The gunshot wound he had sustained during Ethan's rescue had been the deciding factor, the final push his superiors had needed to pull him from active field duty.

And so, with a new rank and a new purpose, Captain North had settled into life as a family man, his days filled with the joys and challenges of fatherhood and the tests that came with being a husband at last.

A knock at the door pulled him from his thoughts, and he looked up to see Ethan peeking around the frame, a mischievous grin on his face.

"Papa, come quick!" the boy exclaimed, his eyes sparkling with excitement. "Mama says the post has arrived, and there's a letter from Uncle Elliot!"

North chuckled, the sound warm and rich as he crossed the room to scoop his son into his arms. "Is that so? Well, we'd best not keep your mama waiting, then." Together, they made their way down the stairs and into the sun-drenched parlor where Amelia awaited, a stack of letters in her hand and a radiant smile on her face.

"News from Yorkshire," she said, holding out a thick fold of paper. "It seems Mr. Barrow has finally taken the plunge and married his sweetheart."

North raised an eyebrow, a grin tugging at the corners of his mouth. "About time, too. I thought he'd never work up the nerve."

"I think he was more worried about how upset his father will be when the new Mrs. Barrow tries to redecorate the cottage."

Owen laughed. "Quite possibly."

"Oh! He sent a note for Mr. Sommers, too. I shall send Ethan round the corner to deliver it."

"Hmm, you could send him now." Owen slid behind his wife, cupping the growing swell of her stomach as he nibbled her ear.

"Stop it, you rogue!" Amelia giggled and turned in his embrace to kiss him properly. It was becoming more and more difficult to do that, and Owen had never yet got over his fascination with the way her body only grew more beautiful as it filled with life. He'd missed this the first time.

But not this time. This time, he wondered in awe at her every day, and the miracle of what she was giving him. He cupped his hands around her stomach and kissed her forehead, pulling back just enough to adore her face. And then he kissed her gently again.

"I'll take it to him," he murmured against her lips. "I'm past due to share a pint with him, anyway."

Owen often sat with the older man, watching the waves roll in or listening to the bells from the ships in port. Sommers had left Yorkshire some six months ago, when Amelia wrote to him from Portsmouth with an offer he could not refuse. With the money from her grandfather's estate, she had not only secured their own future by purchasing a charming little house near the harbor but had found ways to give back to those who had helped them in their darkest hours.

Indeed, she had received the full measure of her inheritance, a thing neither of them could quite believe, even now. There had been no proven links between her fortune and whatever illicit business Ashwood had been involved in... although Ashwood's estate and monies had all been seized by the crown, and the man himself transported.

But Amelia had found a way to redeem the taint of her family's past. She had paid off Mr. Wallis's debt with the bank for the repairs to the roof of his pub. She had bought crates and crates of new books for Mr. Hanley to sell in his bookshop, some of which were earmarked for children who could not afford books of their own.

And she had also bought the little house down the lane when it came up for sale, where old Mr. Sommers now lived there rent-free in comfort and peace, his only "patient" being a six-year-old boy who begged him for fairy stories.

Ethan, their miraculous, precious boy... he had blossomed in the balmy southern climate, his once-fragile lungs growing stronger with each passing day. Though he still had a penchant for rescuing stray kittens and bringing them home to join their ever-growing menagerie, his health and happiness were the greatest gifts North could have ever asked for.

"Oh, I forgot," Amelia said, twisting out of his arms and reaching again for the stack of letters she had brought up. "There is another letter for you."

Owe took it, his eyes widening as he recognized the familiar scrawl of Lieutenant Daniels' handwriting. Eagerly, he broke the seal and unfolded the paper, his gaze skimming over the contents.

"News from Daniels?" she asked.

He nodded, a slight frown creasing his brow as he read between the lines of Daniels' carefully worded missive. "He sends his regards, and updates on his latest mission. Still out there hunting spies, and dashed good at it, too, much to his chagrin."

"Of course he is." Amelia crossed her hands over his shoulder and kissed his temple, her smile tantalizingly close to his cheek as she watched him read. "He was not given that promotion just because of his handsome face. What else does he say?"

Owen scratched his chin. "Mostly accounts of duty... he saw Wesson, and had a letter from Hunt... But there's something more, something he's not saying outright."

"Oh?" Amelia leaned closer, her own face a study in concern as she peered at the letter over his shoulder. "Is he well?"

"Physically, yes. But emotionally..." North sighed, folding the letter and tucking it into his coat pocket. "I suspect our friend is pining for something he believes he cannot have."

Amelia's eyes softened with understanding, her fingers tightening on North's arm in a gesture of compassion. "Poor Daniels. He's always been so closed off about matters of the heart. I had hoped..."

She trailed off, leaving the thought unfinished. But North knew what she had meant to say. There had been a time, back when he and Daniels were still in the field together, when he used to suspect the younger officer of having a sweetheart back home of his own. And, having recovered what he had once lost, he could not help a gentle prod or two in that direction for his friend.

But each time, the lieutenant had politely but firmly shut down the conversation, his eyes shadowing with a pain that North couldn't quite piece out. And so, out of respect for his friend's privacy and feelings, he had learned to let the matter drop, to hope in silence that someday, Daniels might find his own miracle.

"I wish there was something we could do," Amelia murmured, her gaze distant and thoughtful. "Some way to ease his loneliness, to show him that he's not alone."

North turned to her, his hand coming up to cup her cheek with a tenderness that still, after all this time, made his heart skip a beat. "We can pray," he said softly, his thumb brushing over the delicate skin beneath her eye. "And we can be there for him, in whatever way he needs us to be. That's all anyone can do, in the end."

Amelia leaned into his touch, her eyes fluttering closed for a brief, blissful moment. "You're right," she whispered, turning her head to press a kiss to his palm. "And who knows? Perhaps fate has a surprise in store for our dear friend, just as it did for us."

North smiled at that, the memory of their own twisting, tumultuous path to happiness playing out in his mind's eye. If there was one thing he had learned, it was that life had a way of defying expectations, of bringing joy and hope in the most unexpected of places.

"I love you," he murmured, pressing a kiss to his wife's temple. "More than life, more than breath."

"And I love you," she whispered, her hand finding his in the gathering dusk. "Now and forever, until the end of our days."

They settled on the sofa, which they had set to face the sea, and gazed out the window, dreaming together. And that was where Ethan found them half an hour later, with a purring cat in his arms and his ever-present toy soldier working its way out of his pocket.

"Can I sit on your lap, Papa?" he asked.

Owen grinned and held an arm out, pulling Ethan, cat and all onto his lap. He snuggled an arm tightly around his son's waist and kissed the top of his head, as Amelia leaned her cheek on his shoulder. As the sun dipped below the horizon to the west of the harbor, painting the sky in shades of gold and crimson, Captain Owen North held his family close, his heart full to bursting with the knowledge that he was exactly where he was meant to be.

__Lose yourself in Lieutenant Daniels' story, coming in autumn of 2024!__

From Nicole Clarkston

T HANK YOU FOR INDULGING with me and spending a little time with this sweet couple.

I hope you've had a delightful adventure! I would love it if you would share this family with your friends. As with all my books, I have enabled lending to make it easier to share. If you leave a review for *Bess and the Highwayman* on Amazon, Goodreads, BookBub or your own blog, I would love to read it! Email me the link at **Author@NicoleClarksto n.com**

Would you like to read more sigh-worthy romance? I have a swoony, second chance romance for you to try next! Reserve your copy of **_The Debutante and the Spy_** and find out what secrets haunt Robert Daniels. Who is the sweetheart everyone teases him about, and will he ever see her again?

And if you're hungry for more, including a gift ebook of *The Ruin of Lord Aston's Daughter*, stay up to date on upcoming releases and sales by joining my newsletter: https://subscribepage.io/V5dPFd

<u>Reserve your copy of Rober Daniels' story, coming Fall of 2024!</u>